Someone had seen her in Geoff's embrace!

Laurie was certain of it. But who? Suddenly she felt as if her heart had stopped beating. Could it possibly have been Rolf Audley?

She had thought he was away at the hospital, but walking slowly back to the hotel, she noticed that his car had been returned to the garage.

There seemed to be little doubt that it was he who had witnessed Geoff's last desperate attempt to persuade her to marry him. And at that distance, unable to hear what was said, the conclusion an onlooker would inevitably draw was appallingly clear.

Rolf would think that she was in love with Geoff. In fact, nothing could be further from the truth. . . .

OTHER
Harlequin Romances
by MARGARET MALCOLM

Summer's Lease

by

MARGARET MALCOLM

Harlequin Books

TORONTO • LONDON • NEW YORK • AMSTERDAM
SYDNEY • HAMBURG • PARIS

Original hardcover edition published in 1978
by Mills & Boon Limited

ISBN 0-373-02252-2

Harlequin edition published April 1979

Printed in U.S.A.

CHAPTER ONE

LAURIE lay drowsing contentedly in a hammock suspended between two sturdy trees and though it was only early May the sun was as hot as if it was July or August. The bees evidently thought so as well, for they were busily seeking nectar and their steady buzzing contributed to her feeling of well-being.

Not, so she told herself severely, that she ought to be in this mood of contentment. She ought to be worrying out some way to extricate her mother and herself from the financial mess they were in.

For it *was* a mess. The previous autumn Mrs Stephens had seen an advertisement in the local newspaper for what was described as 'A ranch-type house'. It was situated at the top of a narrow lane leading to Armoury Cove on the south coast of Cornwall not a great distance from Penzance and not only was it fully furnished but, for these days, it was remarkably cheap.

'I wonder why?' Mrs Stephens had pondered over this last point.

'There must be a catch somewhere,' Laurie had suggested cautiously.

'Well, let's get the keys from the agent and find out what it is,' Mrs Stephens had suggested gaily.

And that was just what they had done. They both fell in love with Armoury Ranch on sight and for the life of them they couldn't find the catch.

It was true that it was built of timber, but the foundations were solid concrete. The decorations were in good condition and the furniture, though simple, was entirely adequate. There was even a swimming pool. The garden was almost large enough to be described as grounds and were evidently still properly tended.

'It *is* a bargain,' Mrs Stephens had mused thoughtfully.

'Yes, darling, it is. But not for us,' Laurie had insisted regretfully.

'Well, I don't know,' Mrs Stephens had demurred. 'Not as a private house, of course, but as an hotel? No, listen, Laurie! That big lounge, a decent sized dining room and seven—no, nine bedrooms counting the two downstairs in that delightful suite. And plenty of bathrooms——'

'Don't forget, we'd each need a bedroom,' Laurie had reminded her.

'Yes, well, we'd have the downstairs suite.' Mrs Stephens had got it all worked out. 'Two bedrooms, a bathroom, a sitting room—just perfect. Of course, one of the bedrooms is little more than a dressing room, but I'd be quite happy with that. And it would be nice and private with that door cutting it off from the rest of the house, to say nothing of that dear little garden with a fence and a gate we could lock to keep other people out. Yes, it would be perfect!'

'And just how would we pay for it?' Laurie had asked, conscious of a feeling that she was being swept away on the tide of her mother's enthusiasm.

'Oh, *easily*! If we were to sell our house in Penzance—and you know, we've already had several quite good offers for it—and then there's the insurance money——'

Mr Stephens' work had entailed a lot of travelling and he had taken out a large insurance to cover him in case of accidents. When, five years previously, he had been killed in an air disaster, there had been a considerable sum paid to his widow. 'Yes, we could do it!'

'*Just!*' Laurie said warningly. 'And what would we live on until we got going?'

'Oh——' Mrs Stephens had dismissed that with an airy wave of her hand, 'we'd manage somehow.' And then, coaxingly: 'Honestly, Laurie, it's the chance of a lifetime. And it isn't as if we don't know a lot about running an hotel.'

Which was, of course, perfectly true. They both worked in a big, rather impersonal hotel, Mrs Stephens as head cook, Laurie as the secretary. And they were both extremely good at their jobs.

'I still think there must be a catch about it,' Laurie had insisted obstinately.

And that was what she asked the agent when they returned the keys. His answer was reassuringly prompt.

'No catch, I do assure you, Miss Stephens,' he had said. 'The reason why it's going so cheaply is that the present owner wants to make a quick sale.'

'Why?' Laurie had demanded.

'Because, following the tragic death of her husband—he was drowned trying to save a child who'd got into difficulties swimming in the Cove—Mrs Ferris couldn't stand living alone in the home where they'd been so happy,' Mr Truscott had explained. 'Earlier, of course, it had been a family holiday home, but children have a way of growing up and getting married—even, in this case, of living abroad. So she—Mrs Ferris—rarely had any visitors——' and he had waited expectantly. This time it was Mrs Stephens who asked a question.

'Mr Truscott, what can I hope to get for my house in Tregarth Place?'

'H'm. Number sixteen, isn't it? Well——' and he had named a sum which made both Mrs Stephens and Laurie gasp. 'What's more, I have a client who I know will be willing to pay that immediately.'

That had settled it with astonishing speed. Mrs Stephens and Laurie gave up their jobs and had been living at Armoury Ranch ever since.

They had spent the intervening period giving the place that extra cleaning and refurbishing that any house needs when it has not been occupied for several weeks. Then Mrs Stephens had listed all the domestic linen, of which there was an ample supply. Laurie had worked out what they would need to charge for accommodation and had bought the necessary account books and had some very attractive brochures printed. They obtained the necessary licences and they advertised Armoury Ranch in both local and national papers.

It was at this point that the 'catch' revealed itself. They received some enquiries, but not enough and, in any case, hardly any of them became hard bookings.

Why? They puzzled over that. Their charges were not exorbitant. The Ranch was beautifully situated as well as

the Cove with its sandy beach, and there was the swimming
pool. So what was wrong?

'Perhaps it's early in the year yet for people to think
about summer holidays,' Mrs Stephens said hopefully. 'Just
give them time, then they'll write.'

But they didn't, and Laurie and her mother were really
worried. And that was why Laurie took herself to their
pleasant little garden so that she could think things out on
her own—but it didn't, to her surprise, work out like that.
Instead of doing some constructive thinking, she was
possessed with a feeling of optimism and contentment. She
felt convinced, though goodness knew why, that something
would shortly happen which would put everything right. It
did make sense——

She was joined suddenly by their little Siamese cat, who
fortunately approved of their removal from a town house
to the Ranch. Her name on her pedigree certificate was
suitably Oriental, but she was always known as Cherry,
though no one quite knew why.

'Oh, Cherry, do you *have* to?' Laurie protested sleepily.
'This isn't the weather for wearing furs!'

Cherry said unmistakably that she did have to and curled
round on Laurie's chest purring like a kettle on the boil.
Then, as she went to sleep, peace settled over the little
garden. But not for long.

Shatteringly, with no warning whatever, there was an
appalling *crash* followed by an equally terrifying silence.

Laurie tumbled out of the hammock, sleep banished in an
instant, while a disgusted and terrified Cherry shinned up
one of the trees and stared with goggling eyes at the cause
of the disturbance.

And what that was was only too evident. A car coming
down the lane had ploughed through the hedge and had
finished up by crashing into the stone bird bath, shattering
it to pieces.

But where there is a car there is usually a driver. There
was in this case. Laurie, made angrier by the shock of the
accident, raced over to give him a piece of her mind. But at
close quarters she realised that was out of the question.
The driver, a young man, had slumped over the wheel, un-

conscious and with blood dripping from his face.

Laurie's first reaction was: 'Serve him right', but by now, reinforcements had arrived. Mrs Stephens came running out of the house.

'What on earth——' she began. Then: 'Oh, poor young man! We must get him out. Laurie, see if you can find Trewyn——'

But Trewyn, the gardener, had also heard the crash and for a man whose usual speed was, to say the least of it, leisurely, he behaved with commendable promptness. He checked that the ignition was turned off and then put his fingers on the young man's wrist.

'Not dead—yet,' he remarked in a self-congratulatory way. 'We'd best get him out. Good job it's an open car. If you'll hold the door open, ma'am, I'll ease him out, like. And you be ready to take some of his weight, Miss Laurie——'

Only too thankful to have someone who seemed to know what to do, the two women did as they were told. But it wasn't an easy task. For one thing, he was a tall, well-built young man and, unconscious, was a dead weight. Nor was it easy to release the clasp of his safety belt, but at last it was accomplished and they laid him, still unconscious, on a rug on the grass.

'And a nice black eye he'll have,' Trewyn commented as he inspected the badly bruised and cut cheek. 'Right on the bone it is. Still, if that's his only trouble, he's been lucky.'

He ran surprisingly skilful hands over the man's legs and arms and grunted.

'Something wrong with his left leg,' he commented. 'Broken femur, I shouldn't wonder.' He straightened up. 'This is a hospital job, ma'am. Shall I phone them up or will you? Well, perhaps I'd better. I do quite a lot of St John Ambulance work, so they know me there.'

'Oh yes, you see about it, Trewyn,' Mrs Stephens said distractedly. 'And oughtn't we to do something about his cheek? Bandage it——'

'Well, all right,' Trewyn said with a professional lack of enthusiasm for the suggestions of the amateur. 'Take that fancy hanky out of his pocket, fold it crossways and then into a long strip. Tie it—not too tight, to cover that cheek of his.'

He walked briskly to the house and Mrs Stephens knelt beside the supine figure and pulled out the handkerchief with gingerly care. It was large and white and made of very fine silk. Not, in fact, Laurie thought, the sort of handkerchief a man should possess. At any rate, not a *manly* man.

She was still angry with the cause of all this bother. He simply must have been driving badly for such a thing to have happened. Perhaps, even, he had had too much to drink——

'Laurie, you'll have to help me,' Mrs Stephens said urgently. 'I want both hands for the bandage but I can't get it round the back of his head unless it's raised a little from the ground. Not very much——'

Laurie had no choice but to obey and as she slipped her hand under his head, the touch of his crisp, dark hair sent a curious tingling thrill through her fingers. It annoyed her so much that it was all she could do not to take her hand away.

'That's it,' said Mrs Stephens a moment or so later. She stayed on her knees, looking down at the unconscious face. 'What a handsome boy he is!'

'Handsome is as handsome does,' was on the tip of Laurie's tongue, but she left it unsaid. What she did say was: 'Hardly a boy, Mother. He must be in his thirties—quite old enough not to be reckless.'

'Oh, darling,' Mrs Stephens remonstrated. 'That's hardly kind when he's hurt!'

Laurie didn't hear her; she was otherwise engaged. The undamaged eye—a very blue one—was regarding her fixedly.

'Hallo, carrots,' said a surprisingly strong voice. 'I've always had a weakness for girls of your colour, particularly when they have snub noses!' Then the eye closed in an unmistakable and offensive wink, closed again and remained closed. Apparently the creature had lapsed into unconsciousness again.

At that moment Trewyn came out of the house and

announced that the ambulance would be a good half-hour before it could arrive.

'It's got some distance to come,' he explained. 'Lucky it wasn't on another call.'

'But we can't just leave the poor man lying here,' Mrs Stephens protested. 'Can't we get him indoors somehow?'

But Trewyn would have none of it.

'Less he's moved the better,' he said with authority. 'Has he shown any signs of consciousness yet?'

'He opened his eyes and said something,' Mrs Stephens told him. 'But I didn't hear what he said. Did you, Laurie?'

'Not really,' Laurie lied unhesitatingly. 'He seemed to be just rambling——' Not for worlds would she repeat what the outrageous man had said—and done.

'Oh well, no matter,' Trewyn said easily. 'He's breathing all right. Lucky for him he'd got his straps on. Might have crumped himself up proper if he hadn't. Now, about that leg——' He squatted down and was about to investigate when the owner of the leg spoke again, this time in a weak and wavering voice.

'It's broken all right—I felt it go. Besides, I can't move it.'

'Don't you try,' Trewyn cautioned. 'Miss Laurie, if you'll fetch them cushions from your hammock, I'll pack them in to give a bit of support, like. No, I'm not going to splint it,' in answer to a query from Mrs Stephens. 'That's a job for the ambulance men. Besides, to do it proper I'd have to split up his trouser leg and it 'ud be a shame to ruin a good suit. Must have cost him a pretty penny, I'll warrant!'

He was right, Laurie realised. Though it was a casual sports suit the material was an unusually fine worsted and judging by the fit of the shoulders and collars was custom-made by a good tailor. As Trewyn had said, it must have been very expensive. But then everything he was wearing was up to the same exclusive standard. His white, open-necked shirt was made of silk and so were the few inches of sock which were visible. As for his brown, well polished shoes, though Laurie didn't know much about such things, she was reasonably sure that they were hand-made. Clearly a wealthy man, and when she looked at his car, battered and decorated with bits it had torn from the hedge though it was, this opinion was confirmed. No one but a rich man could afford to own one of the most exclusive and speedy models on the market.

Obviously a rich and idle playboy, Laurie decided disapprovingly. All the same, it did mean that he'd be able to pay for the damage he'd done—and she'd see to it that he did!

When the ambulance arrived, the senior of the two men took a look at the recumbent figure and gave a little exclamation of surprise.

'Why, it's Mr Audley! Mr Rolf Audley. Now how in the world did he get into this mess? He's one of the best drivers I know!'

'Oh, you know who he is,' Mrs Stephens said with relief. 'I was worrying about that because his wife or his relations ought to be told what's happened——'

'Isn't married, so far as I know,' the man said cheerfully. 'As for relations—no, I've never heard of any. But the hospital authorities will sort that out, so there's no need for you to worry, ma'am. Now, let's see about this leg——' He investigated carefully and gave his opinion. 'Fractured femur, I'd say. Should be a straightforward job. Splints, Joe, and bandages,' he said over his shoulder to his assistant.

In a surprisingly short time Mrs Stephens and Laurie were watching the ambulance drive away, bearing their unexpected visitor with them.

'You know, I feel I ought to have gone with them,' Mrs Stephens remarked uneasily.

'Oh, but why, Mother?' Laurie asked impatiently. 'He has no claim on us in any way—quite the reverse, in fact.'

'I know, darling,' Mrs Stephens admitted. 'But poor young man, if he's got no wife or relations, surely the sight of a familiar face——'

'But, Mother, yours wouldn't be any more familiar than any of the nurses'. I don't think he looked at you, did he?'

'No, he didn't.' And then, to Laurie's embarrassment, she went on: 'But he looked at *you*, didn't he? And said something. What was it?'

'Something rude about the colour of my hair,' Laurie said shortly, and left it at that. Even her mother wasn't going to hear about that insufferable wink!

Cherry, evidently deciding that she had been neglected long enough, began to shout indignantly that somebody had got to rescue her from the tree where she had taken refuge. But as soon as they tried to get hold of her she retreated further up, her blue eyes alight with mischief.

'Oh, leave her to it,' Mrs Stephens said at last. 'She can get down perfectly well on her own, but she'll keep this up for as long as we're willing to play—and I, for one, am not! I want a cup of tea and you could do with one, Laurie. You look absolutely washed out.'

'Well, I don't feel it,' Laurie snapped, and instantly apologised. 'Sorry, Mother. Yes, I suppose it was a bit of a shock. But before I have tea, I'd like to have a wash and brush up. I feel a bit tousled.'

She went to her bedroom, scrubbed her hands almost viciously and washed her face. Then she went to her dressing table and regarded her reflection critically.

'Carrots, indeed!' That was what she had been called in her school days and perhaps it had been true, but her hair had darkened to a rich auburn and Laurie liked it. Liked, too, the fact that it was so easy to manage. A good brushing swept it back from her face, though curly little tendrils escaped at her temples. Then with a quick twist which she had perfected over the years at the nape of her neck it became one large, natural curl which reached her shoulders. A ribbon at the top end of the curl was the finishing touch which kept everything in place. It was a style which suited her well, as she had been assured on more than one occasion, but all *he* had seen was the colour which, again, had brought her compliments. But—carrots! That was unforgivable!

And then her nose. She leaned nearer the mirror to regard it more closely. It did turn up the tiniest bit, but snub —never! A most unappreciative young man—and a rude one.

Her mother called to her that she was taking the tea out on to the verandah and Laurie, after calling: 'Coming!'

quickly did her hair and powdered her face. Then, after a
moment's hesitation, she added a little blusher to her
cheeks—something she rarely did. Then she went out on
to the verandah, acutely conscious that her mother noticed
the blusher, though she made no comment.

They drank their first cups in silence. Then Cherry, having rescued herself, joined them and was offered a saucer-
ful of milk at which she turned up her nose and instead
lapped up a small puddle of water which Mrs Stephens had
spilt when earlier in the day she had watered the pot plants
on the verandah.

'Unnatural animal,' Mrs Stephens commented.

Laurie didn't reply and Mrs Stephens, after a quick look
at her, became immersed in her own thoughts.

'I wonder how long we should wait before telephoning?'
she asked suddenly.

'Telephone who?' Laurie asked vaguely.

'Why, the hospital, of course,' Mrs Stephens explained. 'I
want to know how Mr Audley is.'

'Do you?' Laurie said without interest. She stood up and
picked up the tea-tray. 'I don't see that it's necessary, myself, but anyhow, I should think it's much too early at
present. Leave it until the evening, Mother, if you must
ring up, and even then probably all they'll tell you is that
he's quite comfortable, which doesn't mean a thing.'

'Perhaps you're right,' Mrs Stephens admitted regretfully. She hesitated and then went on quietly: 'I know
you've taken a dislike to Mr Audley, Laurie, but I haven't.
I think what happened was a genuine accident, and anyway I intend to give him the benefit of the doubt until I
prove to be wrong. That being so, I intend to behave in a
friendly way both by finding out how he is and later, if he'd
like it, by visiting him in hospital.'

Laurie shrugged her shoulders. Usually she and her
mother were on excellent terms, but now she felt that they
were completely out of touch—and all because of that
wretched man.

'That's up to you, Mother,' she said distantly. 'The only
thing is, please don't involve me!'

'But of course you'll be involved,' Mrs Stephens said

matter-of-factly. 'If I go to the hospital, I shall have to ask you to drive me there. There's no other way except walking, and that's out of the question.'

The Stephens had a car—of a sort. It was old and shabby and had only just scraped through its last M.O.T. test and when, finally, it was condemned, the Stephens would be confronted by still another problem—how were they going to find the money to buy a newer one?

Another problem still was that only Laurie could drive, since her mother firmly refused to learn to. She was not mechanically minded and doubted her ability to pass the necessary driving test on the grounds that just the fact that it was a test would make her forget everything she had ever learned about driving. So either Laurie went on her own to do their shopping or still had to be chauffeur if Mrs Stephens came along. That meant that if she was really determined to visit the Audley man, Laurie would inevitably be involved—but only to a limited degree. On that she was determined.

'Very well, Mother, I'll drive you there, but I don't see why I should visit him. I can easily wait in the car.'

Mrs Stephens made no attempt to argue. She simply said:

'Thank you, dear,' in her sweet, gentle voice and Laurie was left feeling that she had been unreasonable and ungracious. But that was nonsense—and another black mark for Rolf Audley.

And this was the day when she had felt that extraordinary conviction that, from now on, everything was going to be all right!

The report that Mrs Stephens got from the hospital later in the day was that the patient was fully conscious and was as comfortable as could be expected. In answer to Mrs Stephens' query as to whether Mr Audley would like her to visit him, the nurse said that she would enquire. She came back almost immediately with the reply that Mr Audley would be delighted to see both Mrs and Miss Stephens the following day, if possible, in the afternoon.

'So he must be getting on quite well if he feels like having visitors,' Mrs Stephens remarked happily as she came away from the telephone. 'I'm so glad!'

'So am I,' Laurie said emphatically. 'The sooner he's on his feet, the sooner he'll be out of hospital and we won't need to bother about him. Except, of course, to make sure that he pays up for the damage he's done.'

'Oh but, my dear, of course he will,' Mrs Stephens said reproachfully. 'I expect that's what he wants us to see him about.'

'To see you, not me,' Laurie corrected firmly. 'I really do mean it, Mother. I don't intend to have anything more to do with Mr Audley.'

'Very well, dear,' Mrs Stephens said placidly. 'Now, what shall I take him as a little gift? So difficult with men. They don't appreciate flowers like women do.'

'Take him something to eat,' Laurie advised acidly. 'Most men are greedy and I don't suppose he's any different from the rest.'

'What a good idea!' Mrs Stephens said appreciatively. 'Yes, I'll take him that fruit cake I made the day before yesterday. That should last him a few days——'

The next day Laurie drove her mother to the hospital, parked the car and settled down—or rather, tried to settle down—with a book. But it was difficult to concentrate. She was, in fact, worried. She loved her mother dearly, but there was no doubt about it, she was far too soft-hearted for her own good. A man like Rolf Audley would be able to con her into accepting that he was in no way to blame for the damage which he had caused. Perhaps, Laurie thought uneasily, she ought to have gone with her mother——

She was saved the necessity of deciding whether or not, even now, she should change her mind about seeing him by the arrival of a young nurse who had evidently been hurrying out to her.

'Miss Stephens?' she asked breathlessly. 'Mr Audley says he'd be most grateful if you could spare him a few minutes to discuss a matter of business. And Sister says please don't keep him waiting because it would be bad for him to be upset.'

In view of such a message, Laurie had no choice but to get out of the car and follow the nurse, but she felt annoyed at being sent what she felt was an arbitrary summons. As for Sister's anxiety, it really seemed rather absurd. After all, he wasn't a little boy to fly into a tantrum because he couldn't have what he wanted the moment he wanted it.

She followed the nurse down a long corridor and when she opened a door, Laurie saw that Rolf Audley had a private room. He would, of course. That was something that money could do!

She went in and found, to her dismay, that her mother was not there.

'It's all right,' said an amused voice from the bed. 'She'll be back in a few minutes and though I look something of a thug with this black eye, I'm not dangerous. No such luck with my leg in plaster. Do sit down, Miss Stephens.'

Laurie sat down on a chair as far away from the bed as possible and regarded its occupant warily.

His cheek was neatly plastered, but he certainly had got a spectacular black eye. It was all colours of the rainbow.

'Does rather spoil my manly beauty, doesn't it?' he said cheerfully. 'If it really revolts you, try concentrating on the other side of my face. It's more or less planned by nature.'

'The message I received was that you wished to discuss some business matter with me, Mr Audley,' Laurie said coldly.

'Business?' he repeated vaguely. 'Oh yes, that's so. But before doing that, I want to offer you an apology.' He paused and regarded her gravely with his good eye.

Laurie waited for him to go on. Certainly he owed her an apology, but she saw no reason why she should help him out in any way.

'I must have given you a terrific shock, bursting into your peaceful paradise the way I did——'

Laurie tensed. If that was all he felt the need to apologise about——

'You did,' she agreed crisply. 'You also did quite a lot of damage to our hedge and to the stone birdbath.'

'Oh, that!' He dismissed it with an airy wave of the hand. 'That will, of course, be put right at my expense as soon as the garage people haul my car away. They'll be doing that tomorrow.'

'I see,' said Laurie, feeling rather as if the solid ground

had vanished from under her feet. She had felt so sure that she would have to fight for their rights.

There was a brief silence.

'Apology accepted?' he asked, quirking one eyebrow at her.

'Of course,' Laurie told him tonelessly.

Another silence.

'You know,' he said doubtfully, 'I somehow have the feeling that I'm in your black book for something more than hedge-crashing. Am I right?'

'Yes,' Laurie admitted frigidly, 'you are.'

'Chapter and verse, please,' he demanded and, when she didn't answer:

'Oh, come, even a hardened criminal is given a chance to defend himself, and honestly, I'm not that! So please tell me.'

'Very well,' Laurie agreed, 'I will. You were abominably rude to me.'

'I was? But my dear girl—my dear Miss Stephens,' he corrected hastily as she frowned forbiddingly. 'When did I have any chance of being rude to you? I was unconscious——'

'Not all the time——' She was beginning to wish that she hadn't admitted that there was something else.

'Well, do tell,' he begged persuasively. 'Otherwise I shall worry myself into having a temperature and Sister will be cross with me.'

'Very well,' Laurie said recklessly. 'You opened your eyes and looked at me——'

'Well, after all a cat may look——' he began, but Laurie wouldn't let him go on.

'You addressed me as "carrots",' she told him stonily. 'And you said you had a weakness for girls of my colour, particularly if they also had snub noses.'

'I said that!' he exclaimed, half sitting up. 'But my dear —my dear Miss Stephens, how could I have done, even in my battered state!' He stared at her fixedly. 'Your hair is a most glorious auburn, and as for a snub nose—never! Delicately retroussé is the way I would describe it.'

And now, of course, he would think that she had been fishing for compliments!

'You also winked at me in a most—most unpleasant way,' she concluded.

'Oh!' He considered that. 'But don't you think that could have been a purely reflex action due to the pain I was suffering?'

Laurie thought nothing of the sort, but she was saved the necessity of telling him so by the arrival of her mother. Mrs Stephens trotted into the room looking thoroughly pleased with herself. Laurie tensed herself apprehensively. She knew that look of her mother's——

'Well, that's all right, Mr Audley,' Mrs Stephens said with satisfaction. 'Sister thinks it's an excellent plan!'

'Just what is the plan, Mother?' Laurie asked, though in her bones she felt she knew what the answer was going to be.

'Why, darling, that when Mr Audley is discharged from hospital, he'll come to us to convalesce,' Mrs Stephens explained brightly. 'It's a very good idea, don't you think?'

'No, I don't,' Laurie contradicted flatly. 'The Ranch is an hotel, not a nursing home. We have no facilities for the care of an invalid. There's no lift and no man who could help Mr Audley upstairs——'

'Oh, but I assure you, Miss Stephens, I shall be very little trouble.' Rolf was very serious now and Laurie realised that having made up his mind, he was unlikely to be deflected by anything she might say. 'You see, Hutton will be with me.'

'Hutton?'

'My chauffeur-valet-cum-general factotum,' Rolf Audley explained. 'I've never yet discovered anything he can't turn his hand to, so I'm quite sure he'll make a good nanny.'

Laurie made one last effort.

'But you're surely ill advised to commit yourself to—I suppose about six weeks in an hotel you know nothing about,' she suggested discouragingly.

'Oh, Hutton will come over tomorrow and make sure that everything is O.K.,' he assured her airily. 'That's all arranged, isn't it, Mrs Stephens?'

'Yes, indeed,' Mrs Stephens confirmed, though she took good care not to meet Laurie's eyes. 'I'll expect Hutton about eleven o'clock, Mr Audley, as we arranged.'

'He'll be there on the dot, Mrs Stephens,' Rolf Audley promised. 'I can't thank you enough for your kindness. I was really worried.'

'Well, you needn't be any more,' Mrs Stephens declared reassuringly. 'And now, Mr Audley, I think we'd better leave you. All this planning must have tired you.'

'A bit, perhaps,' he admitted, and smiled in what Laurie felt was a revoltingly ingratiating way. 'Goodbye for the present, Mrs Stephens, and thank you again. And, of course,' he added after the slightest of pauses, 'you too, Miss Stephens.'

Ignoring him, Laurie stalked out of the room, followed by her mother who looked rather anxious. Neither of them spoke until they were clear of the hospital grounds. Then Laurie said indignantly:

'Mother, how *could* you!'

'Because it was the only thing to do,' Mrs Stephens declared. 'Oh yes, it was, Laurie. That poor young man has no relatives whatever—at least, not in this country. He's got a sister in Canada, but that's no help.'

'Then why couldn't he have gone to a nursing home? I'm quite sure he could afford to.'

'Oh yes, no doubt he could,' Mrs Stephens agreed. 'But quite the wrong atmosphere for a young man who isn't really *ill*. As he said, so depressing to be surrounded by people who are. No, what he needs is a cheerful, homely place——' Then very quietly she went on: 'That's looking at it from his point of view. Have you considered ours?'

'Of course I have,' Laurie said impatiently. 'That's why——'

'Now listen, Laurie,' Mrs Stephens said firmly. 'I *do* want to help Mr Audley. But even if I didn't, I'd still be glad that he and his man are coming. Don't you realise what it means? We're in no position to turn him away. *We need the money!*'

And that, Laurie had to admit, was an argument which she could not refute.

Hutton arrived the following morning exactly on time. He

was a stocky, middle-aged man with a pleasant manner which, while it was not subservient, was certainly not in the least familiar. Mrs Stephens took to him on sight and Laurie knew that so would she have done if he had not come on behalf of Rolf Audley.

As it was, and remembering how positively eager her mother had been to have the wretched man here, she decided that this time she would be present throughout the interview. There must be no unreasonable concessions, no matter how hard up they were.

At first everything went smoothly. Hutton approved of the lounge and the dining room and waxed enthusiastic over the kitchen.

'The nerve-centre of any well run establishment,' he commented, 'whether it be a private home or an hotel. And now, if I may see the bedroom accommodation——'

This, too, he approved, and indeed there was every reason why he should. They were all simply furnished, the curtains and bedspreads were fresh and colourful and all had a view of the sea.

'Charming,' he commented, but Laurie thought she detected a note of doubt in the way he said it.

At the top of the stairs as they were going down, the reason for his manner became apparent. He paused for a moment, shook his head and turned to Mrs Stephens.

'Everything you have shown me I've found entirely suitable—with one exception. These stairs. Even with my help, with his leg in plaster, I don't see how Mr Audley could negotiate them.'

Laurie's heart gave a little jump. Hutton was quite right. It was a tricky staircase—narrow and with deep steps and with two awkward twists in it. So perhaps, after all——

Mrs Stephens murmured:

'Yes, I suppose so,' in a disappointed way, but Hutton still had something more to say.

'Of course, what would be really convenient would be accommodation on the ground floor. Indeed, Mr Audley mentioned that you have a suite so situated. Now, if that was available——'

'It isn't,' Laurie snapped. 'The suite, as you call it, is

Mother's and my private quarters. We don't let it.'

'Oh, I quite understand,' Hutton said gravely. 'And so, I'm sure, will Mr Audley. Perhaps, however, you wouldn't mind me seeing it—in case, at any time, you desire to make different arrangements.'

'We have no intention of doing that,' Laurie insisted firmly.

But it was no use. Mrs Stephens was already leading the way to their rooms and half an hour later she had agreed to let Rolf Audley have the whole suite for the period of his convalescence. She and Laurie could quite easily make do with two of the upstairs rooms.

On his employer's behalf, Hutton expressed warm gratitude for the consideration that had been shown. Then he named the amount that Mr Audley would be willing to pay for the accommodation. It was so colossal that even Laurie's breath was taken away and Mrs Stephens protested that it was too much. But that Hutton dismissed with an airy wave of his hand.

'Not at all, madam. The accommodation is ideal,' he insisted. 'The larger room for Mr Audley, of course, but the smaller one will be most satisfactory for me. I shall be within easy call should he require my services during the night. Besides, you're making the suite available at the cost of personal sacrifice to yourself. That must, of course, be taken into consideration.'

When he had gone, Mrs Stephens turned to Laurie.

'I'm sorry, dear, but what else could I do?' she asked apologetically. And then, as Laurie didn't reply: 'And you must admit that the money is quite wonderful.'

'Yes,' Laurie conceded, 'it is. But what I don't understand is how it was that Hutton was able to tell us what Mr Audley would be willing to pay without reference to him.'

'I don't see——' Mrs Stephens said doubtfully.

'Oh, but surely!' Laurie said impatiently. 'He came already primed with what Mr Audley would be willing to pay. That can only mean that he—Mr Audley—had made up his mind to have our rooms *before* Hutton came.'

'Yes, that is rather peculiar,' Mrs Stephens agreed. 'Because I'm quite sure I didn't tell him what accommodation we'd kept for ourselves.' She pondered momentarily and then shrugged her shoulders. 'Oh well, it's not really of any importance, now is it? He's coming, that's the important thing.'

'I suppose it is,' Laurie admitted grudgingly.

But privately, she was thinking that, if in addition to his other unpleasant characteristics there was some mystery about Rolf Audley, it really *was* the last straw. How could he have known about the suite?

CHAPTER TWO

THE next day the damaged car was towed away, dragging more of the hedge with it. It looked a sorry sight, but Laurie was far more concerned with the condition of the hedge. It must have taken years to grow to the height and depth that it had and it was impossible to imagine that it could ever regain its previous sturdiness. Of course, in a way that didn't matter. Actually nothing had been said about Rolf Audley having the use of the Stephens' little garden, but seeing that the long windows of the sitting room over-looked it, Laurie couldn't visualise herself relaxing at her ease in the hammock—not with those keen blue eyes watching her. Besides, the only way into the garden, other than by a little wicket gate which was always kept locked, was through the sitting room. The same applied to the sec-tion of the verandah which the Stephens had kept for their own use. That, too, was guarded by a locked gate from the rest of the verandah. Evidently the previous owners had treasured their privacy. Probably the mother and father who, though no doubt fond of their family, liked to have something which was exclusively their own. And now Rolf Audley was going to benefit by that.

He was coming in three days' time and as Laurie pre-pared the rooms, largely by stripping them of every single personal possession of her mother's and her own, she seethed with resentment—resentment which was all the more intense because she had to admit that her mother was right. They did need the money, and the huge amount the man was willing to pay to gratify his whims made her feel that she was expected to be grateful.

'The sort of man who thinks that money can buy every-thing,' she thought bitterly as she took down pictures and emptied the bookshelves. And the worst of it was that in this case, it was just what money *had* done.

Hutton came to the Ranch the following day bringing

cases of clothes belonging to his employer and himself. His expression as he looked round the rooms suggested that he noticed how bare they were, but he made no comment about it. Later, he went into some detail with Mrs Stephens as to domestic arrangements and the timing of meals.

He made it quite clear that he expected to wait on his employer, particularly as, for the present, at least, Mr Audley would prefer to have his meals in his own quarters.

'He's a little sensitive about his condition, madam,' he explained. 'He prefers not to excite pity or curiosity. I'm sure you will understand and, of course, it will not occasion additional work for your staff because I shall do the necessary waiting.'

'Yes, I do understand,' Mrs Stephens said sympathetically. 'But there is one difficulty——'

'Yes, madam?'

'Well, of course, I do all the actual cooking, but Miss Trewyn, who helps me, is inclined to regard it as *her* kitchen and she—she might not like it if you——'

'If I invaded the kitchen premises?' Hutton suggested blandly. 'I understand, and I sympathise with her attitude. I've felt it myself on some occasions.' He frowned slightly, then his face cleared. 'If I may suggest it, madam, do you think it would be a good idea if Miss Trewyn and I were to meet before we actually take up residence? A formal introduction might perhaps ease the situation.'

'Yes, it might,' Mrs Stephens agreed, considerably relieved at his understanding. She stood up. 'Miss Trewyn is working out there now—giving the pantry its weekly cleaning, I think.'

Miss Trewyn was the spinster sister of Trewyn, the gardener, and ran his house for him. But since she was an energetic soul this still left time on her hands and she spent almost more time at the Ranch than was necessary.

She was a tall, spare woman of what is usually described as being of uncertain age which meant, as it so often does, that most people knew just how old she was but were too diplomatic to mention it.

She had very definite views on most things and didn't hesitate to voice them, so it was with some trepidation that Mrs Stephens performed the introduction. She need not have worried. Hutton was more than competent to deal with the situation. When Mrs Stephens left them a few minutes later a pleasant relationship had already been established.

'I've never seen anything like it,' Mrs Stephens marvelled to Laurie. 'He got on her right side with no difficulty at all—she was actually laughing over a mild joke he'd made when I left them. And she isn't the laughing sort as a rule.' She sighed contentedly. 'And he was lending her a hand with the pastry.'

'I hope it lasts,' Laurie commented, but Mrs Stephens didn't seem to hear.

'I must say, I find it rather pleasant to have men about the place,' she said reflectively. 'Somehow, a house in which there are only women seems so unbalanced.'

'On the contrary, I think men are likely to have a disturbing effect,' Laurie said sharply, and was vexed to see that her mother was regarding her with interested curiosity. Laurie felt the colour surge to her cheeks. Surely to goodness her mother wasn't anticipating a romance between Rolf Audley and herself? She stood up abruptly. The sooner that notion was scotched, the better! 'Geoffrey rang up while you were talking to Hutton,' she said casually. 'He wants me to have dinner with him in Penzance this evening and I said I would.'

Geoffrey Mellors was a man of about her own age whom she had known for some years. There had never been any suggestion of a romance between them, but they had become good friends. Geoffrey was an easy-going sort of person, cheerful and good company. Laurie enjoyed her occasional outings with him, particularly as there was one trait in his character which made a special appeal to her. He never spoke of his work, preferring to keep their conversation to more interesting topics. He was frank about his reason for this. He worked in the accounts department of a big firm and, as he said, what girl would be interested in hearing about the facts and figures of his daily grind?

As Laurie dressed for the evening she turned over in her mind whether she should tell him of the events of the last few days and decided that she wouldn't. Geoffrey knew, of course, of the venture, but she had never discussed it in detail with him. Still less had she referred to their lack of success so far. That would have acted as a dampener on any outing, particularly seeing how Geoffrey felt about leaving work behind him when he was all set to enjoy himself.

Now, however, there was another reason why she decided not to take him into her confidence. She didn't want to talk about Rolf Audley. He was a disturbing element in her life and she wanted to forget all about him for a few hours at least.

When she went downstairs, her mother looked at her approvingly.

'You look very nice, dear. That yellow dress suits you.' She sighed wistfully. 'It does a woman good to dress up for an occasion!'

Laurie laughed.

'I'd hardly call going out with Geoffrey an occasion— at least, not with a capital letter. Just a pleasant outing. And that reminds me, Mother, it's a dinner-dance we're going to, so I'll probably be home fairly late, so don't worry.'

'Well, do drive carefully,' Mrs Stephens said anxiously. 'We don't want another accident!'

'*Another?*' Laurie said sharply.

'Oh yes, I forgot to tell you. Hutton says that Mr Audley has had a report from the garage and they say that something went disastrously wrong with the steering mechanism. I'm afraid I didn't grasp just what it was—you know how stupid I am about that sort of thing—but apparently if it had happened in traffic there could have been a *terrible* accident and Mr Audley could easily have been killed. Have you got a wrap, dear? It will be quite chilly by the time you're coming home.'

The sudden change of subject was a characteristic of Mrs Stephens' conversation which could produce chaotic results, but this time Laurie welcomed it.

'Yes, I'm taking my velvet jacket,' she said, holding up the article in question and making no mention of the earlier subject.

So it had been a genuine accident. She supposed that meant that she ought to take a more tolerant view of Rolf Audley. But she just didn't want to. Instinct told her that he was a man who was better kept at arm's length, and dislike did just that.

'Anyway, with a car as powerful as that, he ought to be more careful than one usually is to have it overhauled regularly,' she told herself critically as she got into her own car, encouraged to deeper resentment because it was so small and shabby. Why should some people have all the luck and others none? It simply wasn't fair!

Geoffrey was waiting for her at the hotel where they were to dine and dance and she felt a lifting of her spirits as he greeted her. Geoffrey Mellors could certainly not be described as handsome, but he had a pleasant, boyish face and a ready smile which gave character to his face. He would, Laurie knew, entertain and amuse her, and that was just what she wanted. Nor was he the sort of young man who indulged in meaningless kisses and caresses—and he was quite frank about his reason for this.

'I don't want to give any girl a false impression,' he had told Laurie early in their acquaintance. 'One of these days I expect I'll get married, but not yet. The fact is, on the salary I get I can't afford to. At least, I suppose I could if we pinched and scraped and my wife carried on working. But I've seen just what havoc that can cause with even the most promising marriage. So—not for me, thank you. I prefer to wait—for the girl's sake as well as for my own. Not that I shall ever be really rich, but at least one of these days I'll be able to afford to pay for some fun as well as for our bread and butter!'

And Laurie agreed with every word. She, too, had seen the disastrous results of improvident marriages and as she wasn't in the least in love with Geoffrey neither her pride nor her emotions were hurt.

As a matter of fact, at twenty-three, Laurie had never been in love, and as she listened to other girls' accounts of their love affairs, she wondered if there was something unusual about her. Was she naturally cold by nature or was it that, so far, she had not met the right man?

'*Mr Right.*' That was how old-fashioned novelists referred to the man of their heroine's choice. Was it true? Was there only one man with whom one could possibly find happiness? If that was so, then Laurie simply couldn't imagine what he would be like. One would say things like: 'Reasonably good-looking, intelligent, good-tempered and with a sense of humour', but no matter how long a list she made she knew that there was something missing—something that couldn't be put into words.

What was the divine spark which lit up the lives of two quite ordinary people and fused them into one? Of course, the answer was quite simple—*love*. But it was a very special sort of love, and there Laurie had to give up. She couldn't envisage an emotion which entailed—which welcomed—the sharing of one's whole life with another person. Giving up one's individuality—no, it was something that was entirely beyond her and so, in the meantime, friendship with Geoffrey, undemanding and even superficial, suited her perfectly.

Yet as he walked towards her, smiling and clearly appreciating her appearance, an involuntary sense of disappointment possessed her. For the first time since they had known one another she felt that she was seeing him with a clarity that was disturbing. It was as if she had somehow acquired a standard with which to compare him—and he fell short of it. He was so—so ordinary!

'Oh, what nonsense,' she reproached herself crossly. 'There's nobody I could compare him with!'

She wouldn't let herself think any more along those lines and deliberately set herself to making the evening just as successful as she possibly could.

Perhaps she tried a little too hard, for after a while she realised that Geoffrey was looking at her with marked curiosity. And then he put out his hand and laid it over hers—something he had never done before.

'What's happened, Laurie?' he asked softly.

'Happened?' she asked, taken aback.

'Yes, to you,' he explained. 'I've never seen you like this before—you seem a different person!'

'Do I?' she laughed uncertainly. 'I'm sorry!'

'You needn't be,' he told her, giving her hand a little squeeze. 'You're—enchanting. As if something important has happened to you. That's why I asked if it had.'

'Well, I suppose in a way it has,' she fenced cautiously. 'You know how worried Mother and I have been about not as many people booking accommodation as we'd hoped? Well,' as he nodded, 'a day or so ago a man arrived unexpectedly and as a result he and a manservant have reserved accommodation for six whole weeks! Isn't it marvellous? It's just going to make all the difference and it's given me the feeling that perhaps our luck has turned the corner!'

And every word of that was true, even if she hadn't told him the whole story. But what an odd thing that she was making use of Rolf Audley to explain her high spirits! Perhaps, though, in a way it was true. After all, it was because she had been so depressed by the way in which he had so selfishly got everything that he wanted that she had put on this pretence of gaiety . . .

'Two men?' Geoffrey said sharply. 'Strangers?'

'Of course,' Laurie said impatiently. 'As this is our first season, anybody that comes is bound to be a stranger.'

'Yes, of course,' he admitted. 'But doesn't it strike you as a bit out of the ordinary for two men to have turned up out of the blue like that? I don't like it, Laurie. They might be wanting somewhere to lie low for a time—did they say how they came to hear of the Ranch?'

'No,' Laurie said shortly, 'they didn't.' And she added mendaciously, 'Of course, they could have seen one of our advertisements—or a brochure.'

And why in the world, she asked herself, didn't she tell Geoffrey that Rolf Audley had been recognised by one of the ambulance men and, in a way, had been vouched for by him? She didn't know—but she did know that she had no intention of telling him.

'I still don't like it,' Geoffrey demurred. 'I hadn't realised it before, but two women on their own——' he shook his head. 'It could be dangerous.' He paused and then said impetuously: 'I wish to goodness there was something I could do about it.'

'Well, there isn't,' Laurie assured him. 'So don't let's talk about it any more, please! Oh—listen! That's an old-fashioned waltz they're playing. Let's dance, shall we?'

Geoffrey danced well, as he always did, but tonight there was something mechanical about his performance as if his mind was on something else. Nor did that air of preoccupation leave him for the rest of the evening. As a result, conversation lagged and Laurie wasn't sorry when it was time to go home.

Geoffrey saw her into her car and refused her offer to drop him off at his flat, but though she turned on the ignition, he still stood with his hand on the car's open window.

Laurie looked enquiringly at him. He was scowling darkly and staring at her with disconcerting intensity. She must have looked a question, for suddenly he burst into speech.

'If only I could afford it, I'd soon get you out of this mess,' he declared angrily.

Too taken aback to answer, Laurie stared at him blankly.

'I mean—if my boss wasn't such a skinflint, I'd ask you to marry me,' Geoffrey blurted out.

'*Marry* me!' Laurie gasped incredulously. 'But why? You know as well as I do that neither of us——'

'Oh, I know,' he muttered, scuffing one foot on the ground. 'We've just been good friends. But surely that's a good foundation to build on. And anyway, you were different tonight, Laurie.'

'That was just your imagination, Geoffrey,' Laurie said hastily. 'Honestly, I'm just the same as ever I've been.'

'Oh no, you're not,' he contradicted. 'There's a—a sort of glow about you—I don't know how else to describe it. It's as if——' he paused. 'Laurie, you haven't fallen for some other chap, have you?'

'No, I have *not*,' Laurie denied fiercely. 'And I'm sorry, Geoffrey, but I haven't fallen for you, either. So please, please don't——' She bit her lip, reluctant to hurt his feelings but quite sure that she was right not to leave him in any doubt.

He took his hand off the car at that and stood back.

'Oh well, if you haven't, you haven't,' he said, and for the life of her, she wasn't sure whether he was relieved or disappointed at her frankness. 'No hard feelings?'

'Of course not,' Laurie assured him. 'And thank you for taking me out, Geoffrey.'

'Be seeing you,' he said automatically. Laurie slipped into gear and left him standing there. She drove home in a pre-occupied frame of mind.

'*Be seeing you!*' But would they see one another again now that Geoffrey had made that astonishing declaration? Of course, he hadn't actually proposed to her, but he had said that he wished he could. That could mean that when he earned more, as he would, sooner or later, he *would* ask her definitely to marry him. And if, in the meantime, she allowed him to think that she would agree—no, it wouldn't be fair to him or to herself to let such a vague, indecisive state of affairs drift on indefinitely. Geoffrey might change his mind—and yet feel that he was honour bound to her. While she—well, she had never thought of him as anything but a pleasant friend, and tonight she had known beyond all doubt that she could never fall in love with him.

'But as for there being anyone else—what utter nonsense!' she told herself with conviction. 'All the same, I think it would be better not to go out with Geoffrey again —at least not for a long time until he's forgotten this nonsense!'

Rolf Audley's occupation of the Stephens' quarters was carried out with so little fuss that within an incredibly short time one could almost believe that he had always been there and was a permanent fixture.

'But only six weeks,' Laurie cheered herself by saying. 'Then he'll go!'

In the meantime she forced herself to admit that she had got to accept his presence with as good a grace as she could muster. But it wasn't easy, and only by avoiding him as far as possible could she achieve anything like success.

He spent quite a lot of time on the verandah and even in the little garden, for Hutton and Trewyn between them had devised a wooden ramp which covered the two steps between the verandah and the garden down which Rolf's wheelchair could be propelled.

From either of these vantage points he had a good view of the comings and goings to and from the house. As a result, Laurie was aware of watching eyes whenever she went out shopping and though, of course, that didn't really matter, it was irritating.

He was able, too, to supervise the replanting of the hedge that he had damaged, and he saw to it not only that the job was well done but that, once it was planted with well-grown shrubs, Hutton kept it well watered.

'I'm afraid it will be some time before they reach the size of the originals,' he apologised to Mrs Stephens, 'but at least they look reasonably healthy.'

'They do, indeed,' Mrs Stephens agreed. 'And the bird bath is very much nicer than the original one was. I'm afraid you paid a great deal for it, Mr Audley!'

'Well, I never really liked the original,' Rolf said absently, and quickly checked himself. 'So long as you like it——?'

'Oh, I *do*,' Mrs Stephens assured him warmly.

'And Miss Stephens?' Rolf asked.

'Actually, she hasn't said,' Mrs Stephens told him carefully. 'But I assume she would have done if——'

'If she hadn't liked it?' Rolf asked quizzically. 'Yes, I expect she would. And now, tell me how Hutton is getting on with your staff. Well, I hope?'

'Oh, splendidly,' Mrs Stephens assured him enthusiastically, glad that the conversation had turned away from Laurie. 'I've never known Miss Trewyn be so amiable, but that isn't surprising. Hutton doesn't seem to mind what he turns his hand to—and so cheerfully. He's a treasure, Mr Audley, and I feel I ought to pay part of his salary.'

'Oh, Hutton would never hear of that—and nor would I,' Rolf replied emphatically. 'Lucky chap, he can always find something to do to keep himself busy while I——' he glowered at his plastered leg and tapped it irritably with the stick he always used when walking.

'Yes, it must be trying,' Mrs Stephens said sympathetically. 'I expect you're very active as a rule and you miss the sports you're used to.'

Rolf looked at her thoughtfully and shook his head.

'I've only been able to indulge in a very limited amount

of sport for some years,' he told her, and then, seeing her surprise, he smiled. 'Haven't you realised that I'm a hard-working business man, Mrs Stephens?'

'No—no, I hadn't,' Mrs Stephens stammered. 'I really don't know why, though. I had no right to assume——'

'That I'm an idle layabout?' he suggested whimsically. 'Oh, you're not the only person who has formed that opinon of me! Evidently I look the part,' he concluded plaintively.

'Well, if you've got a job—and you like it—then of course you must be missing it now,' Mrs Stephens suggested, rallying gamely.

'I am,' Rolf said shortly. 'In fact, I'm wondering—you see, I'd planned to take a week's holiday, but six weeks! That's a very different matter.'

'Will you lose your job?' Mrs Stephens asked anxiously.

Rolf smiled.

'No. I'm my own boss. But really that only makes mat-ters worse. You see, I prefer to keep the management of the firm in my own hands. It really is impossible to dele-gate the making of decisions.'

'Yes, I suppose so,' Mrs Stephens agreed doubtfully. 'So what are you going to do about it?'

'With your permission, I'm going to work here,' Rolf told her crisply. 'It will mean having my secretary come here daily and perhaps one or two other people from time to time. It will also mean that I have a lot of documents and other things to study, but——' he smiled reassuringly, 'I promise not to make a mess of this delightful room, par-ticularly if you'll let me import a good large desk——?'

Mrs Stephens looked round the room.

'Where will you put it?' she asked practically.

'I thought in the window bay if that small table could be taken away,' he explained, showing no triumph at hav-ing gained his point.

'Well, I really can't see why not,' Mrs Stephens said consideringly. 'It will keep you——'

'Out of mischief?'

Mrs Stephens laughed. She did like this nice man, and for the life of her, she couldn't understand why Laurie was so prejudiced against him.

'I was going to say—happy,' she told him. 'You go ahead with your arrangements. It will be quite all right.'

'Thank you!' he said gratefully, and already his hand stretched out to the telephone.

It was only when Mrs Stephens had left him that it occurred to her to wonder why, for all his frankness, he had not told her what his job was. '*Documents and other things.*' That might mean absolutely anything. She simply couldn't guess.

When she did hear, she was absolutely astonished. Miss Trewyn was her informant and she seemed to have no doubt about the correctness of her information. But then she never did if she made a statement. She prided herself on that.

'You know that big factory on the Penzance Road?' she asked. 'Well, that's his. Toys & Games Unlimited, it's called, but really it's Mr Rolf. It's a family business. His grandfather started it and then his father carried it on. And now, since his death, Mr Rolf has been in charge. And making a very good thing of it, so I hear.'

'I'm sure he is,' Mrs Stephens said abstractedly. 'But toys —I must say that comes as something of a surprise!'

It came as a surprise to Laurie as well when her mother told her. In fact, she burst out laughing.

'Oh, Mother, what nonsense! He was pulling your leg!'

'But it wasn't Mr Audley who told me,' Mrs Stephens explained. 'It was Miss Trewyn. And you know, she's got a positive *thing* about never passing on information unless she knows it's true.'

Laurie did know it, and her expression became serious.

'What an extraordinary thing,' she said slowly. 'And not a very pleasant one.'

'Not pleasant?' Mrs Stephens repeated blankly. 'What on earth do you mean, Laurie?'

'Well—making money out of children, because that's what it comes to.'

'It does nothing of the sort,' Mrs Stephens retorted severely. 'I never heard anything so silly in all my life! What would children do if no one was allowed to make toys? Christmas without them—just think of it! *You* wouldn't have liked it, my dear, let me tell you that!'

'All the same——' Laurie said rebelliously.

'No, Laurie,' Mrs Stephens said with an authority she rarely assumed, 'you're being most unfair—and you know it! The fact is that you're disappointed because Mr Audley isn't the playboy you'd decided he was. And another thing, it was something wrong with the car that caused the accident, and you know that as well. So——' with an air of extreme logic, 'why have you got this absurd prejudice against a very pleasant young man?'

'Because——' Laurie began, and stopped short.

How could she possibly explain that there was something about Rolf Audley which made her instinctively on her guard? His ability to get his own way, that unpleasant feeling that he regarded her as just one more stupid girl who would surrender to his so-called charm——

She shrugged her shoulders.

'Just a case of Dr Fell, I suppose,' she suggested indifferently. 'Still, I suppose I can put up with him for six weeks.'

After Mrs Stephens had agreed to Rolf's requests, events moved swiftly. The little table was removed and the desk put in its place, boxes, bundles of papers and a typewriter arrived—and Laurie met Rolf's secretary.

She arrived on a morning when Laurie was returning from the kitchen garden with fresh supplies for the day. She was wearing shabby old dungarees she kept for such jobs and her hair was tousled with contact with intrusive fruit bushes. Altogether, she was in no condition to welcome meeting one of the most superlatively chic girls she had ever seen.

Sylvia French was tall and slim but that didn't mean that she hadn't got an intriguing figure. She had a pale, clear skin, dark hair and eyes—and she knew how to choose and wear her clothes.

And what clothes! They were what caught and held Laurie's attention, for in her way she was just as well dressed as Rolf himself was. Her white dress, made of a linen-type material, was beautifully cut and styled, emphasising her figure and conveying the impression of expensiveness. All her accessories were black—belt, handbag, high-heeled shoes and a small black scarf over her dark hair. No jewellery except a wrist watch and black pearl studs in her ears. Probably real ones, too, Laurie decided. A present from Rolf? Well, she was certainly the type of girl to whom men did give presents——

'Miss Stephens?' she enquired doubtfully, and Laurie noticed the first flaw in her. A girl who looked as attractive as this one did ought to have a voice to match. This one hadn't. On the contrary, there was a harshly strident quality about it.

'Yes, I'm Laurie Stephens,' Laurie said coolly. 'And you, I expect, are Mr Audley's secretary. He said he was expecting you.'

'Yes, I'm Sylvia French and you're right, he *is* expecting me,' the girl said shortly. 'And having got that satisfactorily settled, I'll be glad if you'll show me the way to his rooms. Mr Audley doesn't like to be kept waiting.'

'What you mean is *you* don't like to be kept waiting!' Laurie thought, but aloud all she said was: 'If you'll follow me——'

In the hall, without setting down the big basket she was carrying, she indicated the door leading to the suite.

'That leads into a small passage off which all the doors open,' she explained. 'The sitting room door is that furthest to the right.'

Sylvia, with a flick of her dark brows which clearly indicated that she thought Laurie should have opened the door for her, went in, leaving it open. That was how Laurie came to hear the greeting between Rolf and his secretary since he had come out of the sitting room to welcome her.

'Sylvia, my dear, you're a sight for sore eyes!' he declared warmly. 'You don't know how I've been looking forward to you coming.'

'You poor dear!' Sylvia said sympathetically. 'You must have been frightfully bored with only——'

The inner door closed and Laurie closed the outer one. She had heard quite enough. Feminine intuition told her that Sylvia French was going to be a troublemaker and, of course, no matter how unreasonable she might be, Rolf

would side with her. They seemed to be on excellent terms
—in fact, Laurie wondered if their relationship was just
that of employer and secretary or whether it was something more personal.

'Well, if it is, serve them both right,' she thought venge-
fully, and took the basket out to the kitchen.

Mrs Stephens looked up from the bowl in which she was
mixing pastry.

'I heard voices,' she remarked. 'Was that Miss French?'

'It was,' Laurie said briefly.

'What's she like?'

'Very well dressed. Very sure of herself and, no doubt,
the perfect secretary,' Laurie told her, setting the basket
down with a thump. 'She and Mr Audley seem to get on very
well together.'

'Oh!' Mrs Stephens digested this in silence. 'Well, that's
just as well, isn't it? I mean, it would never do if an important man like Mr Audley had a secretary who got on
his nerves, would it?'

'I suppose so,' Laurie agreed indifferently. 'Shall I get on
with preparing the vegetables?'

'If you will, dear. Miss Trewyn phoned through to say
she'll be here in time to do the washing up but she had to
wait at home for a parcel to be delivered. Did Miss French
say if she was staying to lunch?'

'No, she didn't. But it wouldn't surprise me if she did.
And——' Laurie added mentally, 'it will be left to the last
minute before either of them thinks of telling us.'

'Oh well, it won't matter if she does,' Mrs Stephens said
comfortably. 'I'm making a steak and kidney pie with
duchesse potatoes and spring cabbage followed by orange
snow and cream. And of course, cheese and biscuits.
There'll easily be enough for an extra person. Just do a
few more vegetables in case, dear.'

It was just as well that they had taken that precaution,
for barely half an hour before it was time for the meal to
be served, Hutton came out to the kitchen.

'Mr Audley was wondering if it would be possible for
Miss French to lunch here,' he said, and though his manner wasn't apologetic, it was clear that he hadn't relished

giving the message. 'He realises, of course, that it's very short notice to give, but——'

'That's quite all right, Hutton,' Mrs Stephens assured him equably, and told him what the menu would be.

'Excellent, madam,' Hutton said with relief. 'But there is just one other thing——'

'Yes?'

'Would it be possible for the meal to be served in the dining room instead of in Mr Audley's sitting room?' Hutton asked, and this time his manner was unmistakably apologetic. 'You see, it's been necessary for Mr Audley to use both the desk and the table to spread out various papers and so on and it would be inconvenient for him to have to tidy everything away to make room——'

'Oh—now, Hutton, that would be rather inconvenient,' Mrs Stephens said worriedly, her forefinger pressed to her cheek. 'You see, we haven't really got the dining room ready yet and I haven't engaged any special waiting staff yet——'

'With your permission, madam, I would do the waiting—just at the one table, of course.'

'Yes——' Mrs Stephens agreed, knowing only too well that it would be the only table in use. 'Very well, Hutton, that will be a great help. I'll see about having a table laid——'

'I shall be glad to do that as well, madam,' Hutton assured her. 'I'll let Mr Audley know that you've kindly agreed to the arrangement.'

He went out and Mrs Stephens looked at Laurie, who had been careful to take no part in the conversation.

'Do you know,' Mrs Stephens said reflectively, 'I got the impression that not only did Hutton not like having to give the message but that he doesn't like Miss French. What did you think?'

Laurie shrugged her shoulders. Having been accused of prejudice where Rolf was concerned, she had no wish to risk a similar charge in connection with Sylvia French.

'Oh, I suppose there could be a certain amount of friction between domestic and office staff,' she suggested casually.

'Jealousy, you mean?' Mrs Stephens looked thoughtful. 'Yes, I suppose there could be if each of them feels that they're invaluable to Mr Audley's comfort. Well, Hutton certainly is. Miss French———?'

'Well, I told you, she's probably the perfect secretary,' Laurie reminded her. 'Anyhow, if there is any friction, it's up to Mr Audley to sort it out, isn't it? It's no business of ours.'

'That's true, of course,' Mrs Stephens agreed. 'All the same, I do like everything to be pleasant.' She sighed and shook her head. 'I'm sure it isn't intentional on Mr Audley's part, but he does seem to be the sort of person who rouses strong feelings in other people. I'm beginning to wonder if it was wise to have him here.'

'Well, we need the money,' Laurie reminded her rather unkindly. 'And at least the extra lunch can be added to Mr Audley's account.'

To which her mother made no reply other than a heart-felt sigh.

It was not until well on into the afternoon that Sylvia French left the Ranch and when she did, unfortunately she encountered Laurie in the hall.

Sylvia had closed the door leading to the suite when she saw Laurie and halted, leaning languidly against the door.

Laurie, aware that now she was wearing a dress which, if it wasn't as chic as Sylvia's, certainly became her, smiled politely.

'Good afternoon, Miss French,' she said pleasantly.

'Oh—Miss Stephens,' Sylvia said curtly, 'I'm glad to have an opportunity of speaking to you. About the lunch you served———'

'I noticed that you left a lot uneaten. Wasn't it to your liking?' Laurie met her eyes squarely. The girl was so obviously out to make trouble that it seemed idle to try to avoid it.

'Oh, no doubt, very good of its kind,' Sylvia said disparagingly. 'But so *hearty*! Even stodgy. And such colossal helpings.'

'We like to give value for money,' Laurie told her.

'Oh, estimable, no doubt,' Sylvia retorted unpleasantly. 'But surely, in view of the absurd amount that Rolf—Mr Audley is paying for his accommodation, you won't have the temerity to charge him extra for my lunch?'

One thing about the possession of auburn hair, as Laurie knew only too well, is that almost invariably a quick temper goes with it. She felt hers bubbling up now, but checked it sternly, since to give way to it would only put her at a disadvantage with this deliberate troublemaker.

'Yes, your lunch will certainly be added to Mr Audley's account,' she said matter-of-factly, 'since no arrangement was made when he first came about having guests. But I shouldn't worry if I were you. I'm quite sure that Mr Audley is perfectly capable of making his own protest if he feels he's being overcharged.'

Sylvia's dark eyes snapped angrily.

'You're being impertinent, Miss Stephens,' she said stridently. 'I'm not used——'

'Oh, that was the last thing I meant to be,' Laurie assured her in a deceptively soft voice. 'On the contrary, I intended being sympathetic.'

'*Sympathetic!*'

'Yes.' Laurie spoke even more softly. 'It must be trying to have to watch each mouthful you eat for fear of getting fat.' She paused deliberately. 'I'm so lucky that way. My weight never varies from one year's end to the next.'

For a moment she thought Sylvia was going to hit her. Her hands clenched and unclenched spasmodically and her face was contorted with fury. Then evidently she thought better of it and pushing roughly past Laurie, she almost ran out of the Ranch.

Laurie watched her go, wide-eyed.

'My goodness, I thought I'd got a temper!' she thought in awe. 'But I'm simply not in her class! All the same, I suppose I ought not to have said——' and she changed her mind. 'Why shouldn't I have done?' she demanded of the empty air. 'She was insufferably rude and she asked for it. But I wonder why she went for me like that? It was almost as if she thought I'd got designs on Mr Audley and she was warning me off! How stupid can people be? She's welcome to him and for two pins I'd tell her so—only I don't suppose she'd believe me. Oh well, she'll soon find out for herself that I'm not interested—but I wonder what version of our set-to she'll tell Mr Audley? Or perhaps she won't say anything at all—and I certainly shan't. I shouldn't have let go like that, but'—with an unrepentant grin, 'it *did* relieve my feelings!'

CHAPTER THREE

AFTER that first day Sylvia French came every day to the Ranch, but always after lunch. Whether that was by her own wish or whether Rolf had been vexed by her lack of appreciation for a meal which he had thoroughly enjoyed no one knew, but certainly it was a relief to Mrs Stephens and Laurie.

So, too, was the fact that instead of coming through the main entrance, Sylvia reached Rolf's quarters through the little garden, which meant, of course, that the gate to it had to be kept unlocked until she left later in the afternoon.

That wouldn't have mattered in the least had it not been that a family who, other than Rolf, were their first guests proved to be very difficult to get on with. Or rather, Mrs Smith and Kevin, an eight-year-old, were. Mr Smith, a quiet, unassuming little man, would have been friendly and easy to get on with had he been allowed to be. But Mrs Smith, a hard-faced, domineering woman, checked the least sign of fraternising with the Stephens. They, since they accepted money in exchange for services, were in her opinion of inferior clay. Consequently anything in the nature of friendliness meant lowering oneself to their level.

Even that would not have mattered too much if she had not had one great weakness. Kevin was the apple of her eye and consequently could do no wrong. Nor was Mr Smith allowed to remonstrate with the child, no matter how outrageously he behaved. As a result, there were few occasions when Kevin didn't make his presence felt.

He was finicky over his food, demanding sausages with every meal and after each meal the tablecloth had to be changed because, when sausages were not forthcoming, he deliberately pushed the food over the edge of his plate. He made a nuisance of himself in the kitchen, getting underfoot and helping himself to cakes or tarts cooling on wire racks.

43

'And how to get rid of him short of manhandling him—which would lead to more trouble—I don't know,' Miss Trewyn confessed glumly to Hutton.

'A proper young pest,' Hutton sympathised with feeling. 'But don't take it too much to heart, Miss Trewyn. That lad will go too far one of these days and in the not very distant future, in my opinion. Just you wait and see!'

'Well, I hope you're right, Mr Hutton,' Miss Trewyn said doubtfully. 'Because I've had about enough of him. Do you know his latest? He sneaked in here when I went out to the dustbin for a moment and not only ate all the cherries off the top of the iced fairy-cakes I'd just decorated but left dirty finger marks all over the icing. Wasted the whole batch. They're only fit for hen food now.'

Hutton tut-tutted sympathetically, but repeated his belief that retribution wasn't far off.

'There comes a time when even the most spiritless worm will turn,' he said wisely. 'You mark my words!'

He proved to be right, and it was Cherry who brought about Kevin's downfall.

He had never seen a Siamese cat before and her unusual appearance was fatally fascinating to him. He chased and teased Cherry at every opportunity. Not that they were many—Cherry saw to that. She had never known anything but kindness from human beings in her short life, but instinctively she knew an enemy when she met one. Keeping a wary eye on Kevin, she quietly removed herself to safety at the least sign of a threat. And the little garden was her usual refuge since, not unnaturally, she still regarded it as her special property.

It was true that she couldn't understand why Laurie no longer frequented it, but she accorded both Rolf and Hutton her modified approval. True, they didn't pet her to any degree, but at least they didn't interfere with her or torment her in any way. As for Sylvia French, by mutual agreement they ignored one another, much to Hutton's secret amusement.

'A couple of cats,' he summed them up. 'And I know which *I* prefer!'

But one day, when Cherry thought she had made good

her escape, Kevin, ignoring the *'Private'* notice on the gate, charged after her and succeeded in firmly catching hold of her slender tail. Cherry gave a shout of pain and outraged dignity and then felt herself suddenly released as one strong hand seized Kevin by his shirt collar while another administered three resounding spanks on his rear.

'You little brute!' said a stern voice. 'I'll teach you to torment helpless animals!' and three more spanks followed in rapid succession.

There was instant pandemonium. Kevin yelled at the top of his voice; Mrs Smith came flying into the garden shouting at the top of hers and Mr Smith followed close on her heels. Hutton came out of the house and Laurie wasn't far behind him.

'You utter coward!' Mrs Smith shrieked hysterically. 'To hit a defenceless little child. Assault, that's what it was. I'll take you to court for this, you see if I don't!'

'By all means, madam,' Rolf replied grimly. He was breathing heavily, partly due to the effort he had made and partly on account of almost primitive anger. 'Your defenceless little child was tormenting an even smaller defenceless little animal, and that I will not tolerate, particularly as the child had no right to be in my garden.'

'*Your* garden!' Mrs Smith retorted scornfully. 'Why yours more than anyone else's, I'd like to know!'

Laurie saw that Rolf was looking quizzically at her and it was she who answered Mrs Smith.

'Mr Audley has the exclusive use of the little garden because he pays for the privilege,' she said coldly. 'And even if the gate wasn't locked, the notice that says it's private should be enough for anyone. Anyone with decent manners, that is,' she concluded recklessly, and heard Hutton's soft 'Hear, hear!' from just behind her.

Mrs Smith's sallow face flushed dingily.

'I've never been so insulted in all my life!' she declared shrilly. 'But what can one expect in a shabby, down-at-heel place like this? No other guests—and small wonder! Oh, I know the signs! On the verge of bankruptcy, that's what it is. And when, on top of that, my boy is assaulted——' she turned on Mr Smith. 'Arthur, we're leav-

ing at *once* and no nonsense about paying for our second
week. They ought to pay us——'

Mr Smith, silent until now, took a deep breath.

'You're quite right, Elsie,' he said sternly. 'We *are* leaving at once. After the way Kevin has behaved and, even
worse, the way you have, I'm too ashamed to stay a moment longer than we have to. So go upstairs and start
packing immediately. And as for what we pay, that's my
business, not yours! No, leave Kevin here. I'll see that he
keeps out of mischief.'

'But, Arthur——' Mrs Smith protested weakly, too
astonished by her husband's revolt to put up any real opposition.

Ignoring her completely, Mr Smith took Kevin by the
shoulder and dumped him on the grass.

'You sit there,' he ordered belligerently. 'And if you so
much as open your mouth, you'll get six more where you
got the others!'

Kevin, deserted by his mother and almost startled out
of his wits by his father's show of authority, did as he was
told. Mr Smith took out his handkerchief and wiped his
forehead.

'I should have done that years ago!' he muttered as if he
was speaking to himself. Then he turned to Rolf, now sitting on the verandah. 'I must apologise to you, sir, for the
inconvenience and embarrassment you've been caused,' he
said formally, 'and for which I accept the blame since—
since——' apparently words failed him and Rolf, genuinely
troubled by the little man's discomfort, could find nothing
to say.

Hutton saved the situation by pushing out a small trol-
ley laden with assorted drinks. Rolf hailed him thankfully.

'Drinks!' he exclaimed. 'Just the thing! What's yours,
Mr Smith?'

'Oh, anything—anything,' Mr Smith said distractedly.
'It's very good of you, but I don't feel I ought to take advantage——'

'Nonsense,' Rolf said briskly. 'How about a Scotch and
soda—or water?'

'Water, please,' Mr Smith said gratefully, and accepted

a well-filled glass from Hutton. '*Kevin, sit still!*' he barked as he sat down in the chair which Hutton had pulled up for him. 'Your health, sir!'

'And yours,' Rolf returned pleasantly but rather abstractedly. He was looking across the lawn to where Laurie was standing at the base of the tree in which Cherry had taken refuge. 'Laurie, won't you join us, and if so—what? Sherry?'

It was the first time he had ever called her by her first name, but somehow it seemed perfectly natural. She came slowly over to the verandah realising that her opinion of him had undergone a remarkable change. Despite the handicap of his plastered leg he had made amazing speed in coming to Cherry's relief. And he had meted out a well-deserved punishment to the culprit. A man who could do that must have *some* good in him.

'Yes, sherry, please,' she said, sitting down on the verandah steps. Just for a moment her eyes met Rolf's and she found herself smiling in response to his enquiring look. Anxious not to hurt Mr Smith's feelings, she lifted her glass and silently toasted Rolf in an expression of gratitude and instantly his whole face seemed to light up as he imitated her gesture.

A little later Mr Smith left them, taking Kevin with him. But before he went, he had one more thing to say.

'Y'know, I've felt for a long time that the best thing for the boy would be for him to go to a good boarding school, but the wife wouldn't hear of it. But now——' he squared his shoulders resolutely, 'that's what's going to happen. My mind is made up!'

He bowed slightly to Laurie, lifted his hand in salutation to Rolf and went off, his hand heavy on Kevin's shoulder.

They watched the two of them until they were out of sight.

'Poor devil,' Rolf remarked feelingly. 'He's in for an uncomfortable time, I'm afraid.'

'Yes,' Laurie said soberly, 'I'm afraid he is. It's rather horrible, isn't it?'

'That marriage should become degraded to such a

travesty of what it ought to be?' Rolf suggested. 'Yes, it is.' He paused for a moment and then asked curiously: 'What do you hope to get out of marriage when it comes your way, Laurie? And what would you be prepared to put into it?'

Laurie jumped to her feet.

'I think I can hear Mother calling for me,' she said breathlessly. 'I must go——'

But a strong hand caught her by the wrist.

'Not until you've answered my question,' Rolf told her inexorably.

'Oh——!' Laurie laughed tremulously. 'I must have due notice before answering a question as important as that!'

'And so far, you've never thought about it?' Rolf suggested.

'Not yet,' Laurie said lightly, and with a quick twist freed herself from his grasp.

But, as she made good her escape, she knew that though she had told him the truth, the time had come when she would have to think very seriously about it.

But the day wasn't ended yet. The Smiths left—mother and son bewildered and subdued, Mr Smith still completely master of the situation.

'And long may it last,' Miss Trewyn said hopefully. 'Nothing will alter the fact that she's a thoroughly unpleasant woman, but at least she won't get *all* her own way now. Funny, the way it goes,' she continued reflectively. 'I've seen it before. A bossy wife and a man who gives in for the sake of peace. Then—bang! there's an explosion—he can't take any more and madam finds she's met her master!'

'But that's all *wrong*,' Mrs Stephens said unhappily. 'That's not what marriage ought to be like. Oh, people can't help having differences of opinion sometimes, I know. But this business of one partner humiliating the other—and it can be either way—no, that's horrible. And look what the effect on the child is!'

'I'd rather not,' Miss Trewyn said feelingly. 'As unpleasant a child as I've ever come across, that young

Kevin is. But let's hope it's not too late to improve him—
thought I have my doubts.' She sighed profoundly and
shook her head. 'Oh well, I suppose I'd better get on with
turning their rooms out. They'll need it, particularly the
boy's. He's a born mess-maker!'

She went off, leaving Mrs Stephens and Laurie to discuss
the matter further on their own—if they wanted to, which
they didn't very much.

'The worst of it is, anything like this leaves such an unpleasant taste in one's mouth,' Laurie said uncomfortably.

'Yes, it does,' Mrs Stephens agreed. 'And I do hope that
nothing like this ever happens again. But how *is* one to
know what people are going to be like? Still,' brightening
up, 'Mr Smith was very nice about paying for their second
week. Of course I wouldn't let him pay the full amount
seeing that they wouldn't be having any food, but he insisted on paying in full for the accommodation.'

'That was very nice of him,' Laurie agreed.

'And there's another thing.' Evidently Mrs Stephens was
determined to look on the bright side. 'What a good thing
Mr Audley managed to rescue Cherry before she'd come to
any lasting harm.'

'I don't know how he *did* manage it,' Laurie admitted
warmly. 'I think he must have been so angry that he forgot
all about his leg being in plaster!'

'Quite likely,' Mrs Stephens agreed serenely. She was
genuinely sorry for any discomfort that Cherry had suffered,
but if the outcome was that Laurie got over her absurd
prejudice against Mr Audley, one really couldn't help feeling that Cherry had suffered in a good cause.

Not unnaturally, Cherry didn't regard the matter so philo-
sophically. Not only had she suffered physical pain but her
dignity had been affronted—and somebody had got to pay
for that! Laurie, being her most willing serf, was the inevitable 'somebody'. She, Cherry decided, should be de-
prived of her company until she was sufficiently repentant.
Consequently she stayed obstinately up her tree, refusing
to be coaxed down until, bored by inactivity, she came
down voluntarily though still resisting all attempts at

consolation. She preferred to march off and remain hidden for the rest of the day.

Nor when nightfall came would she respond to Laurié's urgent whistle.

'Why not leave her out?' Mrs Stephens suggested. 'It's a warm night, she won't come to any harm.'

'No, I don't suppose she would,' Laurie agreed. 'Still, I'll have one more try.'

But her effort produced no result until, as she came near to the little garden, a quiet voice called out:

'She's here with me. Will you fetch her? The gate is unlocked—Hutton isn't back yet.'

Reluctantly Laurie pushed the gate open and walked across the grass, easily able to see her way in the light of the full moon that lit up the whole garden in its silvery light. Only the verandah was in the shadow, giving Rolf's voice a slightly eerie quality as he spoke again.

'She's fast asleep,' he said softly. 'On the softest cushion we could find and dreaming of catching mice or birds, I should think, judging by her occasional remarks.'

'She's a bad lot,' Laurie said lovingly. 'I'm sorry she's been a nuisance to you, Mr Audley.'

'Far from it. I've enjoyed her company,' Rolf insisted. 'I was getting thoroughly bored with my own.'

'Well, as it's Saturday, of course Miss French hasn't come, has she? I suppose that's left you at a loose end——' Laurie suggested tentatively.

'Oh—office work!' he spoke disparagingly. 'There *are* other things that interest me, you know. I suppose you can't spare a few minutes to stay and talk to me, can you? Believe me, I'd appreciate it.'

He spoke so diffidently that Laurie found it quite impossible to refuse. Once again she sat down on the verandah steps and leaned against a supporting post of the verandah roof, completely unconscious of the picture she made in a shaft of moonlight that gave her bright hair a silvery sheen and etherealised her piquant little face.

'What shall we talk about?' she asked.

'Now you've put every idea out of my head,' Rolf complained. '*You* think of something.'

'Certainly,' Laurie said obligingly. 'Have you read any good books lately?'

'I haven't read any books at all,' Rolf told her crossly. 'And well you know why—you emptied all the book-shelves.'

'Well, of course I did,' Laurie defended herself. 'Books are very personal possessions—and anyway, how was I to know if you'd like my choice?'

'How can I say since I don't know what there was?' Rolf demanded. 'Tell me!'

So for a while they discussed books and finding that they had tastes in common, Laurie promised the following day to return some of those she had removed.

A silence fell between them broken only by a cavernous yawn from Cherry.

'Did you——?'

'Have you——?'

'Dead heat,' Rolf commented. 'Ladies first!'

'Oh no,' Laurie contradicted. 'Your turn. I began about books.'

'So you did. All right, I was going to ask if you got rid of the Smiths without any trouble.'

'Yes, we did,' Laurie told him. 'Mr Smith was still very much in command. He was very generous, too. He insisted on paying for the second week they'd booked, though of course, only for the accommodation. We couldn't let him pay for the food they wouldn't eat.'

'No, of course not,' Rolf agreed. 'Well, that's very satis-factory—so why are you so depressed about it?'

'Because it's made Mother so unhappy,' Laurie explained. 'Not only because it was such a wretched business but be-cause——' she hesitated.

'Because——?'

Well, why shouldn't he know? After all, it was some-thing which might conceivably affect him.

'Because she's beginning to have doubts as to whether we're suitable people to run an hotel.' She waited hopefully to be assured that yes, of course they were, but no such assurance was forthcoming.

'Probably not,' Rolf said cheerfully. 'You're far too nice and obliging for your own good.'

'Oh, rubbish!' Laurie demurred, entirely forgetting how annoyed she had been because Rolf himself had benefited to such a degree from her mother's willingness to fall in with his wishes. 'Anyone would think that neither Mother nor I have had any experience of running an hotel!'

'And have you?'

'Mother was the chef at the Black Prince Hotel and I was the secretary,' Laurie explained shortly.

'H'm! Yes, that sounds all right,' Rolf admitted. 'But in fact, neither of you really had an entirely free hand, did you? I mean, Mrs Stephens was limited by the amount available for spending on food while you dealt with facts and figures supplied to you by other people and typed letters which were dictated to you. Isn't that so?'

'Well, yes,' Laurie had to admit. 'But surely——'

'Oh yes, good training so far as it went,' Rolf interrupted. 'But there's a world of difference between that and actually being in charge. *Then*, knowing all the pitfalls, you have to be far tougher or you'd find yourself in Queer Street!'

To that Laurie found nothing to say and after a moment's deliberation Rolf went on briskly:

'I've been reading through your brochure. It's good—up to a point. Well presented, factual and inviting. But it's got one bad fault.'

'Oh?' Laurie sat very erect, her hackles beginning to rise. After all, the brochure was her brain child——

'Yes, you don't charge enough,' he announced with conviction. 'No, listen!' as she made a restless movement. 'People on holiday expect to live above their usual standard. They *want* to because it gives them the feeling that for a short time at least they're superior beings to what is really the case. So, if they're not going to be charged pretty heavily, they conclude that no matter how great the amenities you offer, they won't achieve their ambition. In fact, the more amenities, the less they believe in them if they don't have to pay for them. *Too much for too little!* That's what nine people out of ten would think, believe me!'

'I don't believe you,' Laurie told him stormily. 'We've

gone into it very carefully—what it costs to provide good food, staff salaries, replacements of things that wear out or get broken. All that——'

'How about Mrs Stephens' and your own salaries?' he wanted to know.

'No, of course not,' Laurie retorted. 'We get the profits——'

'I thought as much!' Rolf said triumphantly. 'My dear girl, the profit is what you should get *after* you've charged for all your work. It's your perquisite for taking all the risk and responsibility for running the place. Surely you can see that!'

Whether Laurie could or not, she wasn't going to admit it. He was a hateful, patronising *pig* with far too good an opinion of himself. She remained obstinately silent and after a moment Rolf went on coaxingly:

'Now look, Laurie, I only want to help you and your mother. Oh, I know, I've had no experience in running a hotel, but after all, I've run a reasonably successful business for long enough to know what a thin line there is—or can be—between making a profit and losing out. So suppose we go through your books and papers together——'

It was the last straw! Laurie stooped and scooped a protesting Cherry from her cushion.

'It's extremely kind of you, Mr Audley,' she said stiffly. 'But I do assure you that there's no need for you to concern yourself on our behalf. We shall make out!'

'Will you?' he ejaculated. 'I sincerely hope you do, but let me ask you one thing—*when are your next visitors coming?*'

The answer to that was too humiliating to confess, for it was not for another month! And how in the world, even with what Rolf was paying, they were going to make ends meet goodness only knew.

Forgetting that Rolf himself would be here long enough to find that out, Laurie gathered the remnants of her dignity about her and marched out of the garden in silence.

The next week was a time of small events. Hutton went into Penzance and collected the car, now repaired and showing

no sign of mishap. Several times, with Hutton driving, Rolf
would be out for hours at a time. But even so, Laurie kept
clear of the little garden, though Cherry didn't. Indeed, it
seemed to Laurie's annoyance that she seemed to spend
most of her time there. However Rolf, possibly thinking
that he had gone too far in his efforts to give good advice,
saved them both the embarrassment of Laurie needing to
fetch her at bedtime by telling Hutton to take her to the
kitchen.

Not that Laurie would admit even to herself that he was
being considerate.

'If he hadn't been so tactless about the way we run the
hotel, he wouldn't have had to bother.'

None the less, she kept her promise to let Rolf have some
books, though she didn't deliver them in person. She made
use of Hutton as messenger and in due course received
Rolf's formal thanks through the same channel.

With time on her hands, Laurie went through her account
books and her calculations with scrupulous care and also
studied the brochure of which she had been so proud. It
was vexing, but she couldn't get what Rolf had said out of
her mind. Was he right? Did they offer too much too
cheaply? Did people enjoy being extravagant on holiday?
Against her will she remembered how, in past years, she
had saved every penny so that she could have a dream
holiday. Very well then, so he *was* right. But it was too late
to do anything about it this year. But next year, if they
were still here——

Chewing her pencil, she considered Rolf's other point—
that she and her mother ought to have allowed for a salary
for each of them as well as the ultimate profits.

She went carefully through her list of unavoidable overheads and could find no fault with them—so far as they
went. Then to their total she added the salaries that she
and her mother had earned at the Black Prince. She grimaced at the result. Whether Rolf was right or wrong in
thinking that that was what they ought to have done from
the very beginning, one thing was clear—if they did, then
they had certainly got to charge more.

Frowning, she threw down the pencil and locked everything away in her desk. How exhausting making calculations could be—particularly when they didn't come out on the right side and particularly on a hot day like this!

Perfect holiday weather—and no holidaymakers to enjoy it! Laurie ran her fingers through her hair that clung damply to her head. What a mockery it was, after all their efforts and their high hopes! Wouldn't it be better to admit defeat and close the Ranch at the end of Rolf's stay, then sell it for what they could get? If they took salaried jobs again, they would be reasonably safe——

Then revolt stirred in her. That was a pretty poor attitude to take. Anyway, they had got some bookings and who knew, there might be more, in which case she wouldn't have a moment to spare.

But at the moment she had plenty of time, so, since there was no one else to enjoy this glorious holiday weather, why shouldn't she make the most of the opportunity? She would go down to the Cove——

She changed into bathing rig, slung a wrap round her shoulders and packed a plastic bag with a towel, a comb and a book. Then she went to tell her mother what she was planning to do and added a couple of apples to her bag.

Mrs Stephens, remembering the earlier tragedy in the Cove, looked anxious.

'You'll be very careful, won't you, darling?' she begged.

Laurie laughed reassuringly and hugged her mother with one bare, warm arm.

'Of course I will,' she promised. 'But that other day Miss Trewyn says it was very rough and that really no one ought to have gone swimming. Today it will be as calm as a millpond, and if it isn't, I won't go in. Promise, Honest Injun!'

Mrs Stephens smiled gratefully and Laurie went off. It wasn't too pleasant a walk, for the lane was very rough and stony and her beach shoes didn't give her much protection. None the less, two or three cars had ventured down—to Laurie's regret. She had hoped to have the Cove to herself and evidently that was not going to be the case.

However, though the Cove wasn't very big, the tide was out and the few families there didn't make for a feeling of overcrowding.

Laurie scrambled along a rocky promontory, discarded her wrap and shoes and dived into the sparkling blue water. With a glorious sense of escape she swam out to a tethered raft, hauled herself on to it and stretched out in the sunshine, relaxed and feeling at peace with the world.

She was almost asleep when her peace was shattered, first by the sound of a speedboat and then by the raft tilting uncontrollably in the roughened water.

She scrambled precariously to her knees, but though there were rope loops round the edge of the raft, there was nothing to cling on to on its surface. It could, she knew, be only a very short time before she had to take to the water, for these three men—no, two men; the third occupant of the speedboat was a girl—were coming closer and closer to the raft and they were laughing hilariously. They might quite conceivably think it amusing to cut her off from the rocks.

But almost before she had time to realise that, she was off the raft, swimming for dear life through the turbulent water. Once, twice, the speedboat came perilously near to her, then suddenly its engine cut out and the boat was tossing ignominiously in the roughness it had itself created.

Laurie gained the safety of her rocks and completely ignoring her tormentors' shouts for help, loosened her hair and began to dry it.

'Here, can't you do something?' one of the men shouted. 'We'll be on the rocks if you don't!'

For a moment Laurie hesitated. They *were* in danger—but what could she do to help them? Then to her relief she heard the sound of another speedboat coming towards them. She pointed to it and a moment or so later the crippled boat was taken in tow.

But not before two things had happened. One was that Laurie had recognised the girl who was among her tormentors. It was Sylvia French, and though fear had blanched her face, the malice in her expression was unmistakable.

The other thing to happen was that one of the men grabbed up a camera and grinning offensively, took three rapid snaps of Laurie, her hair in a tangle over her shoulders, furiously angry as she shouted at them.

Shaking with a mixture of shock and wrath, she put on her wrap and shoes and scrambled down to beach level to be met by Tom Weekes, the owner of the two speedboats.

'I'm that sorry, Miss Stephens,' he said with genuine concern. 'Are you all right?'

'I suppose so,' Laurie said shakily. 'But really, Tom——!'

'I know,' he said quickly. 'I did send Fred after them as quick as I could when I saw what they were up to, but it could have been very nasty for you if their engine hadn't conked out when it did.'

'It could,' Laurie agreed feelingly. 'Still, I didn't come to any harm. But who are they, Tom? Because really they're not fit to have a boat out.'

'You're telling me,' he said grimly. 'And believe me, Miss Stephens, they're on my black list from now on. Especially the young woman! She was the one who was egging them on!'

'Was she?' Despite the warmth of the day, Laurie shivered. Nobody had ever hated her before as Sylvia French must hate her. And all for no reason! 'Well, I think I'll be getting home now, Tom. And don't worry, I *am* all right.'

'Thanks be for that, Miss Stephens,' Tom said fervently.

Back at the Ranch, Laurie managed to get up to her bedroom without encountering anybody. She took a warm shower, rinsed the sea water out of her hair and dried it roughly. Then, dressed and with her hair quelled to some extent to its normal smoothness, she went downstairs determined not to tell her mother of her experience.

Fortunately Mrs Stephens had news of her own to impart.

'I had a telephone call while you were out, Laurie,' she said happily. 'A Mr Brownsell. His holiday arrangements broke down at the last minute and he wants to come here for a fortnight. Of course I said he could and he's coming early tomorrow. He had such a friendly voice and was so very anxious not to put us to any trouble. Isn't it splendid?'

'Splendid,' Laurie echoed, but with so little enthusiasm that her mother gave her a quick look full of anxiety. 'Is there a cup of tea going, Mother? The water was a bit colder than I'd expected.'

'Of course. The kettle is almost on the boil. Yes, Hutton?' as he came into the kitchen.

'Mr Audley would be very much obliged if Miss Stephens can spare him a few minutes,' Hutton said as if he was repeating a lesson.

'Not until she's had a cup of tea,' Mrs Stephens said firmly. 'Tell Mr Audley in ten minutes.'

'Yes, madam,' Hutton replied tonelessly, and left them.

'Oh dear, now what?' Mrs Stephens asked helplessly. 'Have you and Mr Audley———?'

'I haven't seen him, much less spoken to him, for several days,' Laurie assured her, but in her own mind she had a premonition as to why Rolf had sent for her. 'Oh well———' drinking the last of her tea, 'I suppose I'd better go and see what it's all about. Send out the St Bernards if I don't come back!' she ended on a would-be jocular note.

'Oh, darling!' Mrs Stephens said apprehensively.

Laurie managed to laugh reassuringly.

'Don't worry, Mother. The man can't eat me!'

None the less, as she reached the door of Rolf's quarters, she instinctively squared her shoulders and as she faced him in the sitting room, her heart sank. She had seen him in a good many moods, but never before in one of such uncompromising anger.

'You wished to see me, Mr Audley?' she said formally.

'I did,' Rolf said curtly. 'Please sit down, Miss Stephens. This may take some time.'

Laurie sat down, deliberately choosing a chair which meant that she was facing him. If he thought she was scared of him———

'I would like your explanation of these two photographs,' he told her, handing over two colour prints.

Before she looked at them, Laurie knew that they must be of her. What she had not anticipated was that, by some freak of the light, her pictured face, instead of looking furiously angry, gave the impression of someone convulsed with laughter as her outstretched hand, actually pointing to the oncoming speedboat, seemed to indicate contempt and ridicule.

'Taken from a speedboat without my permission,' she said coolly. 'It must have been one of those cameras that make instant prints.'

Rolf stared at her unbelievingly.

'You can't brazen it out like that, Miss Stephens,' he told her sternly.

'Brazen what out, Mr Audley?' Laurie asked quietly.

He made a gesture of impatience.

'That when three people were in considerable danger of drifting on to the rocks, you not only refused to help them but you found their plight amusing,' he snapped.

Laurie shook her head. It would have been intensely satisfying to throw something hard and cornery at this infuriating man, but instinct told her that she stood a far better chance of making him eat humble pie if she kept her temper than if she let her natural indignation get the better of her.

'I remember an occasion on which you told me that even a criminal is allowed an opportunity for defending himself,' she reminded him. 'But you appear to have condemned me out of hand.'

'The evidence——' he pointed to the photographs. Then he shrugged his shoulders. 'If you have anything to say in your defence——'

'Oh, I *have*!' Laurie assured him gently, and as simply and briefly as possible she described exactly what had happened, ending with: 'And if you don't believe me, I suggest you should ask Tom Weekes about it. He saw the whole thing.'

'But these photographs——' Clearly he was only half convinced.

'Yes, they're rather misleading, I'm afraid,' Laurie said critically. 'Actually, I was pointing to the boat that was coming to their rescue. Why the result is what it is, I've no idea. Believe me, I wasn't ridiculing them. *I'd* been in considerable danger myself and I was still suffering from shock. As for helping them, what could I have done, Mr Audley?'

To that it appeared he could find no answer and judging

by his expression he didn't like the predicament he found himself in.

Laurie stood up and handed the photographs back to him.

'There's nothing more to be said, is there?' she said quietly.

Rolf seemed to pull himself together.

'Yes, there is,' he said morosely. 'It would seem that I was precipitate in my judgment and that I owe you an apology——'

Laurie waited in silence.

'I do apologise, Miss Stephens,' he said curtly.

'Thank you, Mr Audley,' Laurie said gently, and left him to his thoughts—not very pleasant ones, she imagined.

'Unfair *beast*!' she thought indignantly. 'Believing that horrible girl without question. Because of course it must have been from her that he got the photographs and her version of what happened, though he didn't say so. But she must have known that I recognised her—yes, of course she did! That's why she was so quick to get in first. Thank goodness Tom saw what really happened. Otherwise I don't think he'd have believed me!'

That was what rankled so badly. What right had he to doubt her word? If he was a man of any perception he ought by now to have realised that she was by nature truthful. But then if he didn't realise what an unpleasant person Sylvia was, though he had known her so much longer, how could he be expected to read the character of a girl he hardly knew at all?

'All the same, I'm glad I didn't refer to her by name,' she decided. 'Because that would have made me no better than she is. Not that it really matters. *He* knows that she was lying—I wonder what he'll do about it?'

She decided that she would not tell her mother what had happened, and as Mrs Stephens was very busy she was content with Laurie's casual explanation that there was nothing to worry about. Just Mr Audley had wanted some information——

What she hadn't realised was that by keeping the whole thing to herself she had no vent for her anger at the injustice Rolf had done her. By the time evening came, her resentment had built up to boiling point.

It was childish, she knew, but she wanted someone to sympathise with her and tell her that she had been badly done by.

If only she and Geoffrey were still on their old terms! But twice she had refused invitations from him and she knew he must realise by now that there was no going back to those days.

Consequently, that Geoffrey should choose that evening to borrow a car from a friend and come to plead with her was too much for her self-restraint. Without counting the cost, she greeted him warmly and let him persuade her to go for a drive with him. True, she stipulated that it should only be a short one, but Geoffrey had raised no objection to that.

'It doesn't matter how short a distance we go so long as we have a chance to talk without being disturbed,' he told her. And when, no more than a mile or two from the Ranch, he pulled up in a convenient layby, it was clear that he meant just what he said.

'And now let's have it, Laurie,' he said with an air of authority unusual in him. 'And don't tell me there's nothing the matter, because I know differently. Your hands have been clenching and unclenching ever since you got into the car and you've hardly had a word to say for yourself. So come on, out with it! What's wrong?'

For a moment she resisted, then the temptation was too much for her and out it all came. Geoffrey's reaction was all that could be desired. He was genuinely horrified, furiously angry and as sympathetic as she had longed for someone to be.

'You poor kid!' he said indignantly. 'What a damnable trick to play. What are you going to do about it? Sue them for malicious and dangerous behaviour? I should think you could make a good case of it with Weekes' evidence to back you up. Or don't you know who they were?'

'I don't know who the men were, but I know who the girl was,' Laurie explained. 'Her name is Sylvia French and she's Mr Audley's secretary.'

'Audley?' he repeated, and she felt his arm that had been round her shoulders slacken. 'Not—*Rolf* Audley?'

'Why, yes,' Laurie said wonderingly. 'Do you know him?'

'Know him?' Geoffrey said in a strangled voice. 'He's my boss!'

CHAPTER FOUR

LAURIE was startled but not particularly alarmed.

'Well, does it matter?' she asked matter-of-factly.

'Matter! Of course it matters!' Geoffrey retorted harshly. Gone now was all the sympathy and kindness he had shown and in its place was irritation and—yes—fear. 'Heaven's above, Laurie, can't you see what you've done, getting on Audley's wrong side?'

'If I have, it was hardly my fault,' Laurie pointed out. 'He jumped to the wrong conclusion and if he didn't like having to apologise for his mistake, that's just too bad!'

'Oh, for goodness' sake!' Distractedly Geoffrey ran his fingers through his hair. 'If you knew Audley as well as I do, you'd be scared out of your wits!'

'Would I? Why?'

'Because he's the sort of man who never forgets an injury and he'll regard having to sing small as the worst injury of all. Believe me, Laurie, he'll make you pay for it.'

'I'm not afraid of him even if you are,' Laurie retorted defiantly.

'Well, I am,' Geoffrey said grimly. 'And with cause, believe me! He could sack me at the drop of a hat!'

'But this business has nothing to do with you,' Laurie told him reasonably.

'Oh, hasn't it!' Geoffrey laughed mirthlessly. 'If he found out that you and I——'

He stopped short, but Laurie had no difficulty in knowing what had been on the tip of his tongue.

'You mean,' she said deliberately, 'that if Mr Audley knew that we were—friends, he'd vent his spite on you to pay me out?'

'Yes, I do mean just that,' Geoffrey admitted sullenly.

'Well——' Laurie said briskly, 'there's an easy way out, isn't there? Take me home at *once* and stop at the gates for me to get out. I'll walk the rest of the way and then there'll

63

be no chance of Mr Audley seeing us together. And as for
being friends—my idea of a friend is someone who is loyal
and dependable. You're neither, Geoffrey, so we're not
friends.'

'Here, I say, Laurie, that's a bit unfair!' he protested resentfully.

'You can't have it both ways, Geoffrey,' Laurie snapped
irritably. 'Either you're too scared of Mr Audley to be my
friend or—oh, what's the good of arguing? Take me home
at once before I really lose my temper!'

'Oh, all right,' Geoffrey said sulkily. 'But I must say, I
think you're being very unfair!'

Laurie didn't answer. What was there to say that would
help matters? Geoffrey turned the car and they were on
their way back to the Ranch.

At the gates he stopped and Laurie jumped out. Without
troubling to say: 'Goodnight,' she slipped through the open
gates and ran the rest of the way.

Just as she reached the main entrance a voice called to
her.

'Miss Stephens, Cherry is here with me. Would you care
to fetch her?'

Momentarily Laurie stood still. He didn't sound in the
least unpleasant. On the contrary, there was a distinct note
of friendliness in his voice. But even if Geoffrey had exag-
gerated his arrogance, she knew at first hand how unjust he
could be and she was not yet in a mood for reconciliation.

'I wonder if you'd be so kind as to ask Hutton to bring
her to the kitchen as he has been doing lately?' she asked
expressionlessly. 'I've such a lot of jobs waiting to be done.'

There was the briefest of silences.

'Certainly, Miss Stephens,' he said in a voice as devoid
of feeling as hers had been.

Laurie went indoors feeling vexed with herself.

'I suppose that was meant to be an olive branch,' she
thought, and then remembering his earlier treatment of
her: 'Yes, of course it was. He's probably realised that after
the way he behaved, we've every reason to send him packing—and that wouldn't suit him at all. He's got things just
as he wants them here and he was trying to placate me!

Well, he hasn't managed it—and I wish we *could* send him packing!'

Mr Brownsell arrived early the next morning and Laurie, who received him, took to him immediately. He was, she thought, somewhere in his fifties, but despite his grey hair, there was something youthful about him. Perhaps it was because he had an essentially friendly face that gave the impression of him being a man who liked his fellow human beings. Or it might have been that, despite his years, he had kept a youthfully trim figure. Whatever it was, Laurie found herself smiling in response to his pleasant greeting.

And fortunately he got on well with Miss Trewyn.

'A pleasure to see him eat,' she announced after lunch. 'Didn't leave a scrap on his plates and said it was the best meal he'd had since his old mother died—and she was a notable cook, too. So I reckon he's a bachelor.'

'Yes, perhaps he is,' Laurie agreed. 'Mother will be pleased.'

'That he liked her cooking—or that he's a bachelor?' Miss Trewyn asked innocently.

'Oh, Miss Trewyn!' Laurie chided laughingly. 'You're not matchmaking already, are you?'

'Well, Miss Laurie, the way I look at it is this—a nicer lady than your mother I never met, but say what you will, she didn't ought to be earning her living. She ought to have someone to look after her. And if you ask me, Mr Brownsell is the looking-after sort,' she concluded triumphantly.

'You could be right,' Laurie admitted thoughtfully.

'And you wouldn't mind having a stepfather?' Miss Trewyn asked anxiously.

'Not if Mother was happy.' And then, thinking that they really were rushing their fences, Laurie said teasingly: 'But I thought you had a very poor opinion of men, Miss Trewyn?'

'So I have, as a general rule. But there are some that aren't as bad as others.'

'Hutton, for instance?'

'Oh well, I suppose he's got his good points,' Miss Trewyn conceded grudgingly.

But Laurie saw the colour rise to her sallow cheeks and drew her own conclusions.

'My goodness, there's romance in the air,' she thought. 'Mother—Miss Trewyn! They say these things go in threes, but if they do, the third one won't be me—I'll see to that!'

A little later Hutton himself came into the kitchen and with an exasperated: 'Tut!' Miss Trewyn scurried into the scullery.

'Mr Audley asked me to let you know that it will be a different lady who comes to do his secretarial work,' Hutton gave as his explanation for coming to the kitchen, 'Miss French, as I understand, being on holiday. This lady is Miss Jones and——' with a sudden burst of confidence: 'I think you'll like her, Miss Stephens. She *is* a lady, very different from——' he stopped short, evidently feeling that it was hardly his place, as a good servant, to criticise his employer's secretary. 'Well, anyway, I think you'll like her,' he concluded lamely.

'Oh good,' Laurie replied, and left it at that. 'When will Miss Jones be arriving?'

'About half-past two or three,' Hutton told her.

'Well, I'll make a point of being in the hall then in case she comes in that way, as she probably will,' Laurie promised. 'Then I can show her where to go.'

'That would be very kind of you, Miss Stephens, and I'm sure Mr Audley will appreciate your thoughtfulness,' Hutton said appreciatively, and then, lowering his voice: 'Where's that Maisie got to?'

'Maisie?'

'Miss Trewyn,' Hutton explained huffily. 'No sooner do I come out here than she's off like a scalded cat. Never get a chance to have a word with her.'

So romance *was* in the air!

'I think she'll be leaving about eight this evening,' Laurie told him casually. 'She has quite a long walk to get to her home——'

'So she does!' Hutton looked decidedly more cheerful. 'Well, thank you very much, Miss Stephens. I'm sure I'm very much obliged.'

Miss Jones *was* very different from Sylvia French. Indeed,

two people could hardly be more dissimilar. She was an extremely neat little person, though no one could possibly describe her as chic. She was much older than Sylvia and her brown hair was liberally peppered with grey and though she used make-up, it was only very discreetly. Her face was pleasant rather than pretty and when she spoke, to Laurie's relief, her voice had a lilting quality which was not surprising, seeing that she was unmistakably Welsh.

'Miss Jones?' Laurie asked, smiling.

'Yes, I'm Megan Jones. I've come to help Mr Audley while Miss French is—on holiday,' the newcomer explained.

'I'm Laurie Stephens,' Laurie told her, having noticed and wondered about that rather odd hesitation Miss Jones had made in speaking of Sylvia being on holiday. 'My mother and I run the hotel. I thought it would make it easier for you if I was here to show you the way to Mr Audley's suite.'

'How kind of you,' Miss Jones said appreciatively. 'But then I know from Mr Audley that your mother and you are very kind people. He feels he's lucky to have found somewhere like this to convalesce. His flat is very nice, of course, but it's up several flights of stairs and there's no lift, so it would have been very difficult for him, poor boy, with his leg in plaster, even with Hutton's help.'

There was something almost maternal in the way she referred to Rolf and Laurie felt curious.

'Have you been with the firm long?' she asked as she led the way to Rolf's door.

'Oh yes, ever since I left school,' Miss Jones told her with pride. 'It's the only job I've ever had. Of course, I started at the very bottom, but eventually I became Mr Audley's—the present Mr Audley's father's—personal secretary. Then when he died, I became—well, it's rather difficult to describe just what my duties are. Perhaps Jill of all trades would be the best description. I fit in wherever I'm needed.' She smiled as Laurie opened the door for her. 'It makes for quite a variety of work. Thank you very much, Miss Stephens.'

Laurie went out to the kitchen and told her mother of Miss Jones' arrival.

'She's nice,' she announced with satisfaction. 'Friendly

and gentle—and she sounds as if she's really fond of Mr Audley.'

'Well, you needn't sound so surprised,' Mrs Stephens said reproachfully. 'You're the only person who doesn't think he's nice, and for the life of me, I can't think why.'

'I told you before—it's a case of Dr Fell,' Laurie said shortly.

'Well, I hope you'll get over it soon,' Mrs Stephens said as if Laurie had an attack of measles. Then with one of her rapid changes of interest: 'Do you think she's in love with Mr Audley?'

'I shouldn't think so for a minute,' Laurie said with conviction. 'I should say she's well into her forties, perhaps even over fifty. She must be, because she was old Mr Audley's secretary. Actually, she sounded quite maternal over this Mr Audley.'

'Oh!' Mrs Stephens considered this. 'Then perhaps she was in love with his father and though nothing came of it, she regards Mr Audley almost as if he was her son. I wonder,' she went on thoughtfully, 'how she and Mr Brownsell would get on together. We must see that they have a chance of getting to know one another——'

'Mother!' Laurie protested. 'What an incurable romantic you are! First you conjure up a romance between old Mr Audley and Miss Jones and then you start matchmaking between two people who haven't even met yet! You ought to be ashamed of yourself!'

'I don't see why,' Mrs Stephens defended herself stoutly. 'Here are two people who might find companionship together. So if I can do anything to bring that about—well, I'm going to!'

'You sound as if you regard marriage as the be-all and end-all of life,' Laurie remarked, wondering what her mother would say if she knew that Miss Trewyn had already earmarked Mr Brownsell for *her*.

'Not at all. Some marriages are absolute disasters—look at the Smiths, for instance. But a happy marriage—that's a very different matter. And no one who hasn't had that experience can understand what it means to be the one who's left. You only feel half a person.'

'Darling——' Laurie said remorsefully, putting her arm

round her mother's shoulders and hugging her. 'I'm sorry, I shouldn't have said that.'

'Oh, it's all right, childie,' Mrs Stephens told her briskly. 'It's only that, talking to Mr Brownsell after lunch, I felt so sorry for him. I've had so much happiness to remember and he, poor man, has nothing. Not that he was complaining—he's not that sort. But reading between the lines——' she shook her head.

'Oh, I see,' Laurie said matter-of-factly. If Mr Brownsell had already taken her mother into his confidence to this degree, then she didn't give much for Miss Jones' chances!

'Goodness!' she thought, half amused, half shocked. 'I'm getting as bad as Miss Trewyn!'

During the next few days Mr Brownsell seemed to feel more and more at home. He said quite frankly that he was extremely glad that his original holiday plans had broken down.

'If they hadn't, I wouldn't have come here,' he remarked feelingly. 'And look what I'd have missed!'

'How did you hear of us?' Laurie asked. It was a question that she intended asking of all their visitors since it would help them to know which was the most productive form of advertising.

'I saw one of your brochures,' he explained, and seemed to hesitate.

'What did you think of it?' Laurie asked bravely.

'I thought it was extremely attractive,' Mr Brownsell told her. 'Well written, good photographs—yes, very nice indeed. And yet——'

'And yet——?' Laurie encouraged.

'I don't want to hurt your feelings, Miss Stephens,' Mr Brownsell said diffidently, 'but there was just one thing that very nearly made me decide not to come.'

'Yes?'

'Frankly, I thought you were asking too little for all that you were offering and I wondered what the catch was. Of course, now that I'm here, I know that there isn't a catch,' he went on hastily. 'Though I still feel you're not charging enough.'

Laurie eyed him suspiciously.

'That's almost word for word what Mr Audley said,' she blurted out.

'Audley?' Mr Brownsell said vaguely. 'Oh, the chap with the broken leg, isn't he? What does he know about running an hotel?'

'Nothing really—except that he's a very successful business man apparently and'—with a hint of scepticism—'he seemed to think that qualified him to judge.'

'Oh, he did, did he!' Mr Brownsell said disparagingly. 'Well, speaking as an accountant with several hoteliers among my clients, I don't agree with him. It's a highly specialised industry to which one can't apply general terms. What else did this knowledgeable young man have to say?'

'Oh—that Mother and I ought to include salaries for ourselves as overheads as well as take any profits there may be—not that there are likely to be any this year.'

'No? Well, I understand it's your first year, so that isn't really surprising,' Mr Brownsell said placidly.

'And how about paying ourselves salaries?' Laurie persisted, hoping that once again he'd pour scorn on Rolf's ideas.

He put his fingertips together and tapped them gently against one another.

'That I can't tell you offhand,' he admitted. 'It depends a lot on how you've calculated your other expenses.'

'You mean, you'd have to see all my figures before you'd know for sure?' Laurie asked doubtfully.

'Yes, I do. Any accountant worth his salt would. But please don't think I'm touting for you to become my clients! But there, I expect you've already appointed an accountant, haven't you?'

'No, as a matter of fact, we haven't,' Laurie confessed. 'It seemed rather early to do that.'

Mr Brownsell shook his head.

'There I don't agree with you,' he said gravely. 'I think now is the very time that you need advice. Now look, my dear——' he paused diffidently, 'I don't want you to think that I'm interfering in your affairs, but would you like me to put you in touch with one of my fellow accountants? If you would, I'd be only too pleased.'

'You mean, another firm than your own?' Laurie asked quickly.

'Just that.'

'But, Mr Brownsell, why someone else who would be a stranger to us?' Laurie asked impulsively. 'Why not you, who we do know?'

'My dear, I'd be only too glad to be of use to you,' he assured her. 'But I don't want you to feel that there's any compulsion for you to appoint me. After all, you know very little about me.'

'Enough to be sure that we can trust you,' Laurie told him impulsively.

'Well, well! I must admit that's very gratifying to hear,' Mr Brownsell said appreciatively. 'But I would like you to give the matter a little more consideration before deciding. How would it be if you were to talk it over with your mother? Then, if she likes the idea, we'll have a three-cornered talk about it.'

'Yes, I'll do that,' Laurie promised, feeling considerably elated. Such an arrangement would mean that instead of Mr Brownsell leaving them at the end of his holiday, they would remain in touch with him indefinitely. And who knew what that might not lead to?

When Laurie told her of her talk with Mr Brownsell, Mrs Stephens regarded the idea with mixed feelings.

'It isn't that I don't like him,' she explained. 'Or that I would mind him knowing all our business, but it doesn't seem fair to take advantage of his kindness when he's on holiday.'

'I don't think he minds,' Laurie assured her. 'I think he'd welcome having something to do because he doesn't seem to have any particular interests. I mean, he doesn't play golf and he doesn't swim and I think time hangs rather heavily on his hands.'

'Yes, perhaps it does,' Mrs Stephens agreed. 'You know, Laurie, he seems to me to be a very lonely man. I'd rather hoped that he and Mr Audley would find interests in common, but they almost seem to avoid one another.'

'Oh, I don't know,' Laurie shrugged. 'It's just that Mr

Audley has plenty to do with Miss Jones coming every day, so he keeps to his own quarters. Naturally, they don't have any opportunities of meeting.'

'No, that's true,' Mrs Stephens agreed. 'Well then, Laurie, if you're quite happy about accepting Mr Brownsell's offer, I've no objection. In any case, he'll want your help rather than mine.'

'Oh, he'll want yours as well,' Laurie said quickly. 'I can give him figures, but you know far more about the day-to-day working of the place as well as being the one who decides what we spend on food.'

'Of course I'll do anything I can to help,' Mrs Stephens promised. 'But——' doubtfully, 'I hope he won't be too technical, because I'm simply not a business woman.'

Privately Laurie thought that perhaps Mr Brownsell might find that rather an engaging quality in her pretty little mother, but she only said that she would let Mr Brownsell know of their decision and went off to tell him then and there.

Mr Brownsell looked pleased.

'Good!' he said briskly, rubbing his hands together. 'Let's get on with it, shall we?'

'Yes, let's,' Laurie said as briskly, but added a note of warning similar to the one she had given her mother. 'You do realise, don't you, Mr Brownsell, that you'll need Mother's help as well as mine? You see, though we agreed before we started what must be spent on food it's she who actually portions it out day by day according to how many people there are to feed. So you'll want to know if there's any wastefulness, won't you?'

'That's the last thing I'd expect where Mrs Stephens is concerned,' Mr Brownsell said in a shocked voice. 'All the same, I shall be glad of her help if she can spare the time. But of course, she is very busy.'

To Laurie it sounded rather as if he felt that she didn't do enough to prevent her mother from being overworked, but she let that pass without comment. She was, in fact, patting herself on the back for the way in which she had contrived to make sure that her mother and Mr Brownsell would be in each other's company—occasions on which she resolved not to make a third if it could possibly be avoided.

It took Mr Brownsell three evenings' work before he was willing to give his verdict and when he did, it was remarkably like Rolf's—and yet not like, because he spoke with the knowledge of experience. Mrs Stephens and Laurie listened in silence as, reluctantly, he told them that if they kept on the way they were doing, they could only expect disaster.

'But we can't *make* people come,' Mrs Stephens protested, almost in tears. 'I suppose the real trouble is that we started with too little capital behind us to weather this first year. And that was *my* fault. I thought, because it's such a lovely place, that people would flock here. And they haven't. Oh dear!'

Mr Brownsell's kindly face was troubled.

'I'm afraid you've put your finger right on the problem,' he admitted reluctantly. 'So now we've got to decide what's to be done about it.'

'What can we do about it?' Mrs Stephens asked forlornly.

'A lot,' Mr Brownsell declared encouragingly. 'To begin with, you must realise that you've got a very real asset here. The next thing is—it's absolutely yours. You bought it outright?'

'Yes, we did,' Mrs Stephens said proudly. 'No mortgage or anything like that. I don't like being in debt.'

'Quite right, too,' Mr Brownsell gave her an approving look. 'All the same, a mortgage can be a very useful thing and a perfectly sound one financially. As in this case.'

'You mean, you're suggesting that we should borrow money?' Mrs Stephens said in alarm. 'Oh, I wouldn't like to do that. Besides, who would lend it to us?'

The slightest smile touched Mr Brownsell's lips. Clearly he was both touched and gently amused by Mrs Stephens' jump from what amounted to sentiment to a practical outlook.

'I believe Miss Trewyn is right,' Laurie thought delightedly. 'He *is* the looking-after sort of man! Oh, I do hope——'

But hopes like that had to be left to the future—and chance. For the time being their present problem held pride of place.

'Yes, Mr Brownsell, who *would* lend us money?' she asked anxiously.

'Your bank,' he replied promptly. 'With the Ranch as security, no doubt about that, I'd say.'

'Oh!' Mrs Stephens looked doubtful. 'But suppose we couldn't pay it back? We'd lose the Ranch——'

'No, no,' Mr Brownsell assured her. 'Repayment of the loan would be spread over a period of years so that you would pay it off gradually. Besides, you wouldn't need to borrow anything like the full value of the place.'

'But even then, we've no guarantee that people will come, and I don't see how we can make them.' Mrs Stephens looked at him beseechingly, her pretty face worried and tired. 'Do you?'

'I've a few ideas,' he explained. 'To begin with, though I admit the Smiths—or rather, Mrs Smith, don't come in the category of good, free advertising. None the less, that will surely be an isolated experience. I'm quite sure you'll find other guests will tell their friends about you with enthusiasm—as I certainly shall.'

'Yes, I can see that would be a considerable help,' Laurie conceded. 'But it will take time for it to have any effect, won't it?'

'To some degree, yes. But apart from that, one of the first things on which you'll need to spend some of your loan would be more advertising on a wider and more spectacular scale—now!'

Mrs Stephens sighed.

'I expect you're right,' she admitted. 'But you know, I'm *not* a business woman and it all rather frightens me.'

'And I've been most inconsiderate,' Mr Brownsell said self-reproachfully, gently laying his hand over hers. 'You're tired and I've kept you hard at it when you ought to be resting. Now, I've got an idea. Let's put all this by for the time being, and would you consider letting me take you for a little run in my car? It's a beautiful evening and I think it might do you good.'

'I'm sure it would,' Mrs Stephens said gratefully. 'Laurie——?'

'I won't come, if you don't mind,' Laurie said apologetically to Mr Brownsell who, she thought, looked considerably relieved. 'I've got something to do rather urgently.'

She watched them start with considerable satisfaction, Mr Brownsell carrying a cloak in case her mother felt chilly.

'The pets,' she thought benevolently. 'I wonder if they realise—well, he does, I'm sure of that! The way he looks at Mother as if she's something rather special. Well, she is, bless her!'

She was genuinely glad that there was at least the prospect of happiness for her mother, yet she couldn't help feeling a little ache of loneliness.

'Stop pitying yourself, my girl,' she told herself sternly. 'You've got a job to do!'

And that job was to go and see Rolf.

He was surprised, even startled, when she came into his sitting room.

'Something wrong?' he asked.

'No. Just I want to apologise to you,' Laurie explained.

'Apologise?' He seemed to brace himself as if he expected to be told something unpleasant. 'What about?'

Laurie looked at him reproachfully.

'You're not being very helpful, are you?'

'My dear girl, how can I be helpful when I don't know what in the world you're talking about?' he demanded impatiently.

'Well, it would be rather encouraging if you asked me to sit down,' Laurie suggested plaintively. 'More friendly——'

'Friendly!' he echoed incredulously. And then, urgently: 'My dear Miss Stephens, please do sit down. My wits must be wool-gathering or I would have suggested it.'

'No, it's just that you're naturally surprised that after having been so rude to you, I should speak of us being friendly,' Laurie told him.

'It *is* surprising,' he admitted. 'But very gratifying. But won't you tell me what it's all about?'

But now that it had come to the point Laurie was suddenly tongue-tied. She looked at him appealingly.

'Go on,' he encouraged. 'I don't bite—at least not as a rule.'

'Well——' Laurie hesitated and then took the plunge. 'It's about what I said to you about the way we run the hotel——'

'That!' he exclaimed, frowning. 'If it's about that, then the boot's on the other foot—I should be apologising to you! I honestly did want to help you, but I had no mortal right to think that you'd welcome my interference in your affairs. You were quite right to tell me so.'

'No, I wasn't,' Laurie insisted earnestly. 'Because everything you said was perfectly true.'

'Do you mind telling me what's made you change your mind?' he asked curiously.

'Well, Mr Brownsell, really——'

'Brownsell?' Rolf said sharply. 'Oh yes, your new visitor. Hutton told me you'd got one. But where does he come in?'

'He's an accountant and he's got several hoteliers as clients already,' Laurie explained, conscious that she was gabbling and making rather a mess of it. 'As a matter of fact, he's agreed to having us as clients.'

'I see,' Rolf said briefly.

'You don't approve, do you?' Laurie asked with a touch of her old defiance.

'As to that, I certainly think it's a good idea for you to have appointed an accountant,' Rolf said deliberately. 'Whether this Mr—Brownsell?—is the right man for the job is another matter.'

'Do you know him?' Laurie flashed. 'Have you anything against him?'

'Not a thing,' Rolf admitted. 'But I can make enquiries about him—if you like?'

'Thank you, no,' Laurie said firmly. 'But I'd like you to meet him. Then you'd see for yourself that there just isn't any need to make enquiries.'

'Fair enough,' Rolf said judicially. 'Now, how can we manage that without it appearing too obvious? Do you and your mother play bridge?'

'Yes, but not very well and'—warningly—'we only play for very small stakes.'

'There, and I'd planned to fleece you of every penny you've got! Well, see if you can arrange it. You could make the excuse that I get bored on my own—and that's true enough. I know your mother will think that's a good enough reason to merit her co-operation, but how about this Mr Brownsell of yours?'

'He's not mine,' Laurie denied vigorously. 'He's—well, fifty-ish, I should think. And though I don't know if he plays bridge, I'm quite sure that if he does——' she stopped short, grinning puckishly. 'No, I'm not going to say nice things about him because if I do, it will only make you prejudiced against him.'

'You do think I'm a contrary sort of creature, don't you?' he asked quizzically.

'I think you're used to having your own way——'

'Not always, by any means,' Rolf said harshly. 'In fact, it seems to me that where really important things are concerned—oh well, never mind that. Let's talk about something else. Tell me, is there a romance brewing between my Hutton and your Miss Trewyn?'

'We-ell,' Laurie said judicially, 'there *might* be. But it's early days to say yet.'

'Is it? But do these things of a necessity take a long time to develop?' Rolf asked dubiously. 'I was under the impression that they could be practically instantaneous.'

'You seem to know more about it than I do,' Laurie told him. 'But what I really meant is that when two people are only just finding out whether they care for one another, it's terribly easy for an outsider to spoil everything. By teasing them, perhaps, or taking too much for granted too soon.'

'It seems that you know quite a lot about it,' Rolf said in a surprisingly gentle voice. 'And I should imagine that if the people concerned aren't in their first youth they might be more sensitive than younger ones would be?'

'They might well be,' Laurie agreed seriously, thinking not of Miss Trewyn and Hutton but of her mother and Mr Brownsell. Yes, of course, she must be very careful not to appear to notice any signs of attraction between them.

'Dear me, how serious we have got,' Rolf commented in a jocular manner which didn't somehow seem very convinc-

ing. 'Anyone would think that we have wisdom and experience well beyond average!'

'I don't think it's so much that as wanting people to be
happy and trying to see things from their point of view,'
Laurie said simply, and hearing the sound of an approaching
car, stood up. 'I must go now, Mr Audley. Mr Brownsell
took Mother out for a drive and that will be them coming
back. I want to have some coffee ready for them.'

Too late she realised that in telling him of the little jaunt
so soon after their previous conversation he could hardly
fail to put two and two together, and suppose, even with
the best intentions in the world, he wasn't as discreet as the
situation demanded? It might spoil everything.

But she needn't have worried. Rolf showed no sign of
reading more into what she had said than that it was just
a plain statement of fact.

'Just what she needed, I should say,' he said casually.
'Fresh air after all the hours she spends in the kitchen. All
right, if you must go——' Impulsively he held out his hand.
'Thank you, Laurie. It can't have been an easy thing to do.'

'It wasn't,' Laurie admitted frankly. 'But I'm glad I
plucked up courage!'

She went to bed that night with a feeling of warmth in
her heart and the pleasant memory of a firm handclasp.

'Yes, I'm glad I told him,' she murmured drowsily.

Mr Brownsell was delighted to make up a bridge four. He
turned out to be an excellent exponent of the game, and so
did Rolf. The result was that with Mrs Stephens and Laurie
playing a far less skilful game, the real battle was between
the two men.

Their concentration was something that both Mrs
Stephens and Laurie envied, but to Laurie, at least, it was
rather worrying. She had wanted Mr Brownsell and Rolf to
have an opportunity of becoming friends and instead of
that, they were behaving like enemies.

But once play was finished—with Rolf and Mrs Stephens
narrowly the winners—they were enthusiastic in their
praise of each other's skill. Mrs Stephens and Laurie, going
out to the kitchen for coffee and sandwiches, left them

eagerly analysing the various tactics and manoeuvres that each had pursued.

'Well, thank goodness they're not squabbling like some people do,' Laurie remarked, and her mother looked at her curiously. There had been a surprisingly earnest note in Laurie's voice and she wondered why. But deciding that it would be tactless to ask, she simply said briskly:

'Yes, indeed. Men need male company, particularly when they're both rather lonely individuals as these two are.'

And Rolf said much the same when the little party broke up.

'I can't tell you how much I've enjoyed myself,' he said warmly. 'There's nothing like mental occupation for helping to take one's mind off physical handicaps.'

'I think you owe your thanks to Mr Brownsell rather than to Mother and me,' Laurie suggested ruefully. 'We're very second rate compared with you two.'

This the two men vigorously denied, but Laurie and her mother refused to take their compliments seriously and when, at the very last moment, Mr Brownsell asked Rolf if he played chess and received an enthusiastic affirmative in answer, the two women exchanged amused looks. Chess, essentially a game for two, meant that they would not be needed to make up a bridge four again.

Actually, Laurie's reactions were mixed. She was delighted that Rolf's doubts about Mr Brownsell had been dispelled, but on the other hand, she had enjoyed the evening and it was disappointing to know that it was unlikely to be repeated except, perhaps, at long intervals.

And then, with a sense of shock, she realised that in only a short time neither of the men would be living at the Ranch. Mr Brownsell would be visiting them from time to time on business, but Rolf——

For the first time she counted the weeks that remained before he would be out of plaster and able to return to normal life from the point of view of how *few* weeks there were left rather than how many.

CHAPTER FIVE

As well as spending evenings playing chess with him, Mr Brownsell occasionally took Rolf for a drive in his car. It was almost as roomy as Rolf's own car and he was able to get in and out of it with very little assistance.

On one afternoon, they were out rather later than usual and Miss Jones arrived before they had returned. However, when Laurie explained the reason to her, she didn't seem in the least put out.

'It will do the boy all the good in the world to play truant for once,' she said, and again Laurie noticed that maternal quality in her voice.

'Would you care to have a cup of tea while you're waiting?' she suggested.

'Indeed I would,' Miss Jones replied with evident pleasure. 'Particularly if you'll have one as well—in Mr Audley's sitting room?'

'Very well,' Laurie agreed. It was something she would not herself have suggested, but she was reasonably sure that Miss Jones felt no such diffidence.

When she brought in the tray Miss Jones, sitting in Rolf's own chair, looked up with a smile.

'It surprised you that I've made myself so much at home, didn't it? But then, you see, I've known Mr Audley for a long, long time and I know he wouldn't regard it as a liberty.'

'I think, as well as having known him for a long time, you're very fond of him, aren't you?' Laurie suggested gently as she poured out the tea and handed Miss Jones her cup.

'Yes, I am,' Miss Jones admitted. 'You see——' she hesitated as if unsure whether to continue and then evidently decided that she would. 'You see, I believe I told you I was his father's secretary? Well, some years after Mrs Audley's death, he asked me to marry him and I agreed. But before

80

our wedding day arrived, he died very suddenly and unexpectedly——'

'Oh, Miss Jones!' Laurie said pitifully.

'Yes, it was very hard to bear,' Miss Jones said quietly.
'But in time, one learns to live with one's loss, however
great. And Rolf was very good to me. He was in his late
teens then, but I knew he would have welcomed me as a
stepmother and regretted, as I did, that we would never
stand in that relationship to one another. He's been very
generous to me, very generous indeed. But then he's by
nature generous. I've never known him refuse help to anyone who genuinely needs it.'

She seemed to drift into a sort of daydream, her lips smiling, her eyes tender. Laurie, respecting her need for silence,
had plenty to think about.

For one thing, how amazing that her mother should have
so accurately guessed that Miss Jones had cared deeply for
Rolf's father and regarded Rolf himself almost as a son!
Really, it was almost like second sight!

But what intrigued her even more was the different way
in which people regarded Rolf himself. To Miss Jones, he
was a kind, generous man, willing to help people in need.
To Geoffrey he was the very reverse—mean, arrogant, rul-
ing by fear.

Which of them was right? Unconsciously Laurie shook her
head. They couldn't both be. And yet, different though their
opinions were, they had one thing in common. Neither of
them regarded Rolf as a man to whom they could be in-
different.

Nor, Laurie knew, could she.

The visit to the bank passed off very satisfactorily, though
Mrs Stephens was still inclined to be uneasy over getting
into debt.

'Yes, I know, lots of people have mortgages,' she admitted. 'And this one will give us a chance to make good. But
even so, it will be one of the happiest days of my life when
it's paid off. I'm sorry, Laurie, but I can't help feeling like
that.'

'Well, so do I, darling,' Laurie said sympathetically. 'But

all the same, it will mean that we can get through this first year and without it, we wouldn't have been able to do that, would we?'

'No, we wouldn't,' Mrs Stephens agreed more cheerfully. 'But all the same, we mustn't be extravagant—as regards our personal expenditure, I mean.'

'Of course not. But we mustn't cut down on our hotel standards,' Laurie warned. 'That would be fatal.'

'No, indeed!' Mrs Stephens sounded quite shocked at the mere idea. 'That's just what John—Mr Brownsell—says, and I do think he knows what he's talking about.'

'I'm sure he does,' Laurie agreed.

John! So they were on first name terms already! That was promising, and so was the fact that her mother obviously attached more to his opinion than she did to her own.

'You know, Mother, I have a feeling that this is our turning point,' she went on thoughtfully. 'I think from now on we'll have more and more people wanting to come here.'

'I hope you're right,' Mrs Stephens said with a return to her previous gloom, and Laurie realised that in future she would be wise not to express too much optimism since, perhaps inevitably, her mother's reaction was to express caution, even pessimism.

But to some degree at least, Laurie turned out to be right, for the very next morning two Americans arrived asking if they could have lunch at the Ranch.

'Of course,' the wife apologised, 'we saw from your notice board at the top of the lane that it's a residential hotel, but we hoped you'd be willing to stretch a point——?'

'Yes, we can do that,' Laurie agreed, and added frankly: 'Later in the season it might not be possible, but this is our first year and we have tables to spare in the dining room. Lunch is at one o'clock. Will that suit you?'

'Fine, won't it, Frank?'

'Yes, my dear,' was the dutiful response, and Laurie realised with amusement that the wife was certainly the leading personality of the couple and that Frank was only consulted when a decision had already been made.

'What we plan to do is to go down to the Cove which we

understand is very beautiful, but we'll be back right on time!' with a flashing smile.

'You'll find us ready,' Laurie promised, 'And I wonder—may I know your name?'

'Sure—it's Austin, and we come from Baltimore.'

'Thank you, Mrs Austin,' Laurie said with a smile. Then, as they went off, she dashed out to the kitchen to warn her mother that she would have two more mouths to feed.

'But they won't be here for another hour, so I thought that would give you time—will it?' anxiously.

'Yes, they can have our portions,' Mrs Stephens said promptly. 'It will mean that we have to make do with bread and cheese, but I don't mind if you don't?'

'Of course I don't,' Laurie said rather uneasily. 'But I'm sorry, Mother, I ought to have asked you first.'

'Perhaps you ought,' Mrs Stephens agreed. 'But really, it's my fault. You see, though I've always been careful about not having leftovers if I can help it, now I feel I ought to be doubly careful not to have any waste. It's a sensible way of economising, you see.'

'But suppose anyone wanted a second helping?' Laurie asked mischievously.

'But they won't,' Mrs Stephens told her triumphantly. 'Not with the size helpings I give them.'

Laurie laughed.

'You've got all the answers, haven't you, Mother? Well, I'd better go and lay their table.'

By the time she had done that and put a vase of fresh flowers on the table, the Austins returned, loud in their praises of the beauties of the Cove. Purposely Laurie took them up to one of the bedrooms for a wash and the result was just what she had hoped. Mrs Austin was enthusiastic about the dainty appearance of the room and the plentiful supply of cupboards and drawers.

'Real practical,' she announced approvingly. 'Why, some hotels where we've stayed the space provided was so limited that we had to live in our suitcases, didn't we, Frank?'

'That's so,' Mr Austin confirmed and then, surprisingly, added his own contribution. 'And if you remember, Aline, the towels were so often thin and worn. Not like these!'

'Why, that's so, Frank,' Mrs Austin said in surprise, though less, Laurie thought, because of the quality of the towels than at her husband's show of initiative.

They were just as enthusiastic over their lunch and when they left were regretting their inability to stay over.

'You've got *everything*,' Mrs Austin pronounced. 'And we'd just love to stay but, you see, we're booked up solid from now until when we leave for the States. But we'll be coming over again next year and you can certainly rely on having us with you then!'

'We shall look forward to seeing you,' Laurie said sincerely, but Mrs Austin hadn't finished yet.

'Now, what I'd like would be several of those brochures of yours that I saw in the hall,' she continued briskly. 'Because we shall certainly make it our business to tell our friends about you. Two in particular, Mr and Mrs Hewitt who are over here right now and I know they're not booked up like we are.'

They went off, still singing praises and with half-a-dozen brochures, promising that they'd be hearing from the Hewitts right soon. Mrs Austin was sure of that and Mr Austin agreed with her.

But the Stephens didn't take the assurance too seriously.

'I think she'll do her best to persuade her friends to come,' Mrs Stephens admitted. 'But you can't make people do things if they don't really want to.'

'No, you can't,' Laurie agreed. 'Besides, by now the Hewitts may have made other arrangements. Oh well, it's at least nice to know that we've met with such approval. I almost purred.'

But not only was Mrs Austin as good as her word but that very evening Mrs Hewitt rang up to book accommodation for a week for herself and her husband. She was a somewhat garrulous lady and by the time the conversation ended Laurie knew a surprising lot about the Hewitts' affairs. Not only was she told where they lived and that the Austins were near neighbours—Mrs Austin was described as 'a really lovely person'—but she knew that they had a married son who also lived near and a small granddaughter who was the apple of their eyes.

Then there was a rumble in the background and momentarily Mrs Hewitt paused. Then she laughed goodnaturedly.

'That was my husband! He says to remember this is a
distance call and do I want to ruin him, talking so long?
Well then, Miss Stephens, we'll be with you in time for
lunch on Saturday. 'Bye!' and finally did ring off.

Rubbing her ear tenderly, Laurie told her mother of the
conversation and Mrs Stephens looked surprised.

'But you were on the phone for *ages*,' she protested. 'It
couldn't have taken all that time just to make a reserva-
tion!'

'It didn't, but I was just summarising for you. What she
actually said was——' and almost word for word, she reeled
off all that Mrs Hewitt had said.

Mrs Stephens listened with every indication of considerable interest and when at last Laurie came to a breathless
halt, asked what the little granddaughter's name was.

'She didn't say,' Laurie confessed.

'Oh dear, you should have asked her,' Mrs Stephens said
reproachfully. 'She would think you weren't interested!'

Laurie laughed.

'What a nice person you are, Mother,' she said affectionately. 'I just didn't think of it.'

'Ah well, naturally you wouldn't understand. But I do
because I'm the grandmother age as well. You know,
Laurie,' Mrs Stephens concluded wistfully, 'I do wish you'd
get married so that I could have some grandchildren!'

'Whom you'd spoil outrageously,' Laurie told her
severely. 'But really, Mother, I can't get married just to
provide you with grannie-fodder, now can I?'

'No, I suppose not,' Mrs Stephens sighed resignedly. 'All
the same, it's a pity——'

Laurie fled. She wasn't at all sure that it wasn't on the
tip of her mother's tongue to suggest whom she might consider marrying!

'My Hutton seems quite a bit more cheerful these days,'
Rolf commented to Laurie when she brought back some
more books. 'Does that mean he's making more of a hit with
Miss Trewyn?'

'It could do,' Laurie said cautiously. 'Anyhow, they went

to a dinner-dance together last Saturday. But I expect you know that?'

'No, it's the first I've heard of it,' Rolf denied. 'Hutton evidently doesn't believe in counting his chickens in public before they're hatched—wise man!' He paused meditatively. 'The giddy creatures—how I envy them!'

'Well, it won't be long now before you'll be able to indulge in similar frivolities,' Laurie reminded him encouragingly.

'When I can, will you let me take you gadding to celebrate?' Rolf asked. 'Perhaps not dancing for a while but out to dinner, certainly?'

'Thank you, I'd like that,' Laurie accepted serenely despite the fact that the suggestion had taken her by surprise. 'That is, if you really want to. I wouldn't like to feel it would be—out of——' she stopped short because he was laughing at her.

'Out of gratitude for all the kindness I've had from you?' he suggested. 'No, it's not because of that, though I admit that the fact you have it in you to be so kind to me is a contributory factor.'

'In that case, really it's Mother you ought to take out,' Laurie told him. 'She's been far nicer to you than I have.'

'How you women do like digging up the hatchet,' Rolf complained. 'I thought all that was over and done with long ago. Besides, do you think Brownsell would like it if I suggested taking your mother out?'

'Mr Brownsell!' Laurie repeated in alarm. 'You mean—you've realised——?'

'Not being absolutely blind, of course I have. His interest in the Ranch is obviously something more than a purely professional one,' Rolf told her. 'In fact, there seems to be a positive aura of romance in the air! Your mother and Brownsell, Hutton and Miss Trewyn—only you and I seem to be outside it!'

Laurie felt her colour rising traitorously. What on earth had made him say such a thing, so apparently linking them together!

'But then, you see, I'm not a romantically inclined person,' she insisted with an emphatic shake of her head.

'You mean that so far there isn't anybody special where you're concerned?' he asked bluntly.

'No, there isn't,' she denied firmly.

'I see.' Rolf said, and then, reflectively: 'Do you remember, at the time of the Smith fracas, that I asked you what you considered were the necessary qualities needed by two people in order to make a successful marriage? And you said that was such a serious matter that you needed notice before answering it?'

'Yes, I remember,' Laurie said reluctantly.

'Well, have you come to any conclusions yet?' he persisted. 'Because if you have, I'd like to hear them.'

It was no good refusing to answer because she knew perfectly well that if she did he would somehow compel her to —which might well be more embarrassing than if she capitulated without a struggle.

'I don't know that I've given it much serious thought,' she said slowly. 'But I suppose, really, I do know.'

'Carry on,' he encouraged as she paused.

'To begin with, the two people concerned must—must care very deeply for one another——' she couldn't bring herself to say 'love'. 'Because then their partner's happiness would mean more to each of them than their own.'

'Good point,' Rolf commented critically. 'What else?'

'Oh, they must be able to trust and respect one another. And have similar ideas of what's amusing so that they can share jokes,' Laurie gabbled, wishing to goodness he'd stop looking at her so searchingly. 'And they must share some of the same interests—but not all, because that would mean that they didn't bring any new ideas to one another.'

'So far, so good,' Rolf approved. 'In fact, you've said nothing yet with which I haven't agreed. What else?'

'That's all,' Laurie said firmly.

'Really? I should have thought——'

'Mr Audley, I've quite a lot of work to do even if you haven't,' Laurie insisted sternly. 'I've really no more time for idle chatter.'

'Idle chatter, she calls it!' Rolf apostrophised. 'My good girl, don't you appreciate that it's a topic of vital importance? If more people gave serious thought to it, there wouldn't be so many broken marriages!'

'Maybe not,' Laurie conceded. 'But that doesn't alter the fact that I've got work to do!'

'And that's your last word?'

'It is,' Laurie said cheerfully. But at the door she paused. 'No, there's one other thing. When—if—I ever do get married it must be to someone who wants me to be *me*. Not just a pale shadow of himself.'

She didn't wait for any possible answer from Rolf but shut the door firmly between them. At least she had had the last word!

Until now the swimming pool had not been filled, but now Laurie suggested that it should be.

'After all, it is one of our amenities that people have a right to expect,' she pointed out reasonably. 'And with the Hewitts coming this seems as good a time as any to have it ready.'

What she didn't say was that she had another reason for the suggestion. She realised, though she wasn't sure if Rolf did, that even when his leg was out of plaster it would be some time before he was capable of normal activities. He would almost certainly be told that he must use it to exercise the flabby muscles even though, at first, that would be tiring and even painful. But swimming would not only be helpful, it would be as pleasant a way of taking exercise as could be devised.

So Trewyn was told to sweep and generally clean up the pool in readiness for it to be filled. When that was done, Laurie went to inspect it and was delighted at the difference the sparkling water made.

Before, the pool had looked rather forlorn and useless, but now it had a purpose. The little shelter at the shallow end, complete with two changing cubicles, had a red and white striped awning which pulled out in the same way as those on shop fronts do. There were two white-painted iron tables with chairs to match and room for deck chairs as well. At the deep end was a diving platform with two levels. It was this which tempted Laurie. She went back to the hotel, changed, and went back to take her first dive into their very own pool.

But one thing she hadn't reckoned on. The water, not yet really warmed by the sunshine, was chillier than she had expected and she let out a little squawk as she entered it. But by the time she had swum the length of the pool, she was delighting in the invigorating sting of the water and warmed by her own activity, floated contentedly in the shallows.

'I hope I'll be joining you there soon,' Rolf's voice announced so unexpectedly that Laurie jack-knifed and went under. When, spluttering and breathless she emerged, she saw that he was standing on the edge of the pool, leaning on his stick. Laurie swam over to him and hung on to the rail.

'If it wasn't for your plaster, I'd pull you in, clothes and all,' she told him severely. 'What a thing to do! I might have drowned from sheer shock!'

'Not you,' Rolf retorted confidently. 'You're too much of a mermaid for that! But, joking apart, you swim magnificently, Laurie, as if the water was your natural element. Which is just as well, seeing the experience you had in the Cove——'

'Oh, that!' She was disturbed by the distress in his voice and sought to mitigate it. 'That's all over and done with, so don't think any more about it. I expect really it was no more than a rather stupid prank——'

'You're more generous than I find it possible to be,' he said grimly. 'And though I've done everything I can to bring home the enormity of such behaviour to the culprits, I have an uneasy feeling—in fact, Laurie, I'd be thankful if you'd promise not to swim alone at the Cove again.'

'The culprits', he had said, but that included Sylvia French, and Laurie was sure that it was of her that he was really thinking and wondered if there had been a serious breach between them as a result of the incident.

'Don't you think that's taking a rather extreme view of it?' she suggested. 'I mean, if people have got into trouble once for behaving in a certain way, do you think it's really likely that they'd do the same thing again?'

'Perhaps not,' he conceded. 'All the same—will you promise? Please!'

'Very well,' Laurie agreed briefly, and heaved herself out

of the water. 'Br-rh! But the water is chilly once one stops
swimming. Do you mind if I hurry back to the house?'

'Off you go and—thank you,' Rolf said with such con-
vincing sincerity that Laurie was startled.

He really *was* worried about the possibility of it being
dangerous for her to visit the Cove alone again. But was it
because he was afraid on her account or because he was
anxious to protect Sylvia from a repetition of her earlier
malicious stupidity?

It could be either. Or, of course, both.

The Hewitts arrived punctually on Saturday morning. Mrs
Hewitt was a tiny little woman, pretty and considerably
younger than her husband who obviously adored her. Mr
Hewitt was tall, erect and extremely good-looking. He carried himself in a dignified way as if he was a man used to
having authority but what Laurie found most attractive
about him was his eyes. They were grey, but unlike some
grey eyes, they had a sparkle which, Laurie shrewdly sus-
pected, was a sign of a lively sense of humour.

She was amused to realise that, just as in the case of the
Austins, it was the wife who did most of the talking, though
Mr Hewitt had more to say for himself than Mr Austin had
had. It was he who apologised with rather charming for-
mality for giving such short notice of their intended visit.

'But we felt we just *had* to come after the way Aline
Austin spoke of you,' Mrs Hewitt enlarged. 'And believe me,
she isn't a person to overlook faults. She likes everything
to be just so! So we knew we could take her word for it.'

'That's very reassuring,' Laurie said with a gravity that
she found difficult to maintain. 'And now I expect you would
like to see your room?'

She took them up to one of the nicest rooms which was
not only larger than some of the others but had its own
bathroom. The Hewitts were loud in their praises of everything they saw—and really, Laurie thought complacently,
they had every reason to be pleased. Gay curtains and
matching bedspreads looked so fresh and crisp. Miss Trewyn
had polished the furniture within an inch of its life and the
little bowl of roses made a final air of welcome.

'I'll get the luggage up, Eleanor,' Mr Hewitt announced,

and wouldn't hear of Laurie calling Trewyn to do the job. 'The exercise will do me good after all the driving we've done,' he insisted. 'And so will swimming in that fine pool of yours. I'm looking forward to that.'

'Then I'll leave you to it,' said Laurie, thinking gratefully that these were going to be very different visitors from the Smiths.

As she reached the hall, Mr Brownsell arrived for his week-end visit and they were exchanging greetings when the Hewitts came downstairs. Mrs Hewitt was still talking volubly of their satisfaction with their room when she stopped short in the middle of a sentence and gave a little scream.

'Well, what *do* you know!' she exclaimed delightedly. 'Of all people, John Brownsell! I do hope you remember us, Mr Brownsell? We met when we were all cruising on the *Acantha* and you were so helpful about——'

'Of course I remember you, Mrs Hewitt,' Mr Brownsell assured her so promptly that it sounded to Laurie almost as if he wanted to cut Mrs Hewitt's reminiscences short. 'So you've found this delightful little corner of Cornwall! You must let me show you some of the local beauty spots!'

'Now isn't that just like you, Mr Brownsell!' Mrs Hewitt said warmly. 'So kind and helpful!' She turned to Laurie. 'I must tell you how helpful he was on that Mediterranean cruise I spoke of.'

'Oh, it was nothing,' Mr Brownsell protested hastily, but Mrs Hewitt refused to take the hint.

'Now, that's just your English modesty,' she declared. 'You see, it was this way, Miss Stephens. I was thinking of buying a teddy-bear for our little granddaughter, Sally-Ann, but you hear such dreadful accounts of children pulling the eyes out of cuddly toys and swallowing them or hurting themselves on badly covered wires that I was sort of scared. If Sally-Ann had been hurt on a toy we'd bought for her— well, we'd never have forgiven ourselves. But as we were talking it over, Mr Brownsell, who was also buying something in the ship's gift shop, told us that we could rely on the teddy-bear being quite safe because he knew that the maker had a very strong sense of responsibility about such things and was real insistent that all his toys had a very high standard of safety. That's just word for word what you said, now isn't it, Mr Brownsell?'

'Something like that,' Mr Brownsell admitted with an uneasiness that didn't surprise Laurie. It was only too easy to guess who the maker of the teddy-bear was!

'So,' Mrs Hewitt went on, blissfully unconscious of the mischief she was making, 'just to be on the safe side, I asked him if he knew the maker personally and he said yes, he did and that he was one of his clients as well as a close friend. So that settled it, and Sally-Ann simply loved her teddy! And now, what do you say we go out and have a close-up of that pool? I expect you'll want to get into it as soon as you can, Craig, though of course, you shouldn't bathe until at least an hour after lunch.'

They went off and Mr Brownsell was left to do what he could to put matters right—which judging by Laurie's expression, wasn't going to be easy.

'I'm sorry about that, Laurie,' he said ruefully. 'But how the dickens was I to know that we'd meet again—here of all places?'

'Your meeting them wouldn't have mattered in the least,' Laurie pointed out icily, 'if you and Mr Audley hadn't lied about not knowing one another! That was despicable.'

'Was it?' Mr Brownsell asked defensively. 'I don't think we had any choice.'

'No choice? Of course you had!' Laurie flared. 'Obviously, when I wouldn't let Mr Audley interfere in our affairs, he managed to persuade you to come here and inveigle yourself into our confidence! Oh, it was mean—mean, Mr Brownsell! I can't think how you could have lent yourself to such double-dealing!'

'You mean, you feel Rolf diddled you and you don't like it, don't you?' Mr Brownsell suggested. 'Well, yes, he did. But can't you understand why?'

'No,' Laurie denied flatly.

'Then I'll tell you. It was because he was genuinely concerned. He saw nothing but bankruptcy ahead for you and your mother if you didn't have proper advice. *Genuine concern*,' he repeated, and waited.

Laurie hesitated.

'I suppose you're right. Actually what infuriates me *is* that I let myself be diddled,' she conceded morosely. 'I ought to have guessed, not only because you made friends so quickly which I don't think men do as a rule, but you repeated almost word for word what Mr Audley had said about our finances.'

'That was because we both told the truth,' Mr Brownsell told her bluntly. 'And as for making friends—we thought we'd managed that rather well!'

He sounded quite aggrieved and suddenly Laurie saw the funny side of it all and laughed. Really, it was too absurd. Two grown men behaving like schoolboys with their plotting and planning and thinking themselves so clever!

'That's better!' Mr Brownsell said with relief.

'I bet it was Mr Audley who thought it all up!' she commented. 'It's so typical of him. By hook or by crook he always does get his own way, doesn't he?'

'I'm not so sure about that,' Mr Brownsell said doubtfully, and Laurie remembered that Rolf himself had said that, actually, where really important things were concerned he certainly didn't always get his own way. For the first time she wondered if he had been thinking of any particular occasion when that had been the case.

'There's just one thing, Laurie,' Mr Brownsell said diffidently.

'Yes?'

'About this duplicity of Rolf's and mine—do you intend to tell your mother?'

'Don't you want me to?' Laurie asked with interest.

'Frankly, I'd sooner she didn't know,' he admitted. 'She's such a straightforward, honest little soul. She might find it difficult to understand—and forgive.'

'And that matters?' Laurie asked gently.

'Very much,' Mr Brownsell said earnestly. 'You see, all that I promised Rolf was that I'd come here and find out if he was right in thinking that you—that you——'

'Were making a mess of things,' Laurie suggested, and he nodded.

'But when you got here——' Laurie prompted.

Mr Brownsell drew himself erect and faced her unflinch-
ingly.

'Once I'd met your mother, I knew that there was nothing
I wouldn't do to help her.'

Laurie gave him a flashing smile, but almost instantly became serious again.

'Yes, I do understand, Mr Brownsell,' she said sympathetically. 'But you see, the trouble is that if I don't tell
her, almost certainly Mrs Hewitt will. And of the two, I
think it would be better if she heard about it from me.'

Mr Brownsell gave a sigh which was almost a groan.

'Yes, perhaps it would,' he admitted. 'Oh, confound that
woman! Why, of all people, did she have to turn up here?'

'Fate, punishing you for telling fibs, I expect,' Laurie suggested reprovingly, but then, seeing how downcast Mr
Brownsell looked, she relented and to her own surprise as
much as to his, she gave him a quick, impulsive kiss.

'Don't worry too much,' she encouraged. 'I'll do my best
for you!' and left him, speechless but grateful, to go in
search of her mother. But she didn't rush into a revelation
of the little drama that had just been enacted. First of all,
she commented that the Hewitts had been delighted with
everything, then she remarked casually:

'And would you believe it, they and Mr Brownsell already
knew one another! They met on a Mediterranean cruise last
year.'

'Did they really?' Mrs Stephens sounded only mildly interested. 'Well, these days, that could happen, of course.'

If only Laurie could have left it there! But she knew that
she couldn't and surreptitiously, she crossed her fingers.

'Mrs Hewitt is rather a chatterbox,' she began cautiously.
'And she gave chapter and verse of an occasion when he was
very helpful——'

'He would be,' Mrs Stephens said softly. 'He's like that!
But just what did he do?'

Choosing her words very carefully, Laurie told her the
whole story and as she listened, Mrs Stephens' eyes became
rounder and rounder.

'But why?' she asked perplexedly, when Laurie came to a
halt. 'Why should he and Mr Audley pretend that they didn't
know one another?'

'That was my fault,' Laurie confessed regretfully. 'You see, I felt that Mr Audley was being impertinent, so I wouldn't listen to his advice. And he thought that if I knew Mr Brownsell was connected with him in any way, I wouldn't listen to him either.'

'I see,' Mrs Stephens said thoughtfully. 'So really, one can't blame Mr Brownsell—or Mr Audley for that matter, for having misled us.'

'No,' Laurie agreed, perfectly willing to shoulder the blame if it meant that Mr Brownsell escaped condemnation. 'But he—Mr Brownsell—is worried that you may be annoyed with him even though his motives were of the kindest.'

'Of course they were,' Mrs Stephens retorted with asperity. 'I don't doubt that for a moment.' She took off her apron and prinked her hair before the rather steamy kitchen mirror.

'Where are you going?' Laurie asked curiously as her mother made for the door.

'To find Mr Brownsell and set his mind at rest,' Mrs Stephens said briskly.

'And how about Mr Audley's mind?' Laurie asked mischievously. 'Are you going to set that at rest as well?'

'No, I'm not,' Mrs Stephens retorted decidedly. 'That's your job!' And then, seeing Laurie's rebellious expression, she hammered home her point. 'Oh yes, it is! You've just said that it was your silly prejudice against Mr Audley that was at the bottom of all this muddle, so of course, it's for you to sort things out with him!'

'Oh, all right,' Laurie promised reluctantly.

Mrs Stephens looked at her anxiously.

'Well, why not? I thought you'd got over your dislike of the poor man.'

'Well, perhaps, to some degree,' Laurie admitted cautiously.

'Well, I suppose that's better than nothing,' Mrs Stephens said resignedly, and went off to find Mr Brownsell, leaving Laurie a prey to mixed emotions.

She was delighted at the way her mother had taken the news and only hoped that Mr Brownsell would make the most of his opportunity.

But as for setting Rolf's mind at rest, she wasn't at all sure that she wanted to do that—at least, not immediately. He really did deserve to be made to realise the enormity of his offence—to have treated her like a child, and a not very intelligent one at that! It really was inexcusable.

But Rolf gave her no opportunity of putting any such plan into operation. He sent Hutton to her with a message that he would be grateful if she could spare him a few minutes, and immediately Laurie entered his sitting room she relented. He looked so serious, so distressed, and his first words as he got awkwardly to his feet were not an attempt to justify himself but an admission of his offence.

'Can you possibly forgive me?'

It was said so humbly, so earnestly, that Laurie found herself making the excuses for him that he had scorned to make for himself.

'I think I'll have to,' she told him. 'Because I do see that you were genuinely concerned.'

'I was indeed,' he agreed. 'But that doesn't excuse me for behaving like a bull in a china shop. If I'd been more diplomatic——'

'I don't know,' Laurie said doubtfully. 'You see, the real trouble was that however tactful you might have been, I knew that really you were right. But I couldn't bring myself to admit it.'

Rolf's face cleared as if by magic.

'That's generous of you, Laurie, and more than I deserve. It was a dirty trick to play on you, though I simply couldn't see any other way—I do hope, by the way, that you haven't got it in for Brownsell, because he was a very reluctant accomplice.'

'I realised that—and I let him off very lightly,' Laurie replied. Then her eyes twinkled. 'But the really important thing is that Mother doesn't blame him at all. In fact, she was very worried lest he should be worried that she did. Blame him, I mean.'

'Yes, I got the message even though it was a bit involved. Well, that's fine, isn't it? I only hope I'll be out of this confounded plaster in time to dance at the wedding!'

'There are another ten days before the cast comes off,

4 FREE

Harlequin Romances

Take these ⓸ best-selling Harlequin Romance stories

FREE

 EXCITING DETAILS INSIDE

aren't there?' Laurie said sympathetically. 'But when you're looking forward to something very much, time always seems to *crawl*.'

'You're right there! And I'm not a very patient patient—possibly because, until this happened, I've never had anything other than childish ailments wrong with me. Which means, I know, that I've been lucky, but somehow, at this juncture, that doesn't seem very consoling.'

'It certainly wouldn't console me,' Laurie assured him feelingly. 'I'd be in an absolutely foul temper and everybody would wish I'd never been born! I think you've been very patient—for a man!'

Rolf grinned.

'You'll have me thinking I'm something of a hero if you're not careful,' he warned her, 'and that despite that final jibe!'

'It was mean of me,' Laurie said quickly. 'Because you can't retaliate without being even ruder than I was.'

Rolf laughed outright.

'Let's leave it at that before it gets too complicated, shall we?' he suggested. And then, impulsively: 'You know, Laurie, I believe we're nearer now to understanding one another than we've ever been before.'

'I hope so,' Laurie said, and suddenly feeling shy, made her escape as quickly as possible.

That night, when she went up to bed, she crept quietly along the corridor and listened anxiously at her mother's door.

Mrs Stephens had made a headache the excuse for going to bed early and Laurie was concerned. She could never remember her mother having a headache before and she wondered if it was a symptom of some more serious complaint.

And, listening, she heard an unmistakable sound. Her mother was sobbing as if her heart would break.

CHAPTER SIX

FOR a moment Laurie hesitated outside her mother's door, uncertain whether to go in or not. There were times—she'd experienced them herself—when more than anything one wanted to be alone. Perhaps, for her mother, this was one of those occasions and to go in uninvited would be an intrusion. On the other hand, to take no notice of her obvious distress seemed so heartless.

She compromised by knocking on the door and saying quietly:

'It's Laurie. May I come in?'

There was a little pause and then a husky voice said:

'All right,' and Laurie went in. Her mother was lying on the bed, her face turned into the pillow. Laurie sat down on the edge of the bed and laid her hand gently on her mother's shoulder.

'Darling, is your headache so very bad?' she asked sympathetically.

Mrs Stephens turned her head. Her hair was disordered and her pretty face swollen with crying. But worse even than that, there was no mistaking her expression of desperate unhappiness.

'I didn't have a headache,' she confessed huskily. 'That was just an excuse to get away. Oh, Laurie——' and tears began to stream down her cheeks.

'Then what's wrong, darling?' Laurie said anxiously. 'Is it anything I can help with?'

'No,' Mrs Stephens said dejectedly. 'There's nothing anyone can do.'

'But sometimes it helps just to tell somebody. It gets things sorted out in one's mind.' Laurie coaxed.

Mrs Stephens shook her head.

'I've got it all sorted out and I know just what I've got to do!' Another broken-hearted sob. 'It's John!'

'Mr Brownsell?' Laurie exclaimed. 'What's he done?'

'He—he asked me to m-marry him,' Mrs Stephens confessed, and buried her face in the pillow again.

Laurie could have cried with sheer relief.

'But, darling, that's nothing to cry about,' she said reassuringly. 'Unless—you haven't said you won't——?'

'That's just it,' Mrs Stephens wailed. 'I have! I had to!'

'But why, Mother?' Laurie demanded urgently. 'I thought you—liked him very much.'

'So I do. More than just *like*,' Mrs Stephens admitted softly, her face momentarily clearing only to cloud over again. 'But what else could I do?'

'But why, Mother, why?'

Mrs Stephens sat up and pushed her hair back from her face with hands that trembled.

'Because of the mortgage,' she explained. 'That *beastly* mortgage! Right from the beginning I hated it. But now it's a millstone round my neck!'

Laurie was beginning to understand. Mr Brownsell was some years away from retirement age, but all the same, he was not young enough to relish the journey between the Ranch and his Penzance office twice a day. That would mean that if he and her mother were to be married, she would, of course, live with him in Penzance. And if she did that, with her new home to care for, she couldn't also be at the Ranch.

'*Now* you see what I mean.' Mrs Stephens had evidently read Laurie's dismay in her face. 'We've *got* to make a success of this place. Simply got to—because of the mortgage. And you can't do it on your own. I don't want to sound vain, but my cooking is one of the attractions of the place, isn't it?'

And that Laurie could not deny. Unable to suggest a way out of the *impasse* herself, she asked tentatively:

'What does Mr Brownsell say about it?'

'He says he'll wait,' Mrs Stephens said softly. 'And if it was only a question of waiting until the end of the summer so that we'd at least be able to fulfil our commitments over bookings, that would be all right. But it isn't, it isn't!'

And of course, it wasn't. There would still be the mortgage.

'We could sell the Ranch and pay off the mortgage,'

Laurie suggested. 'We'd come out of it a bit worse off than before, but not all that much.'

'*No!*' Mrs Stephens said firmly. 'That's the last thing we'll do. I was the one who was really responsible for us coming here and I'm not going to back out just to suit myself. That's for sure!'

'But why, Mother?' Laurie asked, though suspicion was dawning in her mind.

'I told you. I started it, I'm going through with it,' Mrs Stephens insisted.

'I suppose it isn't on my account, is it?' Laurie demanded. 'Because, if we gave up, I'd be without a job—or a home?'

'Well, that's a point, of course,' Mrs Stephens admitted, though as if it was a very unimportant one. But she was careful to avoid Laurie's eyes and Laurie drew her own conclusions. She got up off the bed.

'Well, look, darling, you're not to worry about it any more,' she said briskly. 'Because we're going to find a way out. Oh yes, we are!' as her mother shook her head. 'I admit I don't see how at present, but there must be a way, so it's got to be found. And now, I'm going to get you something to eat—nothing very heavy but enough to keep you going. And while I'm getting it, I want you to bathe your face and do your hair. You'll feel twice the girl if you do.'

'Yes, dear,' Mrs Stephens promised meekly as if she was a child and Laurie a grown-up in authority.

Laurie went to the kitchen to find a troubled Miss Trewyn dealing competently with preparations for the next meal. She looked up as Laurie came into the room.

'How's your mother now?' she asked anxiously. 'Not like her to have a headache, is it?'

'No, it isn't,' Laurie agreed and added discreetly, 'But it's a lot better now, I'm glad to say.'

'That's good,' Miss Trewyn commented. But she added thoughtfully: 'Of course, there are a good many things that can cause a headache, aren't there, Miss Laurie?'

'Yes, there are,' Laurie agreed.

'Overwork, for one thing,' Miss Trewyn continued. 'Or anxiety. Or—being unhappy.'

'Any of those,' Laurie admitted briefly, wishing that Miss Trewyn wasn't so shrewd.

'Well, I've made my guess—and I don't think I'm wrong,' Miss Trewyn declared. 'But I'm not one to pry into other people's affairs, believe me! All the same, thinking as I do means that there's something I ought to tell you.' She paused and positively simpered. 'It's about me and Hutton. He's asked me to marry him and I've promised to make him a happy man! And when that happens, I'll be leaving you, of course.'

'Oh, Miss Trewyn!' Laurie exclaimed despairingly. This, on top of her mother's problem, was really the last straw!

'Now, don't you take on,' Miss Trewyn advised reassuringly. 'I've told Hutton that I'm not leaving until—well, until your mother's affairs are more settled. And what's more, I've refused even to let it be known that we're engaged. That would be too unkind as things are!'

So, somehow or other, Miss Trewyn knew exactly what had happened.

'But how could she have known?' Laurie asked Rolf when, seeing that Mr Brownsell had already told him how things were, she discussed the situation with him. 'Mother certainly didn't tell her and nor did I. So how——?'

'Don't ask me,' Rolf shook his head. 'But good servants always do know all about their employers' affairs. I don't know how it's done, but Hutton is always *au fait* with anything concerning me, however discreet I am. It must be a sort of unconscious thought transference, I suppose. Disconcerting, but the outcome of genuine affection, I'm quite sure.'

'Perhaps so,' Laurie admitted, and then, returning to the main problem: 'But what can be done about it?'

'Haven't you any ideas?' Rolf asked cautiously.

'I suggested that we should sell the Ranch at the end of the season, and pay off the mortgage so that Mother would be free to marry Mr Brownsell.'

'And you would be left without a job or a home,' he pointed out.

'Yes, but that's something that worries Mother more than it does me,' Laurie told him. 'I could probably get a job fairly easily. In fact, I'm almost sure that they'd take me back at the Black Prince where I worked before. And as for a home——' she shrugged her shoulders, 'I could get a bed-sitter or something——'

'In any case, Brownsell would be quite happy to have you living with them.'

'No,' Laurie said firmly. 'It's very kind of him, but I don't think it would work. Mother's loyalty would be divided and that might make for all sorts of difficulties.'

'It might,' Rolf agreed.

'Well?' Laurie demanded impatiently. 'Can't you think of anything? After all, you've got something of a gift for——'

'For manipulating and contriving and pulling strings when circumstances can't be coped with by straightforward means?' he suggested wryly as she left her sentence uncompleted. 'Yes, perhaps I have.'

'I'm sorry,' Laurie said repentantly. 'I shouldn't have taken it for granted that you'd feel concerned. After all, it isn't your problem.'

'That's a debatable point,' he said reflectively. 'And as a matter of fact, I have got an idea—somewhat along the same lines as yours but with one radical difference.' He paused. 'Unfortunately, at present it isn't feasible. And it may never be. So there's no point in discussing it.'

'No,' Laurie agreed regretfully. 'Well, thank you for listening to my woes. We'll just have to wait and see, I suppose.' She sighed impatiently. 'Though that seems such a feeble attitude to take.'

He stretched out his hand and took hers firmly in it.

'To tell you not to worry is about the most useless thing I can do,' he said regretfully. 'And yet I've a feeling that we must wait to find a solution.'

'We've got to find one,' Laurie retorted resolutely, encouraged by that firm clasp. 'And you'll do your best to help, won't you, Mr Audley?'

'I will, indeed,' he promised, and then: 'I wonder, seeing that we're to be allies in a good cause, whether you'd feel you could call me by my first name? After all, I've called you by yours for some time—which has been gross impertinence since I did it without asking your permission.'

Rather taken aback by this sudden introduction of such a totally different and rather trivial matter, Laurie didn't answer immediately and Rolf let go of her hand.

'I'm sorry—this is perhaps not the moment to ask for a favour,' he said stiffly.

'Oh, please!' Laurie begged. 'It wasn't that at all. It was just that I was rather surprised. Yes, of course I will, Rolf.'

'That sounds very pleasant,' he told her appreciatively. 'Mind you don't forget!'

'I won't,' she promised, feeling that she had really gained a friend. Yet, only a little later, she lost that sense of re-assurance, for abruptly he gave her some unwelcome in-formation.

'I think it's only fair to warn you that Sylvia French will be coming here to see me and I'd like you to appreciate that it's really essential that she should,' he explained carefully. 'You see, there's a conference coming off in the near future and it's important. It will give manufacturers in my line a chance of discussing ways and means of increasing our ex-ports. I'd naturally planned to attend it, but since I can't, I'm sending someone else in my place. Quite a good chap, but this will be a new experience for him. Sylvia, on the other hand, has always accompanied me to the trade fairs and she can be a tremendous help to Braithwaite.'

'But really, there's no need for you to be concerned on my behalf,' Laurie said coolly. 'Naturally, business must take preference over any personal feelings. I quite under-stand that.'

'Oh, for goodness' sake!' Rolf said impatiently. 'Do you have to take me up the wrong way if you get the least pos-sible chance? I am *not* an insensitive money-grabber as you seem to think, but all the same the prosperity of the firm matters very much to me. It should, you know, because I've got quite a lot of people who are dependent on me for their livelihood. And these occasions are important. For one thing, they give one a chance of seeing what new ideas one's rivals have thought up and I've got to prime Sylvia what to look out for. Oh well, never mind. If you can't un-derstand, you can't.'

'But I do,' Laurie assured him earnestly. 'I was just being rather silly because——'

'Because, in the circumstances, you don't feel very

friendly towards Sylvia,' he interrupted. 'And small wonder. That was why I warned you. I thought you'd prefer to know so that you can avoid meeting her.'

'Well, I certainly won't be looking for trouble, but if you think I'm going to run away——' she flashed defiantly, and then, seeing his quizzical expression, felt suddenly deflated. 'Sorry,' she muttered. 'I lost my temper.'

'Yes, well, I seem to remember telling you that I like auburn hair,' he reminded her, gently touching her bright curls. 'To say nothing of *retroussé* noses. But one does have to remember that a quick temper usually goes with your colouring.'

'One does,' Laurie sighed, and then mischievously: 'But if *I* remember correctly, you referred to my hair as carrots and my nose as snub!'

'So you told me,' Rolf admitted. 'And I must, of course, take your word for it. But don't forget, I'd just had an almighty clump on my head, so it wouldn't be surprising if my eyesight wasn't too good—particularly as one was out of action. But I told you that before and I thought you'd forgiven an insult I didn't even know I'd committed,' he concluded plaintively.

'I've never been quite sure about that,' Laurie told him meditatively. 'And you certainly didn't convince me that your wink was involuntary.'

'Due to reflex action because of the pain I was suffering was my explanation,' he recalled. 'Why don't you believe that?'

'Because it was such an unpleasantly suggestive wink,' she retorted with asperity.

'Oh? Suggestive in what way?'

'As if you thought that I——' Laurie began, and stopped short. It was the first time they had referred to their original meeting since the first day he had been in hospital and she was heartily wishing that she hadn't been responsible for bringing it up again.

'What it was *meant* to express was genuine appreciation,' he told her firmly, and Laurie pounced on the opportunity he had given her.

'So you did know what you were doing and saying,' she

declared triumphantly. 'I was sure you did? So why did you lie about it?'

'Because you had clearly mistaken my intentions and I wanted to put things right,' he explained blandly. 'And, until now, I thought I had!' with a plaintive sigh.

But his eyes were twinkling and Laurie, knowing that she was losing the battle, decided that it was time to put an end to it.

'I see no point in continuing this conversation,' she announced frigidly, and positively flounced to the door.

He said nothing until she had reached it and then he spoke her name:

'Laurie?'

'Well?' she said shortly, pausing with her hand on the door handle. Of course, if the creature was going to apologise——

But nothing was further from his mind.

'Just that, in fairness to myself, I want to put it on record that I still have a weakness for girls with——carroty hair and a snub nose.' And added outrageously. 'Even when they've got peppery tempers into the bargain. In fact, I've come to the conclusion that it's a permanent state of affairs with me. Don't forget that, will you?'

Laurie's answer was to get out of the room as quickly as possible and to slam the door behind her.

Too late she realised that she had given him unmistakable evidence of her temper. In other words, he'd come off best—as he always seemed to if they crossed swords.

'Absurd,' Laurie told herself huffily, and thought of two even stronger words: 'Preposterous—outrageous!'

Because, of course, all three words described her stupidity for attaching any importance whatsoever to Rolf's concluding remarks. He had simply been teasing her. Why, his very use of the word 'weakness' proved that, for it suggested nothing but a passing fancy of which he was even, perhaps, a little ashamed. And not only that—that he had known other girls of her colouring in the past and had found them mildly but not lastingly attractive.

'So, if you've got any sense, not to say pride, my girl,

you'll forget all about it,' she ordered herself sternly. 'And that means most of all that you don't let him guess you've given two thoughts to his nonsense! Understand?'

It was, of course, extremely good advice, but it proved not to be very easy to act upon. And that was because, if one reduced what he had said to its simplest terms, what you had left was that he liked her and didn't want her to be any different.

Which reminded her of what she herself had said—that when—if—she ever got married, it would have to be to someone who wanted her to be herself, not just his pale shadow.

'Oh, my goodness!' she exclaimed aloud. 'But he couldn't have remembered that! He simply *couldn't*. Because if he did, it would mean that——' she shied apprehensively away from the mere idea.

But it wasn't so easily dismissed. However hard she tried to control her thoughts, there were times when they ran away with her.

But that Rolf should be in love with her! That was absurd if you liked!

And that she should be in love with him—even more absurd! Why, they rarely met without ending up with a squabble. That surely proved what nonsense it was!

Sylvia paid her visit the following morning and either by luck or good management, she and Laurie didn't encounter one another. Laurie was inclined to think that it was good management, on Sylvia's part as much as on her own, since, after the berating she had undoubtedly received from Rolf about the incident in the Cove, it was unlikely that she would want to meet the girl whom she probably blamed for getting her into trouble.

But even with the door to Rolf's quarters closed, it was impossible not to hear the sound of her strident voice though one couldn't hear her exact words. Laurie found the sound irritating in the extreme and herself wondered how Rolf could possibly tolerate it at close quarters.

Laurie did the only thing possible. She took herself out of earshot by driving into Penzance and doing some shopping which could quite well have waited. By the time she returned, Sylvia's car had gone and the normal peace and quiet had returned to the Ranch.

But not to Laurie. After her insistence that she wasn't going to run away from Sylvia, that was exactly what she had done. And though that might have been wise, she didn't feel very proud of herself.

Time passed slowly for Laurie during the next week. Even with the Hewitts there, she had time on her hands and didn't know what to do with it. To her there was a feeling of suspense in the air, which was not really surprising in view of all the problems to which there seemed to be no possible solutions.

Mr Brownsell left after his week-end in a mood of depression. Both he and Laurie had tried to convince Mrs Stephens that selling the Ranch was the only practical way out. But with the obstinacy which only a sweet, gentle person like she was can show on occasions, she absolutely refused even to discuss the matter.

'It's out of the question,' she said stubbornly, and from that nothing could move her.

'If only I wanted to get married as well, that would solve everything,' Laurie thought despairingly. 'But I *don't*, so it's no good thinking about it.'

So time dragged on until, at last, it was the day on which Rolf had been told to go to the hospital to have his plaster removed. Hutton drove him into Penzance. Mrs Stephens and Miss Trewyn saw them off, wishing Rolf the best of luck, but Laurie kept out of the way though she watched their departure from her bedroom window.

'But it doesn't mean that I don't wish him luck,' she thought restlessly. 'It would be callous not to.' And then, uneasily: 'Though really, why should he need luck? After, all, taking off plaster is a perfectly straightforward, everyday affair. What *can* go wrong?'

But it appeared that something could. Rolf came home with his leg still in plaster and from Hutton they learned that it had been decided not to remove it for another two weeks.

'Oh, poor boy!' Mrs Stephens exclaimed sympathetically. 'How disappointed he must be!'

'More than that,' Hutton said gloomily. 'He's downright mad! Fair bit my head off, and not just once, either. If I were you, madam, I'd keep out of his way for a bit. He's just not himself.'

'Anyhow, I don't suppose he'll want to see anybody,' Mrs Stephens replied. 'I know I wouldn't. I'd just want to be left to crawl into my own little hole and get over it alone.'

Hutton nodded.

'That's just what he does want, madam,' he agreed. 'Well, there it is. I only hope it won't go on for more than the fortnight.'

'Well, if it does—in any case—if Mr Audley seems to be worrying lest we won't extend his original booking, tell him that's quite all right. He can stay as long as he likes,' Mrs Stephens insisted firmly.

'I'll do that,' Hutton promised. 'As a matter of fact, he has already mentioned that. Said he wasn't going to badger you with a hard luck story into letting him stay on—though goodness knows where we'd go.'

'You must make it quite clear to him that there's no question of badgering. It's a voluntary offer which we're glad to make. Isn't it, Laurie?'

'Yes,' Laurie said briefly.

Hutton went off, but neither Mrs Stephens nor Laurie spoke—Mrs Stephens because she was trying to think hard of something that would cheer Rolf up, Laurie because——

Her mother regarded her with deep concern. What on earth was the matter with the child? Rigid as a statue with eyes that stared blankly at nothing, she had not moved or spoken save for that single word since Hutton had given them the news. Mrs Stephens drew her own conclusion and acted promptly.

'Oh *bother*!' she said loudly, but Laurie took no notice. 'Laurie!' And then, louder still: '*Laurie!*'

Laurie started and put out a hand to steady herself.

'Did you say something, Mother? she asked in a dazed voice.

'I've forgotten the mint for the sauce,' Mrs Stephens explained. 'So silly of me! I wonder if you'd mind getting me some, dear?'

'Yes, all right,' Laurie said automatically, and stumbled to the back door.

Through the window, tears in her eyes, Mrs Stephens watched her go.

'My poor little girl,' she murmured compassionately. 'And to think she never guessed!'

The bed of sturdy growing mint was on the far side of the orchard, but Laurie had all but forgotten her errand. She sat down on the short grass under an apple tree, hugging her knees and wondering what had reduced her to this dazed and bewildered condition.

Because, after all, what had happened? Simply, Hutton had told them that Rolf would be in plaster for a further two weeks. Well, disappointing, of course, but not really devastating. Then why should she feel as if the end of the world had come?

'Because you can't bear it that he should have to put up with even this amount of disappointment, because you'd much prefer to suffer in his place.'

She seemed to hear the words as clearly as if someone had spoken them aloud, though in fact they only existed in her own mind.

'But why? *Why?*'

And that strange new perceptiveness gave her the answer.

'Because you're in love with him, of course!'

When, later, she returned to the house she gave her mother a few sprigs of rosemary instead of the mint she had been asked for. Mrs Stephens thanked her without pointing out the mistake. She knew quite well what had happened to her girl. Her secret heart had told her that she loved a man she had believed she disliked and the knowledge had left her in a state of bewildered enchantment.

'Whatever comes of it, it's something she'll never forget for the rest of her life,' Mrs Stephens thought tenderly with the knowledge of a woman who has known a similar exquisitely disturbing revelation.

She glanced down at the sprigs Laurie had brought in.

' "There's rosemary, that's for remembrance",' she

quoted softly. 'It could hardly be more apt! But for Laurie, there'll be a happier ending. There's got to be!'

Laurie carried her secret locked in her heart, confident that no one but she knew anything about it. And that, of course, was how it had got to be. No one must guess—least of all Rolf. And since she kept out of his way, it was not likely that he would.

But in her own mind, she pondered, her hopes soaring and drooping as she tried to decide whether Rolf's reference to having a weakness for girls of her colouring meant anything more than a mild partiality—or might mean something far more important than that. She didn't know and there was no way in which she could find out, certainly not from Rolf himself.

There was, of course, one other person whom she particularly wished to keep in ignorance of her change of heart —Sylvia French. Laurie flinched at the thought of her knowing. It would be unbearable to see the scorn and amusement in those dark, rather close-set eyes.

Fortunately, Hutton told Miss Trewyn when Sylvia was going to pay another visit.

'And if I know anything about her ladyship, she'll get on his nerves before they've been together five minutes,' he told her glumly. 'And I know who'll have to put up with his temper afterwards! Me! Honestly, Maisie, there are times when I wonder why I stay with him.'

'Because you're fond of him,' Miss Trewyn retorted promptly. 'Same as I'm fond of Mrs Stephens and Miss Laurie. You put up with a lot from people you're really fond of, you know.'

'I'll remember that when we're married,' Hutton told her daringly, and escaped before she could think of a suitable answer.

Miss Trewyn didn't, of course, repeat the entire conversation to Laurie, but she did warn her that Sylvia was coming so that Laurie would be able to keep out of her way when she arrived. She would probably stay about an hour, so that meant there was no need to worry, once she had come, until then.

What Laurie couldn't possibly have anticipated was for

Hutton to have been a true prophet. Sylvia must have 'got on' Rolf's nerves for not more than a quarter of an hour after she had come, the door between Rolf's quarters and the hall opened suddenly and she shot out. What was more, Rolf's voice could be loudly heard telling her that if ever she said anything like that again—when Sylvia slammed the door and turned to face Laurie who had at that moment come into the hall.

It was an embarrassing situation for both of them, but perhaps not so bad for Laurie as for Sylvia, for the bright pink spots in her cheeks and the way she was scowling made it clear that Rolf had been irritable, to put it mildly.

But little as she liked Sylvia, Laurie found herself admiring the way in which she pulled herself together and her lips trembled in a brave little smile.

'Poor darling, he *is* upset,' she said in a far softer voice than was usual with her. 'Such a *terrible* disappointment, this delay over the plaster. He's really hardly himself.'

'I'm sorry,' Laurie said lamely.

'That's sweet of you,' Sylvia said earnestly, dabbing her handkerchief to her eyes. 'I expect you've found him—well, difficult to get on with. But, you know, one *must* make allowances because, after all, in the circumstances, it's only to be expected that he's upset, isn't it?'

'Yes, of course,' Laurie replied automatically, wishing to goodness that Sylvia would go.

Sylvia gave a little start.

'You mean—he's told you?' she asked in surprise. 'Then, in that case, of course you do understand!'

Something in the way Sylvia's eyes narrowed as she spoke warned Laurie that it was far from being by chance that the conversation had reached this point. Sylvia had deliberately manoeuvred it so that it should.

'Naturally, I understand that to a busy, energetic man like Mr Audley it must be extremely trying to be physically handicapped even though it is a temporary state of affairs,' she said coolly.

'*Temporary*,' Sylvia repeated musingly. 'But then that's just it. *Is* it temporary? Don't you see, that's what's worrying him so much?'

'I didn't know that there was any question of there being

lasting trouble,' Laurie exclaimed, betrayed by this new fear.

'Oh, I don't think there is—except in Rolf's mind,' Sylvia admitted frankly. 'But there it is. He's a sensitive man and that being so, he'd feel that, if he's going to be a cripple to any degree, then he ought not to think of getting married.'

'I see,' Laurie choked down the lump in her throat. 'That's —very honourable of him.'

'But rather mistaken, don't you think?' Sylvia insisted earnestly.

'I'm afraid I'm in no position to judge,' Laurie told her stiffly. 'And really, Miss French, I would greatly prefer not to discuss Mr Audley's affairs——'

But Sylvia didn't seem to have heard.

'My poor Rolf!' she sighed wistfully. 'If only I could make him understand! But you see, he's had a lot of bad luck lately and so he can't believe that things can go right for him.' She sighed again. 'There were several things that went wrong for him at the factory—new lines that it turned out other firms had thought of first. And then, of course, there was this place. If *only* you'd been willing to sell it to him!'

'But he's never suggested that we should do that!' Laurie told her sharply.

'Well, what was the good, seeing you were so set on staying here?' Sylvia asked resignedly. 'But I do assure you that when he had that accident, he was on his way to dis-cuss the matter with you.'

'The Ranch had been on the market for some time,' Laurie retorted. 'And nobody other than ourselves had made an offer for it.'

'Oh, I know,' Sylvia agreed—it seemed that she had an answer for everything. 'It was just unfortunate that he didn't happen to have heard that it was for sale. The luck of the game, of course,' she shrugged. 'But of course, this place meant a lot to him. He was old Mr Ferris' nephew, you know, and I'm a distant cousin of Mrs Ferris. He and I spent many happy times visiting them when it was a private house and so naturally it seems ideal as a home to us. Still——' with another shrug, 'when two people are really very much in love, I suppose they can be happy anywhere, don't you think?'

'No doubt,' Laurie agreed in as matter-of-fact a way as she could manage.

Sylvia smiled.

'Well, thank you for listening so patiently to my woes,' she said graciously. 'But really I mustn't keep you any longer. I expect you have a lot to do.'

Laurie didn't answer, and after hesitating briefly and evidently deciding that there was no more she could usefully add to what she had already said, Sylvia went out to her car.

So now Laurie knew! Rolf and Sylvia had planned to get married and had hoped to make the Ranch their home.

The knowledge left her with a strange feeling of emptiness. Not that she had imagined it likely that Rolf would ever love *her*, but at least she had believed that there was no other girl he had cared for and she had allowed herself to dream.

But now the time for dreaming was over. Reality must take its place. She must accept that, however difficult and painful it was. She mustn't even let herself think that she couldn't see how Sylvia could make Rolf happy. Surely she was too self-centred and had too hard a personality ever to consider anyone else's happiness before her own!

'But perhaps she's different with him,' Laurie thought restlessly. 'And if he really loves her——'

It was some time before she realised that there were several discrepancies in Sylvia's story.

If, for instance, he had hoped to persuade her mother and herself to sell the Ranch, why had he not only never mentioned the fact but persuaded Mr Brownsell to come and sort out their financial problems? Or had that been his intention? Wasn't it at least possible that what he had hoped would be that Mr Brownsell would convince them that they would be wiser to sell up before matters got too bad. Only that plan had gone awry because not only had Mr Brownsell found a way out for them but he had fallen in love with her mother and consequently saw everything from her point of view, not Rolf's. Or had his plan been even more subtle than that? Had he foreseen that Mr Brownsell and her mother would be so attached to one another that, if they were to get married, her mother wouldn't be able to continue living at the Ranch?

'I don't know! I *don't* know,' Laurie admitted distractedly. 'He does like to have his own way—and he's got a very complex way of getting it. But if that's what he'd worked out, then I don't think Sylvia knows—and anyway, was she telling the truth? When she came out into the hall, she looked *angry*, not hurt. And the way Rolf spoke to her —even if they had had a quarrel—didn't sound in the least loverlike. It sounded more like a man annoyed with an employee—or is that just wishful thinking?'

Had she known, as Miss Trewyn did, that in Hutton's opinion Sylvia would get on Rolf's nerves in a very short time, Laurie might—almost certainly would— have realised that there were very good reasons for doubting Sylvia's version of what had happened. But she didn't, so all she could do was to decide what she herself must do.

Her first reaction was to wish that she could run away from a situation which it was impossible to control. But second thoughts prevailed. Not only could she not desert her mother but there was Rolf to be considered. He needed to continue living at the Ranch not only for the extra fortnight but afterwards, when, out of plaster, he had got to get his leg back to normal strength.

'And if I really love him—and I *do*—then what he needs matters more than my feelings,' she told herself resolutely. 'It's not going to be easy, but I've simply got to treat him as if we're just friends. No more avoiding him even if he isn't easy to get on with!'

It *wasn't* easy to put the resolution into practice, for Rolf obviously didn't welcome visitors and answered any remarks she made with discouraging abruptness. But she persisted and gradually his manner softened. He even went as far as to apologise for his bad temper.

'I expect you think I've been unreasonable and childish,' he suggested.

'Yes, I do,' Laurie said frankly. 'But I don't suppose you've been able to help it.'

'Did I detect a possibility that you mentally added: "since you're a man"?' he asked wryly. 'You'd have been justified if you had. But then, you see, it's just because I am a man——' he paused, scowling. 'It's no excuse, of course, but when a man most desperately wants to take a certain course yet knows that he has no right to until he can be sure that he's going to be perfectly fit—well, it's pretty frustrating!'

Bereft of words, Laurie nodded. Almost word for word he had repeated what Sylvia had said. She had no choice but to believe it now.

CHAPTER SEVEN

THE days up to Rolf's next visit to the hospital passed with comparative uneventfulness. The Hewitts left after giving a little party and took with them a handful of brochures. Unaware of the unsettled state of affairs, they vowed that not only would they themselves return the following year but that their friends would be told all about the Ranch and would certainly want to come as well.

'And they meant it, too,' Mr Brownsell remarked glumly to Laurie. 'The fact is, you and Lucy between you *will* make a tremendous success of the place. And the more that becomes obvious, the less Lucy will want to leave it. Why was I so confoundedly helpful over that damned mortgage?'

'Because you're too honest to have lied to her when you saw that we would almost certainly make a success of it,' Laurie told him promptly, and added recklessly: 'As Rolf wanted you to!'

Mr Brownsell looked startled.

'He told you that?' he demanded incredulously.

'Good gracious, no! Knowing him, I was able to work it out for myself,' Laurie explained, adding scornfully: 'It was really so typical of him!'

'Now see here, Laurie, you're looking at this from entirely the wrong point of view,' Mr Brownsell told her hastily. 'Rolf honestly believed you hadn't a chance of making good and he wanted to extricate you before you got in still deeper.'

'How very altruistic of him!' Laurie retorted bitterly. 'Seeing that, had we got into a worse mess, we'd have had to sell the Ranch at any price we could get, which would have meant that he could have bought it much more cheaply than he otherwise would have done.'

'Oh, so you knew he wanted to buy it?' Mr Brownsell said morosely. 'Do you happen to know why?'

116

'Oh yes, I know that, too,' Laurie said indifferently.

He looked at her curiously.

'And that made no difference to you?'

'None whatever,' Laurie declared. 'Why should it?'

'Well, I don't know—I should have thought——' Mr Brownsell shook his head. 'Have you told Rolf how you feel about it?'

'Certainly not,' Laurie declared emphatically. 'He and I have never discussed the matter.'

'You haven't?' he exclaimed. 'Then how on earth did you know——?' He passed his hand over his forehead. 'I don't get this!'

'There's nothing to get,' Laurie insisted. 'Simply, as I said, knowing Rolf's mendacious ways of getting what he wants, I was able to put two and two together——'

'And if you ask me, you got the wrong answer,' Mr Brownsell told her bluntly. 'Look here, Laurie, you ought to let Rolf know about those conclusions you've jumped to. Or if you'd rather not, then let me tell him——?'

'Don't you *dare*!' Laurie flared at him. 'Because, if you do, I'll never speak to you again!'

Mr Brownsell hesitated.

'Well, all right, if you feel so strongly about it as that,' he promised reluctantly. 'But I still think——'

'*No!*'

And that ended the matter.

Sylvia paid no more visits but Miss Jones, who had had a week's holiday, returned to duty and there followed an intensive drive on Rolf's part not only to catch up on work he had previously neglected but even to get ahead as far as possible. As a result, Miss Jones showed unmistakable signs of being overworked and admitted, over a cup of tea with Mrs Stephens, that she was beginning to feel her years.

'I'm over retiring age,' she confided, 'and though there's nothing seriously wrong with my health, I do get tired more quickly than I used to. Not——' as she saw the inevitable criticism hovering on Mrs Stephens' lips, 'that I blame Rolf for not realising that. For one thing, I've done my best never to let him see that I'm tired—vanity, I suppose—but

also I do appreciate his reasons for wanting to work hard
at this particular time.'

'Of course,' Mrs Stephens said understandingly. 'There's
nothing like hard work for helping one over a difficult time.'

'Exactly! But it's more than that. He wants to make sure
that once he's out of plaster, he'll be reasonably free to
spend as much time as possible building up that leg of his
to its proper strength.'

'Remedial therapy at the hospital and exercises on his
own?' Mrs Stephens suggested.

'Just that. And you'll see, once he's able to do something
to help himself, just how patient and persevering he'll be,'
Miss Jones said approvingly. 'Oh yes, he'll put his whole
heart into it!'

'So long as he doesn't overdo it,' Mrs Stephens suggested
dubiously.

'He won't,' Miss Jones replied serenely. 'You and Hutton
and I will see to that!'

'We'll have a job on our hands,' Mrs Stephens commented
drily. 'He likes having his own way, you know.'

'Yes, I do know,' Miss Jones agreed tolerantly. 'But I also
know that he's no fool. Beside,' she continued reflectively,
'the Sister in charge of the Therapeutic Department is an
old friend of mine and I've already had a word with her.'

Mrs Stephens chuckled.

'It seems to me that Mr Audley isn't the only one who
likes to have his own way!'

A few more bookings for accommodation were made but
only, Laurie was relieved to see, for the current season.
That suited her for she had at last seen a way out of the
tangle.

While it was true that she couldn't run the Ranch without her mother, equally, her mother couldn't run it without
her. So, if she were to tell her mother that she would prefer
to get a job which wouldn't mean the continued strain of
running the Ranch, then surely she would be willing to sell
out, particularly as she blamed herself for having been
largely responsible for the venture.

The only thing was, Laurie knew that she must be sure of

getting a job elsewhere before she told her mother and she decided that she would go and see Mrs Baxter, the joint proprietor with her husband of the Black Prince, and see what the prospects were of getting her old job back in, say October. She might also be able to arrange to live in, which would save the problem of finding a home for herself.

But in the meantime, she was too busy to take the matter further, for not only had they half a dozen residents to cope with in addition to Rolf and Hutton, but the crops of fruit and vegetables, far too great for immediate consumption, had to be gathered and prepared for deep freezing. If they *had* to stay on, their harvest would be of tremendous value both during the winter months and for the early part of next season. And if they didn't stay on—well, one simply couldn't waste good food.

It was a task which meant being out in the sunshine for long hours and it left Laurie not only tired but with fingers stained with earth and fruit juice. And even when the plucking and pulling was done, everything still had to be cleaned and prepared ready for blanching and packing away in the deep freezers.

'Goodness, Laurie, there's enough for a regiment!' Mrs Stephens remarked apprehensively. 'We'll never get through it on our own!'

'We won't try to,' Laurie assured her briskly. 'If it doesn't look as if we'll use them up here, we can always sell them.'

'Who would want them?' Mrs Stephens wanted to know, 'Most people hereabouts have got garden produce of their own—and deep freezers.'

'Mrs Baxter hasn't,' Laurie reminded her. 'At least she's got deep freezers, but you know she was always complaining how difficult she found it to get fresh garden produce. She'd be delighted to have it.'

'Yes, perhaps she would. But we shall need it here,' Mrs Stephens insisted stubbornly, suddenly changing her tune. 'Because we are staying on here, Laurie. So don't go promising Mrs Baxter——'

'All right,' Laurie promised patiently. 'I'm only saying that whether we stay on or whether we go, the stuff won't be wasted. Oh, my goodness, will nothing get the stains off my hands! I've nearly skinned them scrubbing them with scouring powder without the least effect.'

'You might try bleach,' Mrs Stephens suggested. 'Though the smell of that lasts rather a long time.'

'I'd better not chance it, then, seeing that I've more picking to do,' Laurie decided. 'It would be dreadful if the fruit were to taste of bleach!'

'Perhaps you're right,' Mrs Stephens agreed, though she spoke absently as if she had something else on her mind. As, indeed, she had. 'Laurie, about Miss Trewyn and Hutton—they spend quite a lot of their free time together, don't they?'

'I suppose they do,' Laurie agreed cautiously. 'But I shouldn't worry about them, Mother. After all, they're not teenagers. They're old enough to be sensible.'

'I wasn't thinking about that aspect,' Mrs Stephens denied. 'It was more—well, if it's just a friendship, then that's all right. But if it's a serious affair and they plan to get married eventually, why haven't they told us? Surely it would be the natural thing to do?'

'Oh, I don't know,' Laurie hedged, but Mrs Stephens was quick to draw her own conclusions.

'They are engaged, aren't they?' she stated rather than asked. 'And what's more, you've known about it for some time, haven't you?'

Challenged so directly, Laurie capitulated.

'Well—yes,' she admitted reluctantly.

'Then why haven't I been told?' Mrs Stephens demanded in an injured voice. 'I thought Miss Trewyn liked me.'

'So she does! That's just why she didn't——' Laurie floundered helplessly.

'I'm beginning to understand,' Mrs Stephens said ominously. 'Somehow, she's found out about—about John and me and she's taken it into her head that it would be unkind for her to make a parade of her happiness when I can't. Yes, that's it—I can tell it from your face, child. But you shouldn't have told her. You really shouldn't.'

'But I didn't, Mother,' Laurie protested. 'Truly I didn't. She just seemed to know without being told.'

'But how——?'

Laurie shook her head.

'I don't know. But Rolf says that good servants always *do* know their employers' business.'

'Rolf? So you've discussed it with him?' Mrs Stephens asked sharply.

'Only because Mr Brownsell already had,' Laurie defended herself.

'I see. And what did he suggest that we should do?' Mrs Stephens asked dryly.

'Nothing very definite. Apparently he's got an idea, but he said it was too soon to do anything about it, so he wouldn't tell me what it was.'

'How interesting,' Mrs Stephens speculated. 'Now, I wonder what he had in mind?'

'I couldn't say, Mother,' Laurie said shortly. 'And I've no intention of asking. You know what he's like. Once he's come to a decision it's final. He won't explain until he's ready to.'

'No, I don't suppose he will,' Mrs Stephens agreed, and sighed. 'I must say, though I like a man to know his own mind, there are times when I think they take it too far.'

Rolf's next visit to the hospital was satisfactory. He came back minus the plaster but limping and sufficiently unsure of himself to be glad of Hutton's supporting arm.

But Miss Jones had been right. Once he was able to do something to help himself, Rolf persisted with dogged determination to follow the instructions he had been given at the hospital.

'Properly gone into training,' Hutton reported. 'And, thanks be, he's got the sense not to overdo it at first. I was rather thinking, him being so anxious to get fit, that he'd go at it hell for leather, but no, he's just gradually building up. Only trouble is, they say it'll be a good thing for him to go swimming in the pool.'

'Not on his own at first, surely!' Mrs Stephens said quickly.

'No. With me,' Hutton explained gloomily.

'Well, so what?' Miss Trewyn interjected from the background. 'That's surely no hardship?'

'In one way, no,' Hutton admitted. 'But though I can swim, I'm not that keen on it. I'm not as young as I was and I get puffed easily.'

'Then the exercise will do you good,' Miss Trewyn told him heartlessly. 'I don't like to see a man running to fat—particularly when it's the one I'm going to marry—oh!' She clapped her hand over her mouth and looked apprehensively at Mrs Stephens.

'Now you have let the cat out of the bag, my girl!' Hutton commented with a certain satisfaction.

Mrs Stephens laughed.

'But of course I'd guessed!' she told them. 'And I'm delighted for both of you! I do most sincerely wish you every happiness.'

She shook hands with them warmly and then said briskly:

'And now, off you go and make up your minds when the wedding is to be! Yes, I mean it. Never postpone happiness unless it's absolutely unavoidable.'

But as, rather sheepishly, they went off together, tears came into her eyes.

'I'm not jealous of them,' she told herself firmly. 'I wouldn't be so mean. But I can't help envying them just a little bit!'

Laurie had formed the habit of taking a daily swim in the pool, but she took good care not to be there when Rolf was because she thought it might embarrass him to have her looking on while he made what must, at first, be limited efforts. This was not difficult to manage as Rolf had worked out a time schedule and kept to it rigidly.

But there came a day when Hutton brought her a written message from Rolf.

'Dear Laurie,

Hutton would very much like to take a few hours off today which will mean that he won't be able to accompany me for my swim.

In my opinion I don't think I need a nursemaid, but Hutton says he won't go unless someone else is with me. However, since I understand that he and Miss Trewyn want to go shopping for her engagement ring, I would like to make the jaunt possible.

Would you mind very much taking his place as nanny, life-saver or whatever?

I'd be so grateful.

Yours,

Rolf.'

Laurie folded up the note and thrust it with apparent carelessness into her apron pocket.

'Please tell Mr Audley that yes, of course I'll do as he asks,' she said matter-of-factly. 'He ought not to miss his swim.'

'That's right, Miss Laurie,' Hutton said gratefully. 'I'm very much obliged and so, I know, will Mr Audley be.'

'Not at all,' Laurie replied briskly. 'Half-past eleven is his time, isn't it?'

'That's right,' Hutton confirmed. 'Mr Audley suggested that you should meet him at the pool.'

'Very well,' Laurie agreed, and Hutton went off with the message.

Determined not to keep him waiting, Laurie arrived at the pool before he did and had swum a length before he put in an appearance a few minutes after the appointed time.

'Sorry I'm late,' he apologised. 'I got caught up on the telephone.'

'Not to worry,' Laurie said cheerfully. 'It's too nice a day to mind a few extra minutes in the water. Are you diving in or coming down the steps?'

'Steps,' he grimaced wryly. 'I'm quite sure it would be all right to dive, but I've been advised not to chance it yet.'

'Fair enough.' Laurie swam over to the steps, but though she was on the alert to give him a hand if he needed it since he had discarded the stick he still used, he managed quite well on his own and they swam lazily from one end of the pool to the other. A brief rest and then they swam back to float lazily at the deep end.

'This is *good*,' Rolf said dreamily. 'You know, I feel twice the man that I did half an hour ago.'

'Of course you do,' Laurie told him. 'Being in the water gives you a buoyancy that makes swimming far less effort than walking.'

'What a prosaic explanation,' Rolf complained. 'Now what was in my mind was to convey to you, as delicately as possible, that, quite apart from the sun and the water, I'm thoroughly enjoying your company.'

'Oh, were you?' Laurie replied innocently. 'Well, you wrapped it up so completely that such a thing never occurred to me.'

'No? In that case, next time I want to pay you a compliment, I'll come right out with it so that you can't miss it,' he threatened.

For answer, Laurie turned and swam away from him.

'Don't come if you feel you've had enough,' she called over her shoulder.

But Rolf, whether he thought she meant enough swimming or enough banter, followed her and quickly overtook her. Then as he got a yard or so in front of her, he turned on his back and began to splash his legs vigorously up and down with the result that she swam into a rough patch of water and was all but submerged.

'That was a dirty trick,' she spluttered indignantly.

'Oh, sorry, did I splash you?' Rolf asked with owlish innocence.

'You know perfectly well you did,' Laurie retorted. 'But two can play at that game!' And turning on her back as he had done, she gave him some of his own medicine.

The next moment they were swimming peacefully along side by side, their warfare forgotten, and Laurie found herself, for whatever reason, agreeing with Rolf—it *was* a good day.

When they reached the shallow end they hauled themselves out and spreading out their towels, lay on the sun-baked concrete. The sun glinted on the water, still gently rippled by their passage through it. Birds twittered somnolently in the nearby trees, there was the perfume of flowers in the air. It was really perfect.

'I wish this could go on for ever,' Laurie thought passionately. 'Nothing matters except that we're together and I'm happier than I've ever been before in my whole life!'

Then suddenly, shatteringly, the peace was broken. A bell rang with harsh determination quite near at hand and Rolf sat up with a start.

'What in the world was that?' he demanded.

'My alarm clock,' Laurie explained, yawning as she, too, sat up. 'It's so easy to lose one's sense of time without a watch, so I thought it would be a good idea——'

'I suppose it was, even though the shock of it has taken years off my life.' Then, as she made another move to get up he put out a restraining hand, 'Don't go just yet, though. Not for a few minutes. There's something I want to tell you.'

Laurie sat very still feeling as if, for the moment at least, her heart had stopped beating. There was something so diffident in the way he spoke. Something which made it clear that whatever he had to say was very important—very near to his heart.

'It's about me,' he explained self-consciously. 'Which sounds unpleasantly egotistic, doesn't it? But the fact is, I've been scared stiff that I was going to be a crock for the rest of my life. But today, for the first time, I feel confident that everything is going to be all right and I wanted you to be the first to know.'

'Oh, Rolf!' There was a lilt in her voice and impulsively she laid her hand on his bare, sunwarmed arm. 'I *am* glad!'

He looked at her wonderingly.

'You know, I really believe you mean that!' he said softly, and bending his head, touched his lips gently to hers.

Laurie didn't move. She didn't dare to, for if she had, she knew that she would have kissed him in return in a way that would have told him unmistakably——

But Rolf misunderstood her unresponsiveness.

'Sorry,' he said gruffly. 'I had no right——'

'But I understood,' Laurie assured him breathlessly. 'It was—it was just a sort of champagne kiss, wasn't it? I mean when one feels exhilarated and has something to celebrate. And you have!'

'I certainly have,' Rolf agreed emphatically. And then, softly, 'You're very sweet and tolerant, Laurie. I'll never forget that. And now perhaps we'd better go in before——'

'Yes, perhaps we had,' Laurie agreed breathlessly, not giving him time to finish his remark.

They scrambeld to their feet and for a moment he stood looking down at her.

'Laurie——' he began, but she didn't stop to listen to what he was going to say. She didn't want him to apologise or explain any further. She wanted to cherish that magic moment unblemished. It belonged to her alone, for hadn't he said that he wanted her to be the first to know?

Miss Trewyn and Hutton returned from their shopping expedition looking, as Rolf afterwards said, as pleased with themselves as if they were the very first couple to venture on such an outstanding achievement.

Miss Trewyn was very near to both tears and giggles as she held out her hand for Mrs Stephens to inspect her ring and, of course, approve Hutton's choice. And that she could do in all sincerity for it really was beautiful—a large, single diamond so expertly cut that it flashed and sparkled with the slightest movement of Miss Trewyn's hand.

'It's beautiful,' Mrs Stephens said warmly. 'You must be very proud of it.'

'I am,' Miss Trewyn agreed softly. 'Though I feel sort of guilty because though Frank won't tell me what it cost, I know without being told that it was dreadfully expensive. I never thought to have such a beautiful ring. It's really too good for a working woman like me.'

'Nothing's too good for you, my girl,' Hutton told her masterfully. 'And don't you forget it!'

He stalked out of the kitchen, satisfaction in every line of his carriage. Miss Trewyn's eyes followed him devotedly.

'I never thought I'd be going to marry a man like Frank, either,' she sighed happily. 'Mind, he's got his faults, but they're good ones, if you know what I mean.'

'I do, indeed,' Mrs Stephens assured her. 'And now, what about the wedding? Have you made up your minds?'

'Not until the autumn,' Miss Trewyn said resolutely. 'I said that to begin with and I'm sticking to it. Not but what Frank would buy the wedding ring today. Said it was silly to take two bites at the same cherry. But he's keeping that until The Day!' She hesitated and then went on: 'And that's something I'd like your advice about, Mrs Stephens. It's going to be a church wedding because, say what you like, getting married in a register office, legal though it is, doesn't seem real to me. And I thought, for a church wedding, I'd like to wear something special. Not white, I'm too old for that. Though for that matter, I'd be perfectly entitled to wear it,' she concluded, with a hint of defiance.

'I'm sure you would be,' Mrs Stephens agreed hastily. 'But I think you're right. White would be just rather juvenile. How about a very soft blue with a matching hat and shoes—and, of course, flowers. Either a bouquet or a spray to wear?'

'Yes,' Miss Trewyn said dreamily, evidently conjuring up a picture of herself dressed like that. 'With a long skirt, of course.'

'Of course,' Mrs Stephens agreed.

Miss Trewyn heaved a deep sigh and went to the drawer where a ball of string was kept. She cut off a length, tied the two ends together and linked the ring on to it. She slipped the string over her head and tucked the ring down the neck of her dress. Then she got on with preparing the vegetables.

'Bless her heart!' Mrs Stephens thought affectionately. 'She's as head over heels in love as a young girl, but romance or no romance, she's the most practical soul I've ever met! What I shall do without her I simply can't think!'

Cherry chose that night to create a diversion. By midnight she had not come home and no amount of whistling and tapping her enamel plate had the slightest effect. Laurie searched all Cherry's pet hiding places, but even with a full moon and a torch to help her, there was no sign of the little creature.

'It's no use,' she said at last disconsolately. 'She's done this once or twice before and always on a warm night when there's a full moon. I suppose she gets caught up in a sort of wanderlust, but I never feel happy about it.'

'No, I don't suppose you do,' Rolf said sympathetically.

He and Hutton had taken part in the search, but now, more than he liked to admit, he was glad to sit down on one of his verandah chairs. 'All the same, on these previous occasions she's turned up eventually under her own steam, hasn't she?'

'Oh yes. Round about three or four in the morning,' said Laurie. 'Complaining like mad until someone goes down and lets her in. And I'm always so glad to see her that I simply can't be cross with her.'

'No, I don't suppose you can,' Rolf agreed. 'But look, Laurie, how would it be if I didn't shut this door?' He jerked his head backwards to indicate the door between the verandah and his quarters. 'After all, she's used to coming in this way.'

'Oh, if you'd do that!' Laurie said gratefully. 'And if she does come, will you see that she has plenty of water to drink? She's always very thirsty after these escapades.'

'I'll do that,' Rolf promised.

Laurie's lips quivered.

'I expect you think I'm a fool to worry so,' she said tremulously. 'But I've looked after her ever since she was old enough to leave her mother and—and——' she broke off, biting her lip.

'And you love her,' Rolf said gently. 'You don't need to tell me that. And if you're a fool, then so am I.' He took one of her hands in his and held it tightly. 'I think it's the way that a cat, for all its independence, trusts one to care for all its needs, just as a child does.'

'Yes,' Laurie agreed, her hand tightening in his clasp. 'You know, people say that cats aren't so responsive to humans as dogs are. But they *are*, though in a different way. There's nothing slavish about what they give you, but you can win their devotion if you really want to.'

'I know you can,' Rolf nodded. 'And that's why I'm sure Cherry will come back. This is her home—and she knows it.'

Laurie didn't answer and after a moment, Rolf said briskly:

'And now up you go to bed, my dear. You must be very tired.'

'Yes, I suppose I am,' Laurie admitted restlessly. 'But I don't feel as if I'll be able to sleep.'

Rolf stood up and raising the hand he held, gently kissed it.

'But you'll try,' he coaxed. 'And in the morning you'll see—she'll be back!'

But she wasn't. Nor was there any sign of her during the following day or night.

'Do you know what I think has happened?' Laurie asked drearily. 'I think she's wandered rather far afield and some-one—visitors to the Cove, probably, have seen her and have taken her home because they thought she was a stray. She may be miles away by now.'

'Could be,' Rolf was forced to admit. 'And at least that means that they were kindly if mistaken in their action.' But privately he was thankful that it had not occurred to her that it might have been someone who, appreciating Cherry's market value, had spirited her away. If that was so, there would be very little chance of her ever coming home again.

Laurie, too restless to sleep, got up once dawn had broken. She put on her dressing gown and sat by the open window, trying to face facts. Cherry had never been away for two consecutive nights before. There was no room for hope now.

And then, as the tears streamed down her cheeks, she heard the sound she had been longing for—Cherry's strid-ent yowl announcing her presence and demanding to know why the devil wasn't there anyone about to welcome her?

Barefoot, Laurie raced downstairs and met Rolf in the hall, also in his dressing gown. His hair was rumpled and he was grinning broadly.

'She's back!' he announced triumphantly. 'And gollop-ing up water like a suction pump!'

He led the way through to the verandah where Cherry, her thirst assuaged, was graciously tolerating a thorough grooming by Hutton. And she needed it. Her silky fur was dusty and bedraggled and there were small sticky burrs clinging to it. One ear had a scratch on it and evidently one paw was causing her distress, because every now and then she would interrupt Hutton's ministrations to spread the claws wide and lick between them.

'Proper mess she was in,' Hutton commented, standing

up and starting to comb the fur from the brush. 'Must have walked miles, poor little soul.'

'I think you were right, Laurie,' Rolf remarked as, after a casual glance at Laurie, Cherry began to wash herself. 'I think it was someone with good intentions who kidnapped her. She'd got a pink ribbon round her neck and she doesn't seem to be hungry.'

'That's right.' Hutton was offering Cherry a choice dish of rabbit, but Cherry wasn't in the least interested. 'What she wants now is a good long sleep.'

As if to confirm this, Cherry strolled languidly indoors and, selecting the most comfortable chair in the room, curled round and was almost instantly fast asleep.

'Proper little madam, isn't she?' Hutton commented admiringly. 'Takes it as her right to have the best of everything and sees that she gets it!'

'Yes, but she mustn't take it for granted that she can commandeer your best chair,' Laurie said apologetically. 'I'll take her off your hands———'

'No, don't disturb her,' the two men said in chorus. 'Not now she's settled down.'

Laurie looked at them quizzically.

'Mother says I spoil her, but you two are far worse,' she told them severely. 'That paw she keeps on licking,' she went on anxiously. 'What's wrong with it, Hutton?'

'Got a thorn in it,' he explained. 'I got it out, but it's evidently still hurting her. Still, I reckon she knows how to look after it, but if it's still worrying her later on, perhaps it 'ud be better to have the vet see her?'

'Yes, we'll do that,' Laurie agreed.

She bent down and very gently kissed the top of Cherry's head, evoking a short little rumble of sleepy purring. 'Bless her!' she said softly, and then, for the first time realising how informal her appearance was, she beat a hasty retreat.

'A very nice young lady,' Hutton commented as the door closed behind her.

'Very,' Rolf agreed.

It was soon clear that there was nothing seriously wrong with Cherry except her own conviction that she was an interesting invalid whose fragile constitution merited every consideration—which, needless to say, she got.

Round about eleven Laurie brought her a dish of her favourite rabbit and held it invitingly to Cherry's nose. She sniffed at it without much enthusiasm and said it wasn't worth getting down from her chair to eat it. Laurie set the dish down on the floor and lifted Cherry down.

'Come on, sweetie,' she coaxed. 'You'll like it once you've tried it.'

Cherry finicked critically with a piece of meat, decided that perhaps it wasn't so bad and gobbled down the rest at express speed. Then she strolled out to the verandah, blandly ignoring Rolf's remark that if she had indigestion she had only herself to thank.

Laurie laughed. She felt gay and happy and full of life, not only because Cherry was home none the worse for her adventure but because Rolf had been so sympathetic and understanding.

'In fact, I don't know what I'd have done without him,' she admitted to herself. 'Perhaps, after this, we won't squabble so much——'

She stooped to pick up the empty dish and as she stood up, she brushed against the edge of Rolf's desk, knocking two sheets of paper on to the floor.

Rolf gave a startled exclamation as she picked them up and held out his hand as if to seize them from her.

'It's all right,' Laurie assured him. 'They're not damaged——' she stopped short, her eyes wide.

She was looking at two beautifully executed and coloured pictures of a teenage doll who, tall and slim, was depicted wearing a bikini very much like Laurie's own. Deliberately she looked at the other sheet. The same doll, but this time shown wearing a yellow dress which, again, closely resembled one of Laurie's own. And now, as Rolf sat silent and unsmiling, she paid more attention to the doll's face and head.

Her own bright colour hair, her own face except that—surely hers never wore an expression like that? Seductive and sly and—menacing! And if she wanted further proof that the doll was an unpleasant caricature of herself, across the body of each was a ribbon bearing the words: 'The Lorelei.'

Deliberately she laid the two sheets down in front of Rolf.

'I shall be glad to have your explanation of these two grossly insulting pictures,' she told him icily.

'They're a suggestion from a freelance artist who sometimes works for us,' Rolf explained deliberately. 'He thinks they would make a good selling line—and he's right, in my opinion.'

'You mean you're going to put this—this *creature* on the market?' Laurie gasped. 'But you can't do that! You simply can't!'

'You don't like the idea?' Rolf asked in an expressionless voice.

'Like it?' Laurie flared. 'I think it's an abominable insult!' She looked at him incredulously. 'Surely you can see that?'

'It's not perhaps altogether flattering,' Rolf admitted judicially. 'None the less, it would, I'm quite sure, be a good selling line——'

'And that's all that matters to you!' Laurie retorted bitterly. And when he didn't reply, she went on challengingly: 'I must warn you, Mr Audley, that if you do decide to market this doll, I shall see if it isn't possible to sue you for infringement of copyright!'

'On what grounds?' Rolf wanted to know.

'Oh—for goodness' sake!' Laurie retorted angrily. 'Look, if you were to publish a book of mine without my permission or reproduce a picture I'd painted and sold that, it would be infringement of copyright, wouldn't it?'

'Yes,' Rolf admitted. 'So——?'

'Then surely you would be committing just the same offence by copying *me* without my permission,' she insisted.

Rolf rested his elbows on the arms of his chair and linked his hands.

'That's an intriguing point,' he agreed. 'Though, actually, I don't know the answer to it. I suppose it might stick.'

'Of course it would,' Laurie declared impatiently. 'Because you simply can't deny, it *is* me even to the clothes. And as for calling it Lorelei—why, it's practically my name!'

Rolf picked up a letter.

'This is from Sheldrake,' he explained, 'the artist concerned. He says: "My model was a girl I met recently in a London night club. Should you take the idea up she has no objection to the publicity it would entail for her. In fact, she's delighted at the idea—provided she gets a cut of whatever fee you pay me. A girl with an eye to the main chance, believe me!"'

He laid the letter down and looked questioningly at Laurie.

'Well?'

'But that's nonsense!' Laurie protested hotly. 'Unless I've got a double—and that's hardly likely.'

'Or unless *you* were the model,' Rolf suggested drily.

Laurie stared at him blankly.

'Are you suggesting——?'

'No, I'm not suggesting anything,' he denied. 'But I would like your assurance that you were not the model.'

'No, I was not,' Laurie told him curtly.

'I didn't see how you could be,' Rolf admitted frankly. 'For one thing, it would be completely out of character and for another, Sheldrake speaks of having met this girl *recently* and I, of course, have personal knowledge that you haven't been to London since I came here.'

'Then why did you ask?' Laurie wanted to know.

'Because we had to get that possibility completely cleared out of the way before we try to solve what is, as I think you'll admit, something of a mystery.'

'But is it?' Laurie asked quickly. 'Those photographs of me——'

'I still have them here,' Rolf took the two prints from a drawer and laid them beside the sketches. 'And yes, from either of these, both your general appearance and your bikini could have been copied. But I do assure you, Laurie, they've never left my possession since I first had them.'

Since he had taken her word on trust she had little choice but to accept his. And yet she knew that she wasn't really satisfied. Unconsciously she shook her head.

'You don't believe me?' he demanded sharply.

'I want to—truly I do,' Laurie declared earnestly. 'But you see, there's just one thing——'

'What?'

'That dress,' Laurie said slowly. 'You see, there may conceivably have been other prints made of me in the bikini because I'm almost certain that I heard *three* clicks when those photos were taken. But the dress——' again she shook her head. 'I'm sure no one has ever taken a photograph of me wearing it. In fact, except for that evening when the Hewitts gave their farewell party I haven't worn it for *ages*.'

'Yes, I remember,' Rolf admitted grimly. 'I remember thinking how well the colour suited you, which puts me back as suspect number one!'

'Well, you must admit it's curious,' Laurie said slowly. 'Because who else—oh!' and she clapped her hand over her mouth, her eyes wide and startled.

'Thought of something?' Rolf asked with interest.

'I've just remembered when it was that I'd previously worn it,' she said slowly. 'It was before you came here. A—friend took me to a dinner-dance in Penzance and there was a photographer who was taking instant colour snaps as we danced. My—friend bought the one of us—but I don't remember what happened to it.' Her brows knitted in an effort to recall the incident. 'I remember that it lay on our table for some time and that it was too large to go in my little evening handbag. But no, I can't remember after that——'

'Perhaps your—friend picked it up and put it in his wallet,' Rolf suggested.

'He may have done. Or someone else may have picked it up, though I can't think why. But there *was* a photograph of me wearing that dress——'

'Interesting,' Rolf drawled. 'Though of course it doesn't entirely let me out. But it does suggest that there are some questions which have got to be asked—particularly of Sheldrake. Those photographs must surely play a part in this riddle and I want to know, among other things, why he bothered to tell such a clumsy lie about the London model. I'll go and see him tomorrow!' he concluded determinedly.

'Does that mean you'll have to go to London to see him?' Laurie asked anxiously. 'Won't it be terribly tiring? I mean, I know you're a lot stronger, but all the same——'

For the first time since Laurie had picked up those incriminating paintings, Rolf's expression softened.

'That's very generous of you, Laurie,' he said appreciatively. 'Particularly in the circumstances. All the same, tiring or not, I'm going to get to the bottom of this. For my own satisfaction as well as yours!'

'I hope you do,' Laurie's voice shook. 'Because the thought of my face being seen all over the place with an expression like that on it—I'd die of shame!'

'As to that, Laurie, I give you my word that I'll never market the doll without your permission,' Rolf assured her earnestly.

'That you will never have!' Laurie declared passionately.

CHAPTER EIGHT

Rolf was away for four days, which gave Laurie a lot of time to think things over and try to decide whether there was anything she could do to help solve the puzzle.

One question she asked herself was—what *had* happened to that photograph of Geoff and herself? And it was, she thought, an important question, because if it was answered then surely it would go a long way to proving that the artist, Sheldrake, had lied about the 'London model'.

Of course, the most practical thing to do would be to ring Geoff up and ask him if he had got it or, if he hadn't, who had. But practical though the idea was, it didn't appeal to her. She intended that the break between them should be complete and permanent, and if she rang him up, he might get the wrong impression——

Then, inevitably, she wondered if Sylvia French could have had anything to do with passing on the photographs to the artist. Seeing the trouble it would almost inevitably cause between Rolf and Laurie herself, it was at least a possibility. As regards the bikini photographs, yes, she could have been responsible. She had been present when they were taken—it might even have been with her camera. And after all, it was she who had given the two photographs to Rolf.

But the one of her wearing the yellow dress was a rather different matter. It was true, of course, that since both Sylvia and Geoff worked for Rolf, they must know each other. Had Geoff shown that photograph to Sylvia and had she made some excuse for borrowing it? That was a possibility, for after the way in which she had sent him packing, Laurie felt that it was unlikely that he would treasure a picture of her.

Or had Sylvia also been present at the dinner-dance and had she simply taken the photograph from their table when they were dancing? That could be. There had been rather a crowd present that night and in any case, at that time, she and Sylvia had not met, so it was quite conceivable to suppose that she simply hadn't noticed her.

'I'll have to ring Geoff up and ask him,' she decided at length. 'But I'll have to think up some plausible excuse, even if it isn't true!'

So when she made the call, she explained carefully that she had told her mother about the photograph and that she had said she would like to have it.

She held her breath as Geoff hesitated.

'But I thought you'd taken it,' he said at last.

'No—don't you remember, it wouldn't go into my handbag?'

'That's right,' he admitted. 'Well, I'm sorry, but I haven't got it either. So where it is now, I haven't the least idea.'

'Never mind.' Laurie was disappointed, but she didn't want to give him the impression that the matter was of real importance.

There was an awkward pause.

'If that's all——?' Geoff asked with, surely, a hint of uneasiness. But that, of course, might mean that he, no more than she, wanted to revive their friendship.

'Yes, that's all,' she said slowly—and then remembered her other idea. 'Geoff, did you notice if Sylvia French was at that dinner-dance?'

But the line was dead. Geoff had already rung off.

When Rolf returned, one glance at his face told Laurie that his trip had not produced satisfactory results. He looked both annoyed and disappointed. But since nobody but the two of them knew why he had gone to London, it did not surprise her that she had to wait for an explanation until they had an opportunity of talking without fear of interruption. When that was the case, Rolf came to the point immediately.

'No luck,' he told Laurie grimly. 'I couldn't contact Sheldrake. Apparently he's gone abroad for an indefinite period. What's more, he hadn't left a forwarding address with the hall porter at his block of flats other than that of his bank manager. And though I got that, it didn't do me much good.

Bank managers are proverbially cagey where their clients' affairs are concerned—quite rightly, of course. But he did promise that if I wrote to Sheldrake and gave him the letter, he would forward it. That means a delay, of course, but it was the best I could do.'

'I see.' Laurie couldn't hide her disappointment, but she realised that Rolf had done his best. She saw that he was looking at her curiously.

'Don't you want to know what was in the letter?'

'I'm longing to,' Laurie admitted frankly. 'But it didn't seem worth asking because, if you want to tell me, you will. And if you don't, wild horses won't drag it from you.'

Rolf laughed wryly.

'You haven't changed your opinion of me, have you? Obstinate, self-opinionated and underhanded. That's about the sum of it, isn't it?'

Laurie shook her head.

'Sometimes I feel that. Other times, you have me guessing,' she confessed. 'At least I've realised that you aren't dishonest!'

'Only—what was it? Devious. Something like that. Well, perhaps that's an improvement. I hope so, anyway. But there's no reason why I shouldn't tell you what I said—though I would like you to keep it to yourself in the meantime.'

He looked at her enquiringly and Laurie nodded.

'I said—in unequivocal terms—that I found the idea of him having used a London model for the doll entirely unacceptable and explained why. Then I told him that I couldn't use his idea and warned him that he would be extremely unwise to sell the idea to anyone else because, if he did, he'd be in trouble with you—and me! Not very satisfactory. I'd have preferred to have it out with him face to face. Even the most accomplished liar can give himself away by his expression or even the way he denies the accusation.'

'So now there's nothing to do but wait,' Laurie said dejectedly.

'That's about it,' Rolf agreed. 'Although——' he hesitated, 'I have picked up a few odds and ends of information

as to how he could have got hold of the photographs, but
they're so inconclusive that for the time being I'd sooner
keep them to myself.'

'All right,' Laurie said dubiously. 'The only thing is——'

'Yes?'

'Don't you think that we might find out all the quicker
if we compared notes?'

'Does that mean you've something to tell me?'

'Only in a very negative way,' Laurie explained. 'I phoned
—my friend and made an excuse to ask about the one of me
in the yellow dress.'

'And he said——?'

'First, that he thought I'd taken it and then, that if I
hadn't, he didn't know where it was.'

'I see. Just one more dead end,' Rolf said impatiently.
'And was that all?'

Laurie nodded. There was no point in telling him of her
question to Geoff about Sylvia, because he hadn't even
heard it.

Laurie decided that the sooner she went to see Mrs Baxter
at the Black Prince, the better since until she knew whether
her old job would be available, there was no point in telling
her mother what she intended doing. After all, it wasn't at
all certain that Mrs Baxter would welcome her return.

But as soon as Laurie had explained the purpose of her
visit, she was overjoyed at the prospect.

'The girl we've got at present is *hopeless*,' she announced
emphatically. 'She can't add up accurately, can't spell and
can't even read her own shorthand. She gets on my nerves
half a dozen times a day and I'd have sent her packing by
now except that we might have got someone who was even
worse.'

Mrs Baxter, who was a brisk, competent woman, beamed
at Laurie who was encouraged to bring up the question of
living in. At first, Mrs Baxter looked rather put out.

'My dear, that doesn't mean that you and your mother
are on bad terms, does it?' she asked anxiously. 'I thought
you got on so well together.'

'So we do,' Laurie confirmed quickly. 'But you see,

Mother has met someone she wants to marry, but she won't give up the Ranch because it would mean that I'd have to find a job and somewhere to live.'

'Oh, I see.' Mrs Baxter looked relieved. 'Well, in that case, yes, you could live in. In fact, I'd be glad to have you here. Would you be satisfied with having one of the bedrooms as a bed-sitter? It would have to be on the upper floor, but the one I have in mind is quite pleasant and reasonably big.'

'That would do——' Laurie began, but at that moment the telephone bell rang. Mrs Baxter answered it.

'Mr Baxter? Yes, he's available, but I'll have to fetch him. Will you hold on?'

'Where is he? Can I tell him he's wanted?' Laurie volunteered.

'Oh, will you?' Mrs Baxter said gratefully. 'He's in the bar getting ready for opening time. Tell him it's Mr Forbes about the deliveries.'

Laurie went off on her message to Mr Baxter, who thanked her but grumbled that Forbes ought to have realised that this was bound to be an awkward time.

'I tell you what, Laurie,' he suggested hopefully. 'If you'll stay here in case he keeps me talking beyond opening time —that's only five minutes off—and then open the bar up, I'll be grateful. Probably won't be anyone in, but just in case——? Everything's ready.'

'All right,' Laurie promised, though rather reluctantly. Still, as Mr Baxter had said, it wasn't likely that there would be anyone in so early.

'I'll be as quick as I can,' Mr Baxter promised. 'Help yourself to a drink—on the house.'

When he had gone, Laurie looked automatically round the bar to make quite sure that there was nothing left to be done and having satisfied herself that there wasn't, poured herself out a small measure of sherry.

She sipped it slowly, but the minutes passed all too quickly and it was clear that she would have to deputise for Mr Baxter. What was more, almost immediately the door was pushed open and the first customer came in. And, of all people, it was Geoff!

At first taken aback, Laurie quickly pulled herself together.

'Good morning,' she said briskly. 'What can I get for you?'

But instead of answering her question, Geoff stared at her blankly.

'What on earth are you doing here, Laurie?' he demanded, clearly disconcerted by her presence.

'Helping out for a few minutes while Mr Baxter answers a telephone call,' she explained, and then, as she saw the relief flood into his face, enlightenment dawned on her. 'For goodness' sake, Geoff, you don't imagine I'm here in the hope of seeing you?' she said crossly.

'Well, I did wonder——' he admitted lamely.

'Well, don't any more,' she snapped. 'I was in Penzance with some time on my hands and I thought it was a good opportunity to come and see the Baxters.' Which was perfectly true in a sense, although she had come to Penzance for the express purpose of seeing the Baxters. But to tell him that might have made him more curious to know why and she had no intention of letting the cat out of the bag to anyone, least of all, Geoff.

'Oh, I see.' He sounded relieved, even apologetic, for he immediately offered her a drink which she refused.

'I haven't finished the one Mr Baxter stood me yet,' she explained. 'And since I'll be driving home soon, I think that's enough.'

Geoff accepted that without argument, but he himself ordered a gin and vermouth. They talked in a desultory, rather self-conscious way about nothing in particular until suddenly Geoff stopped short in the middle of a sentence and exclaimed: 'Oh, my sainted aunt!' in a horrified way.

Laurie looked over his shoulder and her heart sank as she saw who it was that had come into the bar.

Rolf.

Laurie was just about to introduce the two men when she remembered that since Geoff worked for Rolf, they already knew one another. She stood silent and ill at ease, for the instant antagonism between the two men was so apparent that it felt like a tangible presence.

It was Rolf who broke the silence. After a brief acknowledgment of Laurie, he turned to Geoff.

'I didn't know you were in the habit of lunching here,
Mellors,' he said coldly.

'I'm not,' Geoff retorted sullenly. 'Their prices are too
stiff for me to do that.'

'Oh, I see. You mean this is in the nature of a special
occasion?' with a glance at Laurie which made it quite clear
what was in his mind.

Laurie gave a little exclamation of annoyance. Then, to
her relief, Geoff volunteered an explanation.

'Since it appears to be of interest to you, sir,' he said
with scarcely veiled insolence, 'my parents are staying here
for a few days and asked me to lunch with them. I trust that
satisfies you that I'm not living above my income?'

'I'm very glad to hear it,' Rolf said coolly.

Geoff sketched a casual salute to Laurie, ignored Rolf
and strolled out of the bar. Almost immediately Mr Baxter
returned and took Rolf's order, but to Laurie there was still
tension in the air. Both men had behaved in a way embarrassing to her, but Rolf had started it. What right had he
to question where Geoff lunched, even though he did employ him? It was intolerable interference on his part, but
even worse was that he had assumed that it was on her account that Geoff was being extravagant.

She saw from his expression that Rolf had spoken to her
and was waiting for an answer, but she hadn't heard what
he had said and she looked at him in a bewildered way.

'I asked you if you would have a drink with me,' he explained suavely. 'Another sherry, perhaps?'

'Thank you, no,' Laurie said brusquely. 'One is enough,
since I'm driving home.'

Just as Geoff had done, Rolf accepted this without argument, and she was just leaving the bar when she almost
collided with someone coming in. She murmured a polite
apology although the fault had not really been hers, when
she realised that the newcomer was Sylvia French.

'You!' Sylvia exclaimed in so low a voice that it was
audible only to Laurie. 'You do turn up all over the place,
don't you? Sometimes one would almost think that there
are two of you!'

'I'm not sure that there aren't,' Laurie retorted recklessly. 'I've been told that I have a double who lives in London and works as a model. It would be rather fun for us to
meet, don't you think?'

She had the satisfaction of seeing an uncontrollable glint
of alarm in Sylvia's eyes before she sailed over to the bar
and greeted Rolf gaily. Laurie didn't hear his reply, but as
she went out into the foyer, she wondered if she had been incredibly foolish in putting Sylvia on her guard.

'Oh, well,' she thought with a shrug. 'It's done—it's no
use regretting it!' And then, ruefully: 'I suppose he's standing her lunch—which must mean that they're still on good
terms. It's incredible that a man as intelligent as he is
should be so blind!'

When Rolf returned to his office he rang through on the
house phone to the accounts department and spoke to the
manager of it.

'Armstrong? Look, I'll be obliged if, without involving
anyone else, you'll bring down young Mellors' personal file
to me as soon as its convenient.'

'I'll do that,' Mr Armstrong promised laconically, giving
no hint of his surprise.

When he laid the file on Rolf's desk, however, he looked
both puzzled and apprehensive.

'Something wrong?' he asked anxiously.

'I hope not,' Rolf replied curtly. 'Just want to make sure
—sit down, Armstrong, this will take a little time. Before I
look at the file, I'd like your personal opinion of the young
man. In strict confidence, of course.'

'H'm!' Mr Armstrong pulled his long nose thoughtfully.
'Well, off the record, he's got brains. But he's also got a
good sized chip on his shoulder.'

'Yes?' Rolf encouraged.

Mr Armstrong shrugged.

'Well, of course, you know how it is. He *is* quite bright—
but not as bright as he thinks he is. Consequently, he feels
he's not sufficiently appreciated and hence the chip.'

'I see.'

'Mind you, you certainly haven't got reasonable grounds
for getting rid of him. Nor, on the other hand, do I think

he deserves further promotion. Not yet, at any rate.'

'So the chip will get bigger,' Rolf said thoughtfully. 'Thanks, Armstrong, that's very helpful. I'll let you have the file back when I've finished with it.'

When Mr Armstrong had left him, Rolf began to study the file. It gave a considerable amount of information about Geoff, although of an impersonal nature—which was why he had wanted Mr Armstrong's private opinion.

It started with the date and place of his birth. Then details of his education. After that came the date when he had joined the firm, having had only one other job previously. Then followed the terms of his appointment and the salary at which he had begun. That had been five years previously. Subsequently he had twice been promoted, each time with an increase in salary. But for the last few years he had done no more than retain the position he already held. As against that, in common with the rest of the staff, he had been paid a cost of living bonus during the last twelve months which had meant a useful increase in his salary.

'H'm,' Rolf said thoughtfully as he saw the figure at which the salary now stood. 'H'm!'—and he locked the file away in one of his desk drawers.

'I didn't know you knew Mellors!'

Laurie stiffened defensively. She was still feeling ruffled by the scene in the bar of the Black Prince, but none the less, she had decided not to make an issue of it with Rolf. It wouldn't do any good because she knew only too well what would happen if she crossed swords with Rolf. He always won!

But when he deliberately sought her out that evening and made that challenging remark, she didn't hesitate to stand up to him.

'No?' in a discouraging voice.

But Rolf persisted.

'Have you known him long?'

'Considerably longer than I've known you,' Laurie told him significantly.

'I see. Does that imply something more than friendship?'

Laurie stiffened resentfully.

'What business is that of yours?'

'I'm interested,' Rolf replied laconically. 'Well, does it?'

Of course it didn't, but some perverse imp kept her from giving him an honest 'No!'

'You mean, are we going to get married? The answer is no—we're not. Geoff is in no position to marry me—or anyone else, as you must very well know.'

'Must I?' Rolf said dryly as he remembered the reasonably generous salary he was paying Geoff.

'Of course you must,' Laurie retorted impatiently. 'He works for you, doesn't he?'

'So it's because I'm such a Scrooge that the wings of romance remain furled?' Rolf asked ironically. 'My dear girl, don't you know that's one of the oldest excuses in the world that a young man makes when he prefers to philander through life?'

'I have no reason for disbelieving Geoff,' Laurie told him coldly.

'And you have for disbelieving me?' Rolf suggested. 'A pity—and if you'll take my advice——'

'But I won't!' Laurie flashed resentfully. What right had he to treat her in this patronising way?

'You will get down to facts and figures with the young man,' Rolf continued, exactly as if she had not interrupted him. 'Find out what he regards as a reasonable income on which to get married—and see if it tallies with your own opinion on the subject.'

'You mean—ask Geoff how much he earns?' Laurie asked scornfully. 'That's the last thing I'd do!' Which was perfectly true, since it was of no interest to her. 'Besides, since you must know, why don't you tell me?'

'Because I'm in a privileged position to know is the very reason why, to me, it's confidential information which I have no right to divulge,' Rolf told her sternly.

'You think it's more ethical to hint and insinuate?' Laurie asked scornfully. 'Because I don't!'

'Have I hinted and insinuated?' Rolf asked with infuriating patience. 'Yes, perhaps I have. None the less, what I've said is no more than the commonsense advice which any man of any experience would give to a girl who——'

'Yes?' Laurie asked with dangerous quiet as he paused.

'Who manifestly knows little of the world,' he finished steadily. 'You've never had the misfortune to have to rough it without the advantage of a good home as your background. Though, come to think of it, I'm not so sure that it is an advantage,' he added reflectively. 'At least without it, one learns not to regard all one's geese as swans.'

'Oh, I don't do that,' Laurie told him with deceptive sweetness. 'I know that there are people who, for example, think nothing of implying slander of people behind their backs! I think you're despicable, Rolf Audley!'

He made no immediate reply, but she saw that his hands slowly clenched until the knuckles gleamed white.

'I've made a mess of this,' he admitted ruefully. 'Yet I had the best of intentions—perhaps that's why. I'm truly sorry, Laurie.'

And the disconcerting thing was that he made that sound as if it was the truth.

Laurie was working in her little office one morning when her mother came in, her face tragic.

'Do you know what's happened?' she demanded, and without waiting for Laurie to reply, she told her, 'Mr Audley has given a month's notice!'

'He has!' Laurie exclaimed incredulously. 'But why?'

'He wouldn't explain beyond saying that he felt it was time he went. But of course, I know the reason. It's perfectly obvious.'

'Is it?' Laurie asked uneasily. 'Not to me!'

'It ought to be clearer to you than to anyone else,' Mrs Stephens declared accusingly. 'It's because of *you*! Oh yes, it is,' as Laurie's lips parted to protest. 'You were against him from the very first! And since he came, you've argued and bickered with him most unpleasantly even though you knew perfectly well that he needed to be here to convalesce! I'm ashamed of you, Laurie!'

'But——'

'There's no "but",' Mrs Stephens declared angrily. 'He's been extremely tolerant of your behaviour—far more so than most men would have been. But evidently he's come to the end of his patience and I for one don't blame him!'

'But——' Laurie began again, but again Mrs Stephens swept her protest aside.

'Now listen, Laurie,' she said severely. 'I've noticed that for the last few days you've not only avoided Mr Audley but you've been in an unpleasantly sulky mood. Does that mean you've quarrelled with him again?'

'Yes, it does,' Laurie said defiantly. 'And I had very good cause to, Mother.'

'Oh, you always have when you lose your temper,' Mrs Stephens snapped. 'And don't blame it on to the colour of your hair. It's sheer lack of self-control!'

'In this case, at least, I had every reason to be annoyed,' Laurie said with as much dignity as she could muster. She could never remember her mother taking her to task like this since she had been grown up and she was dismayed as well as surprised. That her gentle, loving mother should turn on her like this!

'Mr Audley was extremely impertinent to me about a personal matter and I had no choice but to make it clear that I couldn't allow him to speak to me like that.'

'You'll tell me next that he made improper suggestions to you, I suppose,' Mrs Stephens retorted. 'Well, let me tell you, that's something I cannot and will not believe of Mr Audley!'

'No, it was nothing like that,' Laurie admitted wearily. 'But I'm sorry, Mother, that's all I'm going to tell you because it involved someone else and—well, I don't think it would be right to tell you.'

Mrs Stephens looked disconcerted at this flat refusal.

'You realise what this means?' she said worriedly. 'Without what Mr Audley pays for himself and Hutton we just can't make ends meet. Even though I'm a dunce over figures, I know that!'

'Yes, it does mean that,' Laurie agreed. 'And to tell you the truth, Mother, I'm glad!'

'You're glad!' Mrs Stephens exclaimed incredulously. 'You're mad, Laurie!'

'No, I'm not,' Laurie denied bleakly. 'Look, Mother, I think it's time for me to tell you——'

'Tell me what?'

Laurie stood up and faced her mother resolutely.

'That I'm sick and tired of the Ranch and everything to do with it!' she declared passionately. 'I don't mind hard work, but all this worry——'

'But now that we've got this mortgage——' Mrs Stephens reminded her.

'Mother, you've never made a secret of not liking having a mortgage, and I've realised you're right!'

'So what do you want us to do?' Mrs Stephens asked uncertainly.

'Sell the place,' Laurie explained decisively. 'What else is there to do?'

'That's all very well,' Mrs Stephens pursed her lips. 'As you very well know, it would mean that John and I could get married——' She looked suspiciously at Laurie. 'Is that why you want to sell out? Because if so——'

'It's one reason,' Laurie said hurriedly. 'But far from being the only one.'

'But how about you, darling?' Mrs Stephens asked anxiously, her earlier anger forgotten. 'What will you do?'

'Oh, that's all but settled,' Laurie declared airily. 'The Baxters will be quite happy to have me back—and I can live in. So there'll be nothing for you to worry about.'

'Well, I must say you seem to have got it all cut and dried,' Mrs Stephens admitted, torn between relief and anxiety. 'But all this depends on one thing—whether we can find a purchaser for the Ranch.'

'Oh, that won't be difficult,' Laurie assured her confidently. 'We'll sell it all right, and I know to whom—Rolf.'

'Mr Audley?' Mrs Stephens echoed in astonishment. 'But he's never said——'

'He has, to me,' Laurie explained. 'He used to visit here when it was a private house and has always been fond of the place. That day he had the accident he was coming to see if we'd sell out to him.'

'He wanted to buy it as long ago as that!' Mrs Stephens exclaimed. 'How very odd!'

'Not really,' Laurie told her. 'You see, he intends to make it his home—after he's married.'

Mrs Stephens stared at her, as dumbfounded as Mr Brownsell had been at Laurie's indifference.

'But——' she said in bewilderment, 'surely you know——'

'Mother,' Laurie interrupted, 'what I know is that I'm sick and tired of the place and the sooner we can leave it the better pleased I'll be!'

When Mr Brownsell heard the news he was quietly delighted. But to Laurie's embarrassment he regarded the part she had played in bringing about Mrs Stephens' change of heart as having been made at the cost of Laurie's own feelings.

'You're a dear, kind girl,' he said gratefully. 'And I shan't forget this in a hurry. You can be sure of that.'

'Oh, but you mustn't think——' Laurie began hastily.

Mr Brownsell's kindly eyes twinkled.

'My dear, I wouldn't presume to think anything except that you've found a way to help Lucy and me out of our predicament. I don't know how I'll ever repay you, but there is one thing I can do which might be of help to you. How would you feel about me going to the house agent to tell him what's in the wind? Lucy would quite like me to do that, but we both feel we'd like to have your agreement.' He looked at her questioningly.

'I think it would be a good idea,' Laurie said briskly, but her heart was heavy. Somehow the offer brought home more vividly just what she had done—quite deliberately put Rolf out of her life.

'Not that he was ever really part of it,' she thought sadly. 'But at least I'm facing up to that—which is better than pretending that, to use Miss Trewyn's words, he ever "looked my way".'

But if Mr Brownsell was pleased with the turn of events, there were two people who weren't—Miss Trewyn and Hutton. In fact, they were flabbergasted.

'But why?' Laurie asked Miss Trewyn. 'What real difference does it make? I mean, I know it will be dull for you when Hutton goes, but it's only a few months to your wedding day, isn't it? And after that—well, you'd have been leaving here anyway.'

But Miss Trewyn refused to be comforted.

'Yes, I know all that,' she said restlessly. 'But we'd sort of hoped that things would turn out differently. Frank really prefers being here to living in Penzance and how I'll put up with all the noise and bustle I really don't know.' She sighed deeply. 'Not but what Frank has a very nice flat—part of Mr Audley's but sort of detached from it across a corridor.' She sighed again. 'Oh well, I suppose I'll get used to it. But as I say. It'll be very different from what we'd hoped.'

'Well, perhaps after all, you'll be able to live here,' Laurie consoled her. 'Who knows?'

Miss Trewyn brightened instantly.

'Oh, Miss Laurie, does that mean——?' she asked hopefully.

'It means nothing except that if that's what you want, then I hope your dreams come true,' Laurie said hurriedly.

'Well, that's nice of you,' Miss Trewyn said appreciatively. 'And I must say, I hope yours do, too!'

But that, of course, would never happen.

When Rolf had first returned to his office he had only worked for mornings, returning to the Ranch in time for lunch, but now he kept full office hours. Even, sometimes, he would telephone through to say that he was working late and would be dining out. On these occasions he was usually quite late back.

Laurie assumed that he was with Sylvia French—and promptly told herself that if he was, it was no business of hers. But it wasn't so easy to keep a curb on her imagination as she pictured them sitting *tête-à-tête*, discussing their joint future.

That was why, when Geoff rang her up, she quite welcomed hearing from him, with the result that Geoff, who had sounded rather uneasy as if he wasn't sure what sort of welcome he would have, became more at his ease. In fact positively expansive.

'I've got something important to tell you,' he announced briskly. 'Something I think you'll find interesting.'

'Oh, what?' Laurie asked, intrigued.

'Not over the telephone,' he told her cautiously. 'This is something I'd like to tell you face to face.'

'How—mysterious,' Laurie said slowly, feeling as if a light in her brain was flashing a warning. 'But really, Geoff——'

'Oh, come on, be a sport!' Geoff urged. 'I promise you won't regret it. What about dinner somewhere quiet this evening?'

'No, I can't manage that,' Laurie refused. 'Miss Trewyn is off duty this evening, so I shall be busy.'

'Confound the woman,' Geoff grumbled. 'She would be! Well, what about coming out for a drink after dinner time then?'

Laurie hesitated. She knew that by the time dinner was over and all the clearing up done, to say nothing of setting the tables for breakfast the following morning, she would be really tired and in no mood to go out celebrating, which was, she supposed, what Geoff wanted to do.

'Look, Geoff, I won't be free until half-past nine at the earliest. Then I'd have to change—I think it would be a much better idea for you to come here.'

'Oh, heavens, no!' he refused crossly. 'With Audley on the premises the Ranch is about the last place——!'

'Mr Audley will be out until late, so you needn't be afraid,' Laurie snapped, and rang off.

Geoff didn't ring back, so she presumed that he would do as she had suggested. And if he didn't, Laurie shrugged her shoulders—what did it matter even though he had aroused her curiosity? But Geoff arrived at twenty to ten and one look at him made it obvious that he was bursting to tell her his news.

'Let's go down to the pool,' he suggested. 'We're not likely to be disturbed there.'

'All right,' Laurie agreed. 'But just wait a minute——'

Quickly she prepared a tray with two glasses, a bottle of chilled lager for Geoff and one of home-made lemonade for herself.

'Carry that, please, Geoff,' she requested briskly. 'I'll switch on the pool lights as we go through the hall.'

'No need to do that,' Geoff told her as he picked up the tray. 'The moon's almost full——'

But Laurie had no use for moonlight. It could be seductive and induce one to behave with a recklessness which one would afterwards regret. So, ignoring Geoff's suggestion, she firmly switched on the lights.

Even so, the pool looked very attractive with the lights, as well as the moon, reflected in its placid surface.

Geoff set the tray down and poured out the drinks. For a moment or so they sat in silence, sipping contentedly at their cool drinks. Then Laurie said briskly:

'Now, what's this mysterious news?'

'Well——' Geoff set his glass down. 'I've got a new job!'

'You *have*?' Laurie was so surprised that she spilt some of her lemonade. 'You mean you're leaving Mr Audley?'

'I mean just that,' Geoff declared with considerable satisfaction. 'And you can hardly blame me after that episode at the Black Prince, now can you?'

'Perhaps not,' Laurie admitted. 'Though you did your share to make things awkward.'

'Not until he'd started,' Geoff retorted sulkily. 'What damn business was it of his where I had lunch?'

None at all, Laurie had to admit, as she'd made clear to Rolf

'Well, never mind about that,' she said hurriedly. 'Tell me about the job. Is it a better one than you've got at present?'

'I'll say,' he declared enthusiastically. 'Better pay right from the beginning and better prospects as well. The only thing is, it means living abroad. Will you mind that, Laurie?'

'Why should I mind?' Laurie asked uncomprehendingly. 'It's got nothing to do with me!'

'Oh yes, it has,' Geoff declared masterfully. 'I'm asking you to marry me!'

For a moment Laurie was too taken aback to reply.

'Well?' Geoff demanded.

'I'm sorry, Geoff, but no, it's out of the question,' Laurie said firmly.

'Now look here——' Geoff began, and stood up. He began to pace up and down. Suddenly he came to a halt in front of her. 'Is it because of the stupid way I sort of half-proposed to you—said that if I could afford to, I'd ask you to marry me?'

Laurie shook her head, but Geoff took no notice.

'I've often felt what a heel I was to take that line,' he said regretfully. 'But at the time I felt it was the only thing to do. You see, actually, I've been earning enough to get married on, only it would have meant cheeseparing, no spare cash for having a good time or saving for a rainy day. And I just couldn't face it even with you. But now everything will be different. So won't you say "Yes"?'

Laurie shook her head again. She didn't enjoy hurting her old friend, but she knew that it was out of the question to do as he wished. She had nothing to give him.

Geoff was silent for a time. Then he asked harshly:

'You're not by any chance carrying a torch for Audley, are you?'

Laurie stood up, her head in the air.

'I'm not carrying a torch for anyone,' she declared emphatically. 'Please understand, Geoff, I mean that. And I don't see that there's any point in us staying here any longer.'

She turned to go back to the house, but Geoff quickly blocked her way.

'Oh, don't you!' he said angrily. 'Well, you're wrong there!'

And before she realised what was in his mind, he had caught her in his arms and his lips were demanding hers, possessively, even brutally.

Perhaps she should have been very angry, but instead a strange apathy overcame her. She stood rigid and unresponsive in his arms and after a while Geoff let her go.

'All right, I get the message,' he said sulkily. 'I just haven't got what it takes where you're concerned. Forget it!'

He strode off, but Laurie, peering across to the far end of the pool, didn't move. Just as Geoff had left she had been almost certain that she had seen a shadow move on the far side of the lights.

Someone had seen her in Geoff's arms. She was all but certain of that. But who? She felt as if her heart stopped beating. Was it possible that, after all, Rolf had returned earlier than he had expected to?

She walked slowly back to the Ranch and saw that the doors of the garage where Rolf kept his car were closed, though she knew that Hutton had left them open in anticipation of his return.

There seemed to be little doubt that it was he who had witnessed Geoff's last desperate attempt to persuade her to change her mind. And at that distance, unable to hear what they said, the conclusion that an onlooker would inevitably have drawn was appallingly clear.

CHAPTER NINE

IT didn't occur to Laurie to give Rolf an explanation for the scene he had witnessed between Geoff and herself. She thought that he would probably have believed her, but that was just the point. Rolf already had an unfair prejudice against Geoff. How could she possibly explain without appearing to blame Geoff—which would simply serve to increase that prejudice? Admittedly, Geoff had lost his head and behaved stupidly, but that was her business, not Rolf's, particularly as she was reasonably sure that such a thing would never happen again. No, it was no concern of Rolf's, nor did she think that, so far as she was concerned, he would be interested.

It was also probable that by now Rolf was aware that Geoff was changing his job and had realised that any authority he had ever had over him as an employee now simply didn't exist. What was more, the sooner that Geoff left Toys & Games Unlimited, the better. The two men were utterly incompatible. Rolf would never be able to give Geoff a square deal and Geoff would never be able to bring himself to kow-tow to Rolf's notions of discipline.

So Laurie kept the whole matter to herself and since Rolf made no reference to it either, perhaps she might have forgotten all about it but that, in all innocence, Megan Jones brought the matter up.

With Rolf now spending more time at the office they saw less of Megan at the Ranch, much to Mrs Stephens' regret. She and Megan had formed one of those quiet, unemotional friendships which are the prerogative of middle age and it was clear that something had to be done if the friendship was not to founder.

'I'm going to ask Megan here for a week-end,' Mrs Stephens told Laurie. 'This coming one if she can manage it because John won't be here. He's going to Oxford to pay a visit to an old aunt of his who isn't at all well, so I'll be able to spend more time with her. Megan, I mean.'

'Nice,' Laurie said briefly. She was, in fact, pleased at the suggestion. Without the need to keep her mother company she would feel free to spend what spare time she had away from the Ranch, which was just what she wanted—needed—to do. With the knowledge that their time at the Ranch was now limited, it was impossible to put one's heart into running it.

Megan arrived early on Friday evening and after one look at her Mrs Stephens was doubly glad that she had issued the invitation. Megan, she thought, looked both tired and tense and was very ready to sit quietly in the kitchen watching Mrs Stephens and Laurie completing preparations for the evening meal.

'Had a busy week?' Mrs Stephens asked tentatively, breaking off from her work to make Megan a piping hot cup of tea.

'Busy—and rather demanding,' said Megan, sipping her tea. 'This is delicious, Lucy. I don't know anyone else who can produce such a hot cup of tea. I can barely drink it. Just right!'

'Good,' Mrs Stephens said absently, her mind still occupied with Megan's appearance. 'Why particularly demanding?' she asked.

Megan smiled. From some people such a question would be an impertinence, but from Lucy, bless her, it was the outcome of genuine interest. Knowing this, she had no hesitation in answering.

'We've got a vacancy in the accounts department and we need to get it filled as quickly as possible,' she explained. 'I've been helping Mr Armstrong who runs the department to vet the applicants so that Rolf only has to deal with a short list.'

'That's a responsible undertaking,' Mrs Stephens commented.

'It is,' Megan agreed, 'and I feel an additional responsibility because I was so confident that the young man who's just left us was the right choice.'

'And he wasn't?'

'No, decidedly not. Yet he had good qualifications, well

up to our standard, he had a pleasant manner and he seemed to be enthusiastic about the work. That was the trouble,' she added broodingly. 'He was too keen. He didn't like taking orders and he resented any criticisms of his work. One way and another it made him very difficult for the rest of the staff to work with.'

Laurie listened with her ears pricked. She was preparing vegetables at the sink so that her back was towards the other two women and she could listen to what they were saying without appearing to be particularly interested. But of course she was. It could only be Geoff to whom Megan was referring and of whom she was giving such an unflattering description. And Megan, she was sure, was not speaking from prejudice as Rolf had done. Or had he?

In view of what Megan was saying, wasn't it at least possible that he had legitimate reason for dissatisfaction with Geoff?

Not that that excused him for having initiated that unpleasant scene in the bar. If he wanted to question Geoff he should have waited until they were alone, not embarrassed her by compelling her to listen to their conversation.

And afterwards—he had been so unpleasantly patronising with his advice. What right had he to assume that she was just an ignorant little twitterpate, incapable of making intelligent decisions?

Yes, she had good reason to be thoroughly annoyed with him, she decided stubbornly. And yet——

The weather, which had been glorious for months past, suddenly changed its tune. Great black clouds, sent scurrying across the sky on a wind strong enough to be called a gale, and rain which came lashing down, made venturing out of doors seem sheer folly.

Yet Laurie, staring out at the bleak scene, felt a sense of claustrophobia at being confined to the house and as soon as the rain eased a little, she put on a mackintosh, sou'-wester and gumboots and set out despite her mother's protests.

She had to duck her head against the wind as she crossed

the garden, but once she reached the lane its high banks and hedges gave her some protection. Then as she reached the Cove, she met the full blast of the storm.

For a moment she lost her breath, then, seeking the leeward side of a big outcrop of rock, she watched, fascinated.

It was no more than half-tide but as the great, foam-crested waves came thundering in, Laurie could taste the salt spray on her lips. Huge masses of water beat against the rocky promontory from which she had dived earlier in the year, spurting up into white fountains only to sink back again as if sulking at the resistance they had met.

It was a magnificent sight, turbulent, ever-changing and with a suggestion of defiance about it which found its echo in Laurie's mood. She didn't consciously make the comparison, was hardly even aware that it existed, but as she stood there, her senses buffeted by the sight and sound of Nature in a fury, she was overwhelmed by a sense of her own insignificance.

Why, after all, did it matter in the vast scheme of things that she should be feeling disappointment and unhappiness? It was childish to expect that her life would always be lived in the sunshine or that those dreams of hers would ever be fulfilled.

Gradually her mood of rebellion and defiance died away to be taken by one, not of resignation—that was beyond her—but by a realisation that somehow or other she had got to learn to build up a new life for herself. A life which, even if it wasn't as rich as it might have been, could at least be worthwhile.

It wouldn't be easy. She had no illusions about that, but the very fact that it would mean a stiff fight was stimulating. She'd got to make out—she'd got to.

It was at that moment that she was suddenly convinced someone was watching her. She turned swiftly, but she could see no one else on the beach. Then she raised her eyes and saw that she had not been mistaken. Someone was watching her—a man. He had found a comparatively sheltered spot on the cliffs above her and he was watching her through binoculars, but though they masked his face to some extent, she knew who it was. Rolf.

With a sharp exclamation she turned and made her way as quickly as she could up the beach to the lane. At all costs she must get away before Rolf had time to get down from his vantage point. But her speed was her undoing. She stumbled over a large stone half covered in sand and felt an agonising stab of pain in one ankle. Perforce she stood still, balancing on one leg while she tentatively rubbed the injured ankle. Though it was painful she didn't think it was a serious injury, but the delay gave Rolf time to scramble down beside her. Quickly Laurie set down her injured foot so that, though she could not put any weight on to it, Rolf would not know that she was in trouble. She faced him defiantly.

'Why were you spying on me?' she demanded challengingly.

'Why are you down here on your own when you gave me your word not to take risks?' he flung back at her.

'Oh, that!' Laurie said contemptuously.

'Yes, *that*!' he said angrily. 'I thought you were the sort of person who could be trusted to keep a promise once you'd given it.'

'But that was something quite different,' Laurie insisted, picqued into defending herself. 'It was because, after the way those people behaved so stupidly, you were afraid that something like that might happen again. But today there was no possibility of anything like that happening.'

'There are more ways than one in which an accident can happen,' Rolf told her significantly. 'And on a day like this——'

'Oh, rubbish!' Laurie said impatiently. 'You're making a mountain out of a molehill! Simply, I wanted to get out of the house for a little while and I came here in the hope of being alone. But nobody but Mother knew I was out!'

'That's just the point,' Rolf retorted. 'Nobody knew— but, by chance, someone might have seen you and followed you.'

'But nobody did,' Laurie pointed out triumphantly.

'*I* did—and someone else might have done as well.'

Laurie shrugged her shoulders.

'No doubt you feel that I should feel flattered by your

concern,' she said indifferently. 'But in fact, I regard it as an impertinence!' And momentarily forgetting her injured ankle, she began to walk away from him, but two paces and she had to admit defeat. Walking was out of the question.

'You've hurt yourself?' Rolf asked sharply. 'Ankle? Is it very bad?'

'I've twisted it a bit,' Laurie admitted, setting her teeth and fighting to keep the tears back. 'It will be better in a few minutes—please don't wait for me.'

But Rolf stood stock still beside her, waiting silently as the minutes passed.

'Well?' he demanded at length.

'I can manage,' Laurie insisted defiantly, taking a step forward only to give a sharp cry at the pain which resulted.

Instantly Rolf's arm was round her and the next moment she was swung up into his arms.

'Put me down!' she demanded furiously. And when he took no notice, she beat against his chest with her clenched fists. 'Do you hear me? Put me down at once!'

For answer, Rolf's hold on her tightened and he gave her a little shake.

'Keep still, you obstinate young idiot,' he said roughly. 'Do you want to have us both down?'

'But—but Rolf, you can't carry me all the way back,' she protested, her defiance wilting. 'I'm too heavy——'

He turned his head to look down into her face as it lay against his shoulder.

'As a matter of fact, you're not nearly heavy enough,' he told her disapprovingly. 'You ought to weigh considerably more than you do for your height. What have you been doing to yourself, young Laurie? Not eating enough?'

'One never does eat as much during the hot weather,' Laurie equivocated. 'But if it's of any interest to you, as well as my usual cereal, toast and marmalade and coffee for breakfast, I had a boiled egg this morning.'

'Good,' Rolf said absently, only to go on with his questioning. 'Anything worrying you?'

'A bit,' Laurie admitted.

'What?' he wanted to know.

She didn't answer immediately. Despite the roughness

of the lane, now that she had surrendered to the insistence
of his strength, she had been growing increasingly conscious
of a sense of security and wellbeing. She didn't want to talk,
least of all to answer questions to which she couldn't give
truthful answers. But there was, she realised, one answer
which would probably satisfy him.

'I expect you know that Mother and I have decided to sell
the Ranch?'

'Yes, I know.'

'Well, supposing we don't find anyone to buy it? We'll
really be in difficulties then,' she explained, and waited
anxiously for his reply.

She felt him give a little start of surprise.

'But hasn't Brownsell or your mother told you?' he asked
in surprise. 'That's all settled. I'm buying it. The contract
date is October the tenth.'

'No, I didn't know,' Laurie admitted, unconsciously sag-
ging in his arms. 'But of course, it's really more Mother's
business than mine and I expect he thought she would tell
me.'

'Possibly,' Rolf agreed shortly, and left it at that.

They were crossing the garden now and to Laurie's surprise, instead of going in through the main entrance, he
carried her through the little private garden and so into his
own quarters, not stopping until they were in his bedroom.

'Now then, off with that mackintosh,' he ordered, setting
her down so that, standing on one foot and with his support, she could slide out of the wet garment. Then, without
warning, he picked her up and laid her gently on the bed.

Instantly Laurie jerked herself up on her elbow.

'But I can't——' she protested in dismay.

Rolf stood over her, grim, determined and very sure of
himself.

'Don't be a little fool,' he said harshly. 'You've got to put
that ankle up without delay, and with the best will in the
world I can't carry you upstairs. Understand?'

'If you'll fetch Mother——' Laurie mumbled, sinking
back thankfully.

'Certainly,' Rolf promised. 'Just as soon as I see how bad

the damage is—no need to alarm her more than necessary.
Now then, off with those boots!'

He took the one off her uninjured foot first and that was
comparatively easy. Then he paused.

'This is pretty certain to hurt you,' he warned. 'But I
don't think it would be any easier if I were to cut the boot
off. Are you going to let me try?'

'Go ahead,' Laurie told him stoically.

'Yell if you can't stand it,' Rolf muttered, and got to
work.

He was as gentle and careful as it was possible to be, but
when the boot was finally off, Laurie was very near to faint-
ing and Rolf's face was wet with perspiration.

'You've got guts,' he told her gruffly, and Laurie felt as
proud as if she'd been awarded the Victoria Cross. 'Now
then, off with your stocking——'

When that was off, he inspected her ankle. It was swollen
and inflamed and she winced as he felt it with long, sensitive fingers—she had never noticed before what fine hands
he had got——

'H'm!' He stood erect. 'A nasty sprain, but I don't think
there's anything broken. We'll see what a cold water com-
press will do and I'm pretty sure there's a crêpe bandage in
my first aid kit.'

He fetched a basin of cold water, folded a clean handkerchief, soaked it and bound it firmly round Laurie's ankle.
She winced at the chill of it, but admitted that it was giving
her some relief.

'Good,' Rolf said with relief, soaked the handkerchief
again and replaced it. 'Now we'll put the bandage on——'

He did this neatly and efficiently and Laurie thanked him
in a subdued voice, but he brushed her thanks away.

'My good deed for the day,' he said lightly. 'Didn't you
know I'm a Boy Scout in good standing? Well, I am! Now
then, a cup of tea and some aspirin and while you're having
them, I'll go and tell your mother that you're *hors de com-
bat* and she can take over.'

He brought her a piping hot cup of tea and stood over
her while she sipped it and swallowed the aspirin. Then he
went off to find Mrs Stephens. When they came back it was
clear that Rolf had contrived to give her the news without

alarming her unduly. In fact, she spent far more time praising Rolf for the way in which he had coped with the emergency than in commiserating with Laurie.

Then, without any reference to her, they discussed what the best arrangement for the night would be, and to both of them it seemed that there was only one answer—that Laurie should have Rolf's bed while Mrs Stephens had Hutton's and the two men slept upstairs in two of the empty bedrooms.

'But, Mother——' Laurie protested.

'Don't be silly, darling,' Mrs Stephens said briskly. 'It's by far the most sensible thing to do and if Mr Audley doesn't mind, there's nothing more to be said.'

'I could get upstairs—somehow,' Laurie insisted stubbornly.

'I'm not so sure of that,' Mrs Stephens told her dispassionately. 'But anyway, you're going to need to be in bed for a couple of days. Have you thought how much more trouble it would be to take trays upstairs than to bring them in here?'

Laurie subsided at this practical point of view and Hutton, returning at that moment, was informed of the plan. He took it in his stride and he and Rolf selected the essentials they would need to make the transfer and took them upstairs.

When they had gone, Mrs Stephens brought Laurie's night clothes and helped her to change. Then she slipped a soft little woolly cape round Laurie's shoulders and told her that the most sensible thing she could do would be to have a sleep.

Laurie, pleasantly drowsy now as the aspirin took effect, didn't argue. Really, it was very pleasant to be fussed over and with the pain in her ankle at least tolerable now she was really quite comfortable. Her eyelids fluttered—and then opened wide as she heard Rolf speak to her mother.

Then he was standing by the bed, smiling down at her.

'Comfy?'

'Yes,' she said shyly. 'Really quite comfy.'

His expression changed, but she was too sleepy to read its meaning. Then he said softly:

'You look a positive infant with that woolly thingummy

and your hair loose.' And bending over, he kissed her lightly. 'Pleasant dreams, Laurie!' and he was gone.

Laurie lay very still. Once before he had given her what she had described as a 'champagne kiss'. This one had been quite different. It had expressed the sympathy he felt for her—but it was also the sort of kiss he would have given to the child he said she looked like.

Yet it had been very sweet——

Laurie snuggled her head into the pillow that smelled faintly of the very masculine hair fixative that Rolf used. Her eyes closed and she drifted into sleep.

By morning her ankle was considerably better, though twice during the night she had been disturbed by the pain of it. She did her best not to make any noise, but each time her mother had woken up and come to her. Feeling how hot the ankle was, she had renewed the cold water treatment and the second time she had made tea for them both and insisted that Laurie should have another dose of aspirin.

'Of course it won't do you any harm,' she said firmly in answer to Laurie's protest. 'I know you don't like taking drugs of any sort, but it's hours since you had the last dose. So come along, there's a good girl!'

So Laurie, feeling that in fact she was still a child, did as she was told and after a while, went to sleep again until her mother woke her with morning tea and biscuits.

After that, the ankle was inspected again and it was clear that both the inflammation and the puffiness had decreased.

'You're doing nicely,' Mrs Stephens pronounced with relief.

'Then can I get up?' Laurie asked eagerly, only to be met with a flat refusal.

'No, indeed, you'll do nothing of the sort—at least not until Dr Morris sees you.'

'Dr Morris!' Laurie exclaimed. 'But surely you haven't——'

'But surely I have,' Mrs Stephens retorted briskly. 'Mr Audley and I talked it over and decided that he'd better have a look at you. So I telephoned him—or rather, Mr Audley did. And he'll be along just before lunch. Now I'll get you washed and you can do your hair and then you'll be ready for breakfast.'

Laurie grumbled at the prospect of enforced laziness, but the knowledge that Rolf had played a part—probably a leading part—in summoning the doctor served to quell her protests. For one thing, she'd already learned the hard way that it was useless to argue with Rolf, and for another—it was rather nice to feel that he was concerned on her behalf.

'Mr Audley says he'd like to see you for a few minutes before he leaves for the office,' Mrs Stephens announced as she tidied away the odds and ends and straightened the bedclothes.

'Oh? All right,' Laurie said casually, but as soon as her mother had left her, she took her handbag off the bedside table and took out her powder compact and lipstick. No more being told that she looked like a child if she could help it!

So when Rolf came in bearing a tray and followed by Mrs Stephens, Laurie smiled at him in an easy, assured way and when she had answered his questions about her ankle, began to thank him for his help the previous day. But he interrupted her impatiently.

'Don't be silly,' he said shortly. 'I only did what anyone would have done for someone in your plight. There's no need for you to feel you're in my debt.'

'But I don't—at least, not in an uncomfortable way,' Laurie protested indignantly. 'But you *did* help me and it would be horrid of me not to thank you! So you needn't be so superior about not wanting to be thanked—so now then, Rolf Audley!'

For a moment he stared at her as if he couldn't believe his ears. Then he grinned broadly.

'Yes, you're better,' he admitted. 'Almost your usual self, in fact! Now then,' briskly, 'is there anything I can get in Penzance that will help to pass the time for you? I'll be back for lunch today.'

'So that you can see the doctor?' The question popped out before she had time to think of the possible consequences, but if she had hoped to disconcert Rolf, she was disappointed.

'Just that,' he admitted coolly. 'Well, is there anything?'

'A paperback?' Laurie suggested after a moment's thought. 'A nice gory whodunnit?'

'You bloodthirsty little monster!' Rolf said reprovingly. 'I should have thought that a nice girl like you would have preferred something romantic.'

'Then I can't be a nice girl, can I?' Laurie suggested pertly. 'Because I find other people's romances so boring. Don't you?'

'Perhaps,' he conceded. 'All right, a blood-and-thunder it shall be!'

But when he returned at lunch time, as well as the book he had brought her a bunch of deep red roses and a box of juicy fruit sweets.

'Oh, how lovely!' Laurie said, smelling the roses appreciatively. 'And sweets! Do you know, I think it's rather fun being laid up. One gets so nicely spoilt——' her eyes were mischievous. 'And one is forgiven for all one's past misdeeds!'

Rolf didn't reply, but she heard the sharp intake of his breath and wondered why what she had said disturbed him so. Then the doctor and Mrs Stephens came in and he went out of the room.

After examining it, Dr Morris was reassuring about the ankle. He approved the treatment which Laurie had had, saying that it was just what he himself would have prescribed.

'You're going on nicely,' he told Laurie. 'And provided you behave sensibly, you'll be able to get up in a day or so. Though you'll still have to keep off your feet at first. X-ray?' in answer to a question from Mrs Stephens. 'Well, yes, if there's any doubt about a complete recovery. But my personal opinion is that it won't come to that. Lucky girl!'

He left a few minutes later with a parting injunction to Laurie to be sensible.

'Do as your mother—*and* that young man of yours— tells you to——' he chuckled as he saw the colour flood her cheeks. 'He's not the sort to stand any nonsense, as you probably know!'

'But he's——' Laurie began, but Mrs Stephens had

already hustled the doctor out of the room. When she came back, Laurie rebuked her indignantly.

'Mother, how could you let Dr Morris go away thinking that Rolf and I——'

'But my dear Laurie, what does it matter?' Mrs Stephens asked. 'Dr Morris won't give it a second thought. Besides, if you'd told him he'd made a mistake, think how embarrassed the poor man would be! You really must stop worrying about trifles, dear!'

A week later Laurie drove into Penzance, despite her mother's protests.

'I shan't do any more walking than I've done already,' she pointed out. 'Just from the Black Prince car park to the hotel and back. Honestly, it will be all right. And I could do with a little outing.'

She did not say so to her mother, but she knew that she had a real need to get away from the Ranch and back to normal activities, and the longer she put it off, the harder that would be. For a week she had lived in a cosy little world, petted and pampered and with no responsibilities. Mrs Stephens and Miss Trewyn had waited on her hand and foot. Megan Jones had come out to see her several times, bringing little gifts each time—talcum powder, chocolate, grapes. And Rolf—he had come in to see her at least once a day and, once she was up, his visits had increased in length. Of an evening he would spend perhaps a couple of hours with her, and they always found plenty to talk about. She discovered a new Rolf—companionable, interesting and as good a listener as he was a talker.

'And it won't do,' Laurie told herself restlessly. 'He's getting to mean too much to me, and the longer it goes on, the harder it's going to be——'

She paid her visit to Mrs Baxter, making more definite arrangements over the date when Laurie would be able to start work at the Black Prince and the terms of her appointment.

This satisfactorily concluded, Laurie left the hotel, but she didn't immediately go to the car park. On the opposite side of the road from the Black Prince was a toyshop that she had known and loved from her childhood days. Smiling reminiscently, she crossed the road and joined the admiring group of children. There was a dolls' house on display, complete down to the very last detail. It had electric lights which really lit, water in the bathroom and kitchen and in all the rooms, beautifully dressed dolls working and playing.

At last she tore herself away from the main window to look at the slightly smaller side one—dolls of all sorts and sizes from cuddly baby ones to the bigger girl sizes. Suddenly she caught her breath and the colour drained out of her face. In the centre of the window was a display of some half dozen dolls which were labelled: 'Underclothes and dresses available.'

They were young girl dolls attired in bikinis. Their auburn hair was arranged in one long curl and in their eyes was a sly, seductive look. If further identification was needed, across the chest of each doll was a ribbon printed with the words: 'The Lorelei.'

Laurie felt physically sick. Despite Rolf's promise, he had gone ahead with marketing the doll. What was more, seeing how recently it was that he had made that promise, it must have been a rush job. Or else perhaps it had already been in course of manufacture. In either case, what else could she read into the presence of these dolls but the most cynical sort of treachery?

But he had, she remembered, said that he was sure it would be a paying line and he had evidently decided that her threat to sue him if he went ahead with manufacturing them wasn't worth bothering about. To do such a thing would mean she would need money behind her, since lawsuits were expensive things, particularly if one lost the case. And he knew, of course, that she hadn't got that sort of money. But he had!

None the less, she wasn't going to let the matter rest there. At least Rolf was going to hear what she thought of his duplicity! She marched purposefully into the shop, to be met with the sight of another display of the dolls on the counter.

'I want one of those dolls,' she announced in a voice that she hardly recognised as her own. 'And I would like to see the clothes you say you have.'

The assistant picked up one of the dolls and handed it to her.

'Nice, aren't they?' she said conversationally. 'Kind of cute. Expensive, of course, but then it's a quality job and you have to pay for that. I'll get the clothes.'

She went off and came back with a box full of cellophane bags each containing a dress, a slip and a pair of panties.

Laurie turned them over carefully. Even through the wrappings she could see that the garments were well made and of good material. Rolf had certainly spared no expense!

But though most of the dresses were attractive, to Laurie one stood out unmistakably.

'I'll have this yellow one,' she told the girl.

The bill was a heavy one, far more than Laurie could really afford, but she had no intention of asking Rolf to take her word for it that the dolls were on sale. She was determined to have undeniable proof.

She went back to the Black Prince car park and drove to Rolf's factory on the outskirts of the town. There was ample room to park and clutching her parcel, she went through the swing doors of the main entry, only to be halted by a commissionaire.

'Can I help you, madam?' he asked politely.

'I would like to see Mr Audley,' Laurie told him crisply. 'At once, please.'

'Have you an appointment?' the man asked, still polite but with the evident intention of being obstructive.

'No—but it really is urgent——'

'I'm very sorry, madam,' and he really sounded as if he was. 'But Mr Audley is very busy this morning and I've had strict instructions——'

'Something the matter, Roberts?' a woman's voice asked, and to Laurie's relief she saw that Megan Jones had come into the hall. 'Why, Laurie!' she exclaimed. 'Can I help you?'

'I want—need to see Mr Audley at once,' Laurie explained urgently.

Megan nodded without asking questions.

'All right, Roberts. Miss Stephens is a friend of Mr Audley's. I'll take the responsibility of interrupting him. This way, Laurie.'

She led the way to one of the lifts and pressed the button for the third floor. Despite her preoccupation Laurie realised that this was the office floor and almost immediately they came to a door which Megan opened. It led into a small ante-room from which there was another door.

'Just a minute, please, Laurie,' said Megan, and opened the second door into what was evidently Rolf's sanctum, for almost immediately she heard his voice.

'Laurie? Yes, of course, Megan.' He sounded surprised, which was only to be expected, but there was no hesitation in the way he spoke. He was standing up at his desk as Megan ushered Laurie in and he smiled a welcome.

'Why, Laurie, this is——' he began, and stopped short, his genial expression giving place to one of apprehension. 'Something wrong?' he asked sharply.

For answer she put the parcel down on his desk and tried to undo it, but her fingers fumbled with the adhesive tape and after a moment, Rolf put out a hand.

'Let me.'

Quickly he cut the tape with his penknife and took off the wrapping paper. Then he looked at her enquiringly.

'Open it,' she said in a choked voice.

Rolf lifted the lid and gave a sharp, wordless exclamation. For a moment he stared at the contents. Then he dragged his eyes from the doll and looked at Laurie. His face was unnaturally white and when he spoke, his voice was unsteady.

'Where in the world did you get this?' he demanded incredulously.

'In the big toyshop in the town,' Laurie told him contemptuously. 'Really, it was rather silly of you, don't you think, to have them on show there! I mean, I was almost bound to see them, wasn't I?'

Rolf drew a deep breath.

'You're assuming that I'm responsible for putting the dolls on the market?' he asked harshly.

'Yes,' Laurie said bluntly, and then, as he shook his head, she went on impatiently: 'Oh, *please*! It's bad enough that you've broken your promise, but to deny that you have is utterly despicable!'

'Laurie, listen to me,' he said urgently. 'On my word of honour I am not responsible for this—this outrage. Nor at present do I know who is—but I intend to find out! Do you believe me?'

For answer, she pointed to the doll on his desk as if that was all the proof she needed of his perfidy.

'No? I'm sorry. I should have been—proud and glad if you'd taken my word for it. However'—he shrugged his shoulders—'that apparently being out of the question, we'll get down to proof.'

He went over to a cupboard and took a box from it. This he set on the desk and indicated the chair on the opposite side of the desk from his own.

'Please sit down,' and then, as she hesitated, went on drily: 'Oh, I know, this isn't a social visit, but surely it's only common sense for you to spare your ankle as much as possible. Thank you!' as she complied, however reluctantly. 'And now, will you please examine these dolls' heads?'

There were half a dozen heads in the box, rather grim-looking since they were eyeless and had no hair.

'Now look at the nape of their necks,' Rolf went on. 'And tell me what you see.'

'A little mark of a tiny Noah's Ark,' Laurie replied after investigation 'And the letters GTL.'

'Games & Toys Unlimited. The firm's trade mark,' Rolf nodded, and sat down opposite to her. 'It appears in some form on every article we produce. It also appears on our notepaper——' and he flipped a sheet over to her to substantiate his claim. 'We use it as well on any advertising matter and you'll find the same sign above the entry to this factory. Now then——' He picked up the doll she had bought and handed it to her. 'Look at the nape of the neck of this doll and tell me if you find the same mark. Go on——' grimly as she hesitated. 'Or are you afraid to? Well?'

'It's a different mark,' Laurie admitted in surprise. 'A shield with the letters BT on and a crown above it.'

'Bright Toys—the trade mark of Arnold Bright, my greatest rival,' Rolf explained, and waited for her reaction.

'All right,' Laurie said argumentatively, 'so the dolls weren't made here. But how could anyone else have made them without your——'

'Connivance?' Rolf suggested grimly as she hesitated for a word. 'Don't bother to spare my feelings, Laurie! Well, I don't know the answer to that, but I certainly intend to find out!' He stood up and went to a small safe which he opened with a key which he wore on a safety chain. He took out an envelope and from it extracted the Sheldrake paintings and the two photographs of Laurie. 'I brought these over from the Ranch the first time I was able to come to the office and put them in the safe, to which, I should add, only one other person other than myself has a key—Megan Jones. Perhaps you think she's the culprit?'

'No!' Laurie said unhesitatingly. 'Of course not! You'll never make me believe that!'

'Good!' said Rolf as he put the pictures back into the safe and locked it.

He came back to the desk, but instead of sitting down again, he stood over her, an angry, menacing presence. 'No, in your mind I'm still cast as the villain, aren't I?' he went on bitterly. 'And I may tell you, I'm sick and tired of the part! And so,' he continued decisively as she sat silent, 'I've made up my mind to put an end to it! Please listen carefully, because I shall require your co-operation whether given willingly or not. To begin with, I shall write to Arnold Bright and tell him just what's happened. Knowing him, he won't be easy to convince against his own interests. That's where you come in. I shall ask him to come here to meet you. Without that, I doubt if he'll believe that there's been any skulduggery about the dolls. Well?'

'All right,' Laurie promised reluctantly. 'If you think it's really necessary.'

'I do!'   .

'Very well, then.' Laurie stood up. She felt tired to the point of exhaustion and her ankle was throbbing painfully. 'I—I think I'll go now. There doesn't seem to be anything left to say——'

'There isn't,' Rolf agreed curtly, and opened the door for her.

It closed behind her with a finality which echoed in Laurie's thoughts. If, even now, Rolf was lying, then she had finished with him. But if he had told the truth, then he would never forgive her for doubting him.

Either way, this was the end even of friendship.

CHAPTER TEN

It was almost a week before Rolf rang Laurie from his office asking her if she could go there on the afternoon of the following day to meet Arnold Bright who, he had claimed, was responsible for the manufacture and distribution of the Lorelei doll.

Laurie promised that she would. Actually, the arrangement suited her very well since she knew that her mother would be out for most of the day.

'There's just one thing,' Rolf went on. 'Do you mind wearing that yellow dress? It would, I think, finally convince Bright that there's been some jiggery-pokery going on.'

'Very well,' Laurie agreed, quite seeing his point. 'About three o'clock?'

'That's what I had in mind. Thank you for being so co-operative, Laurie.'

'Not at all,' Laurie replied briskly. 'I'm extremely anxious to get this unpleasant business cleared up.'

'Not more anxious than I am,' Rolf retorted, and rang off.

As she, too, rang off, Laurie stood irresolutely for a few minutes. Then, hardly knowing why, she went to what had been Rolf's quarters. He and Hutton had left the Ranch two days previously—leaving a disconsolate Miss Trewyn behind—and all their personal possessions had gone with them leaving the rooms with an impersonal, deserted appearance. But the desk he had had brought from the office was still there and Laurie sat down at it, leaning her arms on it and burying her face in her hands.

Tomorrow she would know the truth—and she wasn't sure if she wanted to or not. As she had already realised, it didn't really matter much, one way or the other, since either she or Rolf would be proved in the wrong and neither would relish that. Still, as they had both felt, the whole thing had *got* to be cleared up.

The following day she saw her mother off—Mrs Stephens was going to visit what would be her new home to see if there were any changes she would want to make, and later Mr Brownsell would meet her and they would dine somewhere together. With a sigh of relief, Laurie knew that there was no possibility of her returning until quite late.

Nor did Miss Trewyn present any difficulty. She was only at the Ranch for a few hours that morning and though she offered to stay if Laurie didn't like being on her own, she was easily reassured that Laurie had plenty to do and would be too busy to feel lonely.

'Well, I'm just as glad you feel like that, Miss Laurie,' she admitted. 'The fact is, I want to give the cottage a thorough do. I expect you know that Mr Audley is going to make a sort of flatlet upstairs for Hutton and me. We're to have one of the bedrooms that's got its own bathroom and another bedroom next to it is to be turned into a sitting room. All nice and private.'

'I'm so glad for you,' Laurie said sincerely.

'But of course, I know what'll happen once I leave the cottage! That brother of mine will turn it into a pigsty in next to no time and I won't be able to do more than pop over now and again. Oh well, we'll see. Perhaps with me out of the way he'll get married. There'll be one or two widows I could name looking his way, I don't doubt!'

Laurie, feeling that after Miss Trewyn's own romance, nothing was impossible, agreed gravely that that might be the answer.

After Miss Trewyn had left, she had a scrappy lunch, fed Cherry having first shut all the doors and windows to prevent her from roaming, went upstairs and after having a shower, changed into the yellow dress. But looking at herself in the mirror, she frowned. Really it wasn't suitable for daytime wear, so she added a lightweight coat before driving into Penzance.

This time she was met by a smiling Roberts who had evidently been told to expect her. Knowing the way to Rolf's office now, she went up in the lift unescorted and found not only the door of the ante-room open but also that of the inner office. Rolf must have heard her coming, for he was waiting at the door to meet her. At that moment, the nearby church clock struck three.

'Good afternoon, Laurie,' he said. 'Mr Bright has only just arrived. Come and meet him.'

He stood back for Laurie to precede him and followed her in to make a formal introduction.

Arnold Bright was a tall, spare man, some years older than Rolf. He had a clever, alert face and there was a certain shrewdness about it which convinced Laurie that he would make a formidable opponent.

However, he greeted her pleasantly enough, but as Laurie took off her coat, his expression changed to one of consternation.

'Well, I admit a personal likeness might be a coincidence, but with the dress as well——' he shook his head. 'Well, let's get down to brass tacks, shall we?'

They sat down at a round table and then Laurie noticed for the first time that Megan had slipped quietly into the room and was already sitting down with a notebook and pen in front of her.

'H'm, keeping a record of proceedings?' Mr Bright commented drily. 'Perhaps you're right. Now then——' he opened his briefcase and took out an envelope from which he extracted two paintings and *three* photographs.

Rolf had already laid an envelope on the table at the place where he was sitting and from it he, too, took out two practically identical paintings—but only *two* photographs. Unmistakably all the paintings were the work of the same artist. The photographs were identical.

'Cards on the table, I think,' Arnold Bright said briskly. 'You first or me?'

'Me, I think,' Rolf suggested, 'since I came into the affair before you did. Well, it began with an unpleasant incident in the Cove which happened to Miss Stephens. She was swimming there and some fools in a motor boat circled so close to her as to cause the water to become dangerously rough. Indeed, if Miss Stephens was not a very strong swimmer she could have been in serious difficulties.'

'Nasty,' Mr Bright commented with a sympathetic glance at Laurie. 'But I don't quite see——'

'You will,' Rolf promised grimly. 'It's a case of cause and effect. The two photographs of Miss Stephens which I have were taken by an occupant of the boat. Afterwards they were shown to me in an attempt to shift the blame from the real culprits to Miss Stephens on the grounds that the boat's engine had cut out and there was danger of it drifting on to the rocks. It was said that Miss Stephens had refused to take their plight seriously and that she had in fact welcomed it. Her expression was claimed to substantiate the accusation, though what she could have done to help was, in the circumstances, nothing.'

'Sounds as if someone had got it in for Miss Stephens,' Mr Bright commented.

Rolf, who had paused briefly, nodded his agreement and Laurie, who until then had been compelled to admit that his account had been absolutely fair and accurate, waited anxiously for what he would say next.

'Fortunately, there was a reliable witness of the whole incident,' he resumed evenly. 'And so it was proved beyond doubt that far from mocking the people in the boat, Miss Stephens was pointing out that another boat was coming to their rescue. The same witness also saw how Miss Stephens had been harassed by the boat's manoeuvres and the culprits have been warned off the beach.'

'Better luck than they deserved to have got off so lightly,' Arnold Bright commented, and looked shrewdly at Rolf. 'You know, Audley, something tells me that the person who gave you those photographs was a woman—and a spiteful one at that!'

But Rolf didn't seem to hear the question, for he ignored it and Laurie thought bitterly:

'He heard all right! But even now, he's doing his best to shield Sylvia!'

'The photographs were taken by one of the occupants of the boat, and a short time after that I received some paintings—these——' he indicated the paintings. 'They were submitted from a freelance artist who sometimes submits ideas to us. His name is Sheldrake——' He looked questioningly at Mr Bright, who nodded with an air of satisfaction. 'After a discussion with Miss Stephens in which she made it clear that she found the idea of marketing such dolls intolerable, I gave her my word that I would not do so. That promise I kept.' He paused again as if to emphasise his final statement. 'However, Miss Stephens saw a display of the dolls in a toyshop here and jumped to the inevitable conclusion, namely that I was responsible.' He glanced briefly at Laurie, but she could read nothing into his impersonal expression. But he had called her belief 'inevitable'. Perhaps, after all, he wasn't blaming her. 'I had already written to Sheldrake—a letter which his bank manager promised to forward. In it I not only turned down his idea but told him in unequivocal terms that I didn't believe his story about the London model and why. Further, I told him that if he tried to sell his idea to anyone else, he would not only be in trouble with Miss Stephens but with me. To that I have had no reply, so whether he had the letter of not, I can't say. However, I think he had since, unless he knew that I'd turned his idea down, he would hardly have offered it to you. That's about all, except that, when I recognised your trademark on the doll, I immediately wrote to you.'

'Yes—well——' Mr Bright began as Rolf looked at him enquiringly. 'Mine isn't such a long story, but it fits in. I was approached by an attractive young lady who represented herself as Sheldrake's agent during his absence abroad. She told me the same story about the London model and I accepted it as being true. As a matter of fact, we were looking for a new line and time was running short. I was glad of the opportunity of using Sheldrake's idea. He's worked for us before with very satisfactory results. I thought——' with an apologetic look at Laurie, 'that Lorelei was attractive in an intriguing way, so we went ahead at top speed, in all ignorance that there would be unpleasant complications as a result. I think that's about all——'

'Did—the lady—say how she got hold of the photograph of Miss Stephens in the yellow dress?' Rolf asked, and Laurie listened breathlessly. Geoff meant nothing to her now, but they had been good friends and she hoped for that reason that he hadn't been involved.

'Something about having picked it up at a dance she'd been to,' Mr Bright said vaguely. 'I didn't take much notice at the time because it didn't seem to be important. Well, that's it,' he concluded. 'Where do we go from here?'

'Isn't that for you to say?' Rolf suggested, and Mr Bright nodded.

'I suppose it is,' he agreed ruefully, and turned to Laurie. 'I take it that there's no possibility of you withdrawing your opposition, Miss Stephens?'

'None whatever,' Laurie told him emphatically.

'No——' with a glance at Sheldrake's work, 'I can't say I blame you!' He pondered, tapping his fingers on the table top. 'I shall stop production of these damned dolls at once. I shall also withdraw those which have already been distributed—though that won't be too easy. However, I shall, I promise you, do my very best.'

'Yes?' Rolf said in a way which suggested that he was satisfied—so far. And then, as Mr Bright remained silent, he said bluntly: 'How about compensation to Miss Stephens for the distress she has been caused—and may yet be caused?'

'H'm, yes, compensation,' Mr Bright said thoughtfully. 'What had you in mind, Audley?'

'Just a minute,' Laurie intervened, dangerously quiet. 'When you speak of compensation do you mean—*money*?'

'Why, yes, Miss Stephens, just that,' Mr Bright confirmed.

'It's out of the question,' Laurie said decisively, and when she saw the surprise on the faces of the two men she went on passionately: 'Do you think I'd accept money that you'd never have thought of paying me if it hadn't been for these horrible dolls? Don't you see, I'd be making a profit out of them—and that would be intolerable!'

'Then what do you want?' Mr Bright asked, completely at a loss.

'For you to do what you've already promised to do,' Laurie explained unhesitatingly. 'You'll see that's done, won't you?' she appealed to Rolf, who agreed briefly. 'And after that, I want to forget all about it.'

Arnold Bright looked enquiringly at Rolf, who shrugged his shoulders.

'If that's Miss Stephens' considered decision——?'

'It is!'

'Then it must be accepted,' Rolf declared, giving no hint whether he approved or not.

Arnold Bright sighed, replaced the pictures in his case and stood up.

'I'll attend to this immediately,' he announced. 'And I'll let you have my promise in writing at once.'

'Good,' Rolf replied laconically, and stood up as well.

Mr Bright turned to Laurie.

'I should like to express my regrets to you, Miss Stephens, for the distress you have been caused,' he said formally. 'And to thank you for your generosity,' he added as an afterthought.

Laurie, literally beyond words now that it was all over, bent her head in acknowledgment.

The two men walked towards the door. Suddenly Mr Bright paused.

'Do you reckon Sheldrake was in on this? Or did that girl make it up about being his agent?' he asked curiously.

'I don't know,' Rolf admitted in a strained voice. 'Is it of much importance?'

'Perhaps not. I just wondered. She was an attractive piece to look at,' he added reflectively. 'Pity her voice doesn't match!'

So, though her name had not been mentioned, that proved that Sylvia had been the 'agent'.

Rolf made no reply, but as he reached the door, Mr Bright paused again.

'Do you think we can be sure she doesn't get up to any more mischief?' he asked.

'I'm reasonably sure we can,' Rolf said unemotionally. 'For one thing, she has now left my employ. For another, she is about to get married and her interests will be totally different. She'll have no cause to want to make trouble!'

Laurie would not let herself think of that final significant statement of Rolf's and fortunately she had a lot to keep her occupied for her mother and John Brownsell were to be married in two weeks' time and there was a lot to do in preparation. True, there were a few alterations or additions that needed to be dealt with in the new home before the wedding, but despite the prospective bride's protests, Laurie and Megan had insisted on going through her wardrobe and had told her firmly that it simply wouldn't do. She must have a trousseau.

'Oh, what nonsense!' Mrs Stephens protested. 'John and I aren't youngsters. What I've got will do perfectly well. Perhaps one or two new dresses, but that's all.'

But it was two to one and in the end Mrs Stephens not only capitulated but began to enjoy the mild extravagance into which the two conspirators inveigled her. The result was several shopping expeditions during one of which she bought her wedding day finery.

Actually she rather wished that she hadn't suggested a blue outfit for Miss Trewyn's wedding later in the year, as otherwise that was the colour she would have chosen for herself. As it was, her choice fell on a charming pale grey dress which had a muted suggestion of pink about it. With it she chose a close-fitting hat entirely covered with little feathers which blended both the pink and grey colouring of the dress. And while she was utterly shocked at the price, she knew that Laurie's enthusiastic praise: 'You look absolutely lovely, Mother!' was more or less justified. She *did* look her best, and what was more, there was no suggestion of mutton dressed as lamb about the outfit.

Laurie, as bridesmaid, chose a dress that was basically pale green but patterned with little pink rosebuds. It was attractive but lacked the unmistakable chic of her mother's dress—which was just what Laurie intended. This was her mother's day and nothing must be allowed to detract attention from her appearance.

It was a quiet wedding. An elderly uncle of Mrs Stephens' who, with his wife, had come all the way from Norfolk for the occasion, gave Mrs Stephens away. A cousin of Mr Brownsell's acted as his best man and, apart from Laurie and a few other somewhat distant relatives on both sides, Megan Jones, Miss Trewyn and her brother were the only invited guests. Rolf had been invited but had been unable to accept as he was to be away on a business trip. Privately Laurie thought it was simply a tactful excuse so that he would avoid the embarrassment of meeting her socially. But whether it was an excuse or not, Laurie was thankful that he was not there. They had not seen one another since the day when she had gone to the office to meet Arnold Bright, and that was how she wanted it to be.

After the ceremony there was a pleasant little reception at the Ranch, complete with an elaborate wedding cake made by Miss Trewyn as her wedding present.

When the newly married couple had left for their short honeymoon and the guests had drifted off to catch trains or drive, in some cases, considerable distances, there was the cleaning up to do at which Cherry assisted with enthusiasm having a special liking for smoked salmon sandwiches and pâté de foie gras.

'Fond of her tummy, that young lady,' Miss Trewyn commented tolerantly. 'Well, she'd better enjoy herself while she can!'

'While she can?' Laurie repeated. 'How do you mean?'

'Well, she'll miss you and she'll miss the Ranch when she goes to live with your mother,' Miss Trewyn explained. 'I know Mrs Brownsell's fond of her, but she won't get the fussing you give her. And though the house has got a nice enough garden, it's not to be compared with all the space she's got here. To say nothing of the traffic——'

'Oh *goodness*!' Laurie said in dismay.

'Well, don't worry too much,' Miss Trewyn consoled. 'Because what I reckon will happen is that she'll find her way back here. Almost bound to, I'd say.'

Which didn't exactly set Laurie's mind at rest.

During the next few days Laurie and Miss Trewyn began methodically to pack up her mother's personal belongings that were to go to the Brownsells' home and her own which would go to the Black Prince.

When that was done, the two of them turned their attention to the preparations for Miss Trewyn's wedding which was to take place a few days after the Brownsells returned from their honeymoon.

It turned out to be a much bigger affair than the Brownsell wedding had been because though neither bride nor groom had many relations, Miss Trewyn had lived all her life at the Cove and consequently was known by all the other local people. And liked, too, which is quite another matter. As for Hutton, he had quite a lot of friends among other members of Rolf's employees. And of course Rolf, now back from France, would be there. He was, much to Hutton's gratification, to be best man.

Laurie wished that she could have avoided attending the wedding, but that was out of the question. Miss Trewyn's feelings would have been badly hurt by what she would undoubtedly have felt was a slight.

But at least Laurie consoled herself that Rolf would be too occupied with his duties to have any time to spare for her. Indeed, it turned out that it was not until they had seen the happy couple off that they found themselves next to one another. Not that Rolf seemed to be particularly aware of the fact. He simply took her nearness for granted.

'Nice wedding,' he commented easily.

'Very,' Laurie agreed cordially. 'And do you know, though it's usually the bride who attracts all the attention, I thought Hutton just about stole the picture. I've never seen a bridegroom look so quietly confident and with such a look of absolute contentment.'

'Yes, he was superb,' Rolf replied with, surely, just a hint of envy in his voice. 'I only hope that when—if ever—my turn comes, I'll put up as good a show.'

Laurie contrived to laugh.

'Oh, I'm sure you will,' she told him lightly. 'I can't imagine any circumstances which would disconcert you!'

'Can't you?' He looked at her with a curious intensity. 'I hope you're right! Excuse me, I must go and have a word with the caterers. Be seeing you, Laurie!'

'Not if I can help it,' Laurie told herself stoically as he strolled off leaving her unaware that they had been under the scrutiny of two pairs of shrewd eyes.

'I'm absolutely exasperated with them,' Mrs Brownsell declared, and sounded as if she was just that. 'They're head over heels in love with one another—anyone with half an eye can see that—except the two of them! I'd like to knock their silly heads together!'

Megan Jones puckered her lips reflectively.

'I don't know that that would do much good, Lucy
But——'

With the Trewyn–Hutton wedding over, Laurie closed the
Ranch and went to stay for a short time with her mother
and her stepfather. She took Cherry with her and in a very
short time it was only too clear that the new Mrs Hutton
had been right. Cherry didn't like her new home and said so
with unmistakable clarity. She frankly sulked, refusing to
take any notice of the blandishments lavished on her. On
the third day she was missing and despite frantic searching
could not be found.

Until no hope seemed left, Laurie made no reference to
Mrs Hutton's opinion that Cherry would make her way
back to the Ranch, but as soon as she did, Mrs Brownsell
seized on the idea.

'But of course! Why didn't we think of that before!' she
exclaimed. 'Well, that settles it, Laurie. You'll have to go
over there and see if that's what's happened. You'll probably find her in Mr Audley's sitting room.'

'But, Mother, how can she be?' Laurie protested. 'Every
door and window is shut and locked. I know they are, I
checked them very carefully. She simply couldn't get in.'

'Cherry can get in anywhere she has a mind to,' Mrs
Brownsell said resignedly. 'You know she can.'

Laurie did know it, but she still had another objection to
make.

'Well, she may be able to, but I can't. You know you've
handed over all the keys to our solicitor so that he can give
them to Rolf when he takes over the Ranch.'

'Not yet,' Mrs Brownsell explained triumphantly. 'I'm
not handing them over until next week in case there's anything we've forgotten.' And then, as Laurie still didn't seem
at all enthusiastic: 'Good gracious, Laurie,' she added
crossly, 'anyone would think you didn't care tuppence for
Cherry despite all the fuss you've always made over her.'

So, reluctantly, Laurie capitulated and drove over to the
Ranch. She was alone, because as Mrs Brownsell had
pointed out, someone must stay behind in case, after all,
Cherry turned up.

She drove round to the back of the Ranch where she had always kept her car and then came back to the garden to call entreatingly in the hope that Cherry, unable to get into the house, would be glad to surrender.

But when there was no sign of the truant, she went reluctantly into the house. She paused in the hall filled with an unpleasant sense of rejection. It seemed that even in the short time that the house had been unoccupied, it had changed. It was not only that, closed up, the air was heavy and oppressive. The atmosphere of home had gone and in its place was something that to Laurie felt like unfriendliness, even downright hostility. Involuntarily she shivered and for the first time realised that she was alone and defenceless if—if anything happened.

'Oh, nonsense,' she told herself crossly. 'What *could* happen?'

She began a meticulous search for Cherry, leaving the front door ajar in case she turned up, but she set a chair against the door so that if anyone else tried to come in she would at least be warned.

But when at last she was satisfied that she really was only wasting time, she went back to what had been Rolf's quarters for a final look since that had always been Cherry's favourite haunt.

It was just as she had come to the conclusion that Cherry simply wasn't here that she heard an ominous and unmistakable sound. Someone was trying to open the front door further and in doing so, was pushing the chair back over the polished floor.

With a catch of her breath, Laurie looked round desperately for some sort—any sort—of a weapon, but there was literally nothing and she was only too well aware that the open door leading to these rooms from the hall was almost certain to attract the invader's attention and there was no way of escape. The door leading to the verandah had been locked and she hadn't got the key.

Nor was she reassured by the fact that the intruder was taking good care to make as little noise as possible. She could barely hear the slight scuff-scuff of his cautiously moving feet.

And then, at the door of the sitting room, the sound ceased.

Laurie stood petrified, her hand at her throat suppressing a scream. Perhaps if she made no noise he—whoever he was—would go to some other part of the house first——

Then suddenly the door was flung open and Laurie could no longer suppress her scream.

A man stood there. A man who dropped the stick he was holding and held out his arms. Laurie, sobbing and laughing at one and the same time, ran to him.

'Oh, Rolf, Rolf, I thought you were a tramp or a burglar!' she told him hysterically, and clung desperately to him.

Rolf's arms tightened protectively.

'Hush, darling, hush,' he said comfortingly. 'There's nothing to be afraid of—you're quite, quite safe, sweetheart!' And picking her up, he carried her over to the sofa and held her even closer.

Then there was no need for words between them, for, as she still clung to him, his lips sought hers and it was so easy, so heavenly to respond in a way which told him her secret beyond any chance of misunderstanding.

Later, though she had no idea how much later, she asked him wonderingly:

'But, Rolf darling, why didn't you tell me before?'

'My little love, because if I made the least attempt to advance, you were off like a scalded cat!' he told her frankly.

'That's not very polite,' Laurie complained.

'No, but it's the truth, my love,' he insisted. 'Why were you so perverse, Laurie?'

'Because I thought you were going to marry Sylvia French,' Laurie explained—and how marvellous it was to be able to say that without fearing that it was true!

'Sylvia?' Rolf exclaimed incredulously. 'Where in the world did you get that idea? No, don't tell me——' resignedly. 'I know—from Sylvia herself, confound her! Look, my sweet, we're going to get this sorted out once and for all—and then we'll forget all about it. The fact is, Sylvia was a menace when we were children. We both used to spend at least part of our holidays here and she attached herself to me like a limpet and flew into a rage if I tried to shake her off.'

'Oh, poor Rolf!' Laurie said sympathetically, and then, after a moment's thought, 'and perhaps poor Sylvia as well.'

'Well, perhaps,' Rolf conceded doubtfully. 'Anyway, I was thankful when, later on, she went to live in France for some years to finish her education. Her parents were pretty well off in those days. Then suddenly everything changed for her. Her parents were both killed in a car crash and Sylvia was not only left an orphan, she was just about penniless because her parents had lived right up to—and beyond—their income.'

'How terrible,' Laurie said in horror.

'Yes, it was,' Rolf agreed reflectively. 'The sort of thing that makes one feel one *must* do something to help. So, when she came back to this country and couldn't get a job, I, like a fool, gave her one. And I must say, in all honesty, that she put all she'd got into it. But, unfortunately, she read far too much into the fact that I'd come to her rescue. She took it for granted that eventually we'd get married. I did my best to make it clear that I had no such intention, but it wasn't any good because she didn't *want* to believe that I wasn't interested.' He paused, frowning. 'I've never been in such a spot in my life! Of course, if there had been another girl in whom I was interested, it might have been easier to convince her. But at that time there wasn't. Then I met you—and there *was*.'

'No wonder she hated me so.' Laurie's voice shook at the memory.

'She did that all right,' Rolf agreed grimly. 'I was terrified on your account, literally scared out of my wits. And with reason. I knew she'd do her damnedest to make trouble between us and, my heavens, she pretty well succeeded!'

'Well, it was partly your fault,' Laurie told him judicially.

'I like that!' Rolf retorted indignantly. 'What did I ever do to encourage her?'

'That first day she came to work here,' Laurie reminded him, 'I heard you say that she was a sight for sore eyes and that she didn't know how you'd looked forward to her coming.'

'Well, so I was glad to see her,' Rolf admitted. 'But not for her sake. Simply, I was bored with inactivity and her coming here meant that I could get down to work!'

'All the same, what you said was open to misconception,' Laurie insisted. 'And she really is beautiful, you know. How could I help thinking——?'

'Misconception, my foot!' Rolf retorted indignantly. 'Even if you were such an idiot as to get the wrong idea, honestly, you ought to have realised that I'm not! As for being beautiful—all right, I admit, she is a good looker— but her voice! Tintacks and nutmeg graters aren't in it! Fancy living with it! And that reminds me, just to close the account, it's Sheldrake she's marrying—and good luck to him. He'll need it!'

'Yes,' Laurie agreed thoughtfully, 'I think he will. Do you think he knew what she was trying to do?'

'I doubt it,' Rolf said consideringly. 'I should think it was simply that he wanted to please her—he'd been keen on her for some time—and didn't realise all that lay behind it. Certainly I don't think he knew she would go to Bright representing herself as his agent. And I don't suppose she'll ever tell him. Nor shall I. It might break up their marriage —and that's the last thing I want to do. The more securely she's tied up with another man the less likely she is to bother us! Well, that's it. Satisfied?'

'Yes,' Laurie said magnanimously. 'And I'll forgive you!'

'You'd better, my girl,' Rolf told her masterfully. 'Because if you don't——'

She never heard what terrific threat he was going to hold over her head, because at that moment the telephone bell rang. When she answered it, she heard her mother's voice.

'Oh, darling, such good news!' Mrs Brownsell announced joyfully. 'I've found Cherry!'

'Oh, good!' Laurie said thankfully. 'Where was she?'

'In the airing cupboard,' said Mrs Brownsell. 'She'd tucked herself under a blanket that was airing there.'

'How odd,' Laurie said slowly. 'I looked in there several times—I even took the blanket out. And she certainly wasn't there then.'

'I suppose she must have slipped in later,' Mrs Brownsell suggested reasonably. 'You know how elusive she can be!'

'Yes, but——' Laurie paused. A disturbing suspicion had occurred to her. 'Mother,' she asked sharply, 'was Cherry really lost at all? Or did you just pretend that she was?'

'Laurie dear, what an extraordinary idea,' Mrs Brownsell said reproachfully. 'Why on earth should I do such a thing?'

Laurie's only answer was to ring off. She knew only too well that she was right—and why her mother had behaved as she had.

When she rejoined Rolf her lips were tightly pressed together and there was a patch of bright colour in either cheek. Rolf looked up enquiringly.

'It was Mother,' Laurie told him, breathing heavily. 'She's found Cherry.'

'Oh good,' said Rolf, holding out his hand. 'Come and tell me all about it. Where was she?'

Laurie dropped down heavily beside him.

'She was never lost,' she declared belligerently.

'But——' Rolf looked puzzled.

'I'm sure of it,' Laurie insisted. 'It was just a put-up job! Mother was too glib for it to be anything else!'

'But why——?' Rolf wanted to know.

'Why?' Laurie repeated furiously. 'Because she knew that *you* were going to be here and she thought, if we were to meet unexpectedly—if I was almost scared out of my wits we'd—we'd——' she choked, unable to go on.

'Oh—yes, I see what you mean,' Rolf said consideringly. 'You may be right, but after all, what of it? We have——'

'What of it?' Laurie almost shouted, bouncing up and down in her agitation. 'It's absolutely shameful! I've been thrown at your head!'

'Yes, perhaps you have,' Rolf conceded with infuriating calm. 'But that's no reason why you should bounce about like a ping-pong ball! Do stop, there's a darling. It really is most uncomfortable. And quite unnecessary. After all, I've been equally thrown at yours!'

'You have?' said Laurie, taken aback.

'Oh yes,' he explained calmly. 'How do you think it comes about that I'm here?'

'Mother——?'

He shook his head.

'No, Megan. She insisted that she'd accidentally left some important papers here that she needed to have at once, and she bullied me into coming here to get them. And I bet——' he added admiringly, 'that when I get round to looking for them, I'll find them just where she said they were! I know Megan. Nothing if she's not thorough!'

'You mean to say that the two of them put their heads together——' Laurie exploded. 'And you don't *mind?*'

He shook his head, smiling at her.

'Well, I *do!*' Laurie insisted resentfully. 'I think it was outrageously interfering of them and I'll never speak to either of them again!'

'Oh yes, you will, my love,' Rolf told her firmly. 'What's more, once we're living here, you and I, they'll be our most honoured guests any time they choose!'

'*No!*'

'*Yes!* It may have been interference, but I'm grateful for it.' He gathered her close and his lips brushed hers. 'Don't you see, beloved, it's because of them that I've got my heart's desire?'

'Oh!' Laurie was still tense, but she spoke in a subdued voice. 'Do you mean *me?*'

'Just you.'

Laurie considered this.

'Well, all right. I'll forgive them for your sake——'

Rolf smiled, but he waited. And Laurie capitulated without further ado.

'And for my own,' she said softly.

As Rolf's lips claimed hers, Laurie realised that, once again Rolf was getting his own way.

But what did it matter when it was her way as well?

The wonder of love is timeless. Once discovered, love remains, despite the passage of time. Harlequin brings you stories of true love, about women the world over – women like you.

Harlequin Romances
with the
Harlequin magic...

Recapture the sparkle of first love...relive the joy of true romance...enjoy these stories of love today.

Eight new novels every month – wherever paperbacks are sold.